ALLISON & BUSBY
TWENTIETH CENTURY CLASSICS

What is it that makes us pick up and read a book again and again? The memory of that first immersion when everything but what we were reading paled into insignificance? When the book ate with us, walked with us, travelled with us, slept with us, and, when it was finished, we grieved as for the loss of a close friend. For us that book and what it had to say to us remains as true now as it did when we first connected with it.

There comes a time when we realise that we haven't seen it let alone read it for years, and when we try to get it in the bookshop find that it is out of print and there are no plans to reprint. Second-hand copies are in short supply so the book is lost to us. It is that sense of loss which stimulated me into starting up the Allison & Busby Twentieth Century Classics, reprinting old favourites which still speak to me as strongly as they did when I first picked them up.

These are not the books you are going to find in other series, the national classics which have been in print for ever; these are my favourites, books I think should be in print, books that I really believe you will want to read and enjoy, books that will speak to you as they have to me.

If I am right and these are books you enjoy reading then why not write to me with your own out-of-print favourites and I will see whether they too can be included in this new Allison & Busby Twentieth Century Classics list.

PETER DAY

City of Spades

Also by Colin MacInnes
and published by Allison & Busby

Absolute Beginners
Mr Love and Justice
To the Victor the Spoils
Absolute MacInnes: the Best of Colin MacInnes
(edited by Tony Gould)

CITY OF SPADES

Colin MacInnes

a&b

This edition published in Great Britain in 1993 by
Allison & Busby
an imprint of Wilson & Day Ltd
5 The Lodge
Richmond Way
London W12 8LW

A catalogue record for this book is available from the British Library

ISBN 0 74900 116 X

Printed and bound in Great Britain by
Mackays of Chatham PLC, Chatham, Kent

FOR RICKY

CONTENTS

PART I

Johnny Fortune hits town

1

Pew tentatively takes the helm

'It's all yours, Pew, from now,' he said, adding softly, 'thank God,' and waving round the office a mildly revolted hand.

'Yes, but what do I *do* with it all, dear boy?' I asked him. 'Why am I here?'

'Ah, as to that . . .' He heaved an indifferent sigh. 'You'll have to find out for yourself as you go along.'

He picked up his furled umbrella, but I clung to him just a bit longer.

'Couldn't you explain, please, my duties to me in more detail? After all, I'm new, I'm taking over from you, and I'd be very glad to know exactly *what* . . .'

Trim, chill, compact, he eyed me with aloof imperial calm. Clearly he was of the stuff of which proconsuls can even now be made.

'Oh, very well,' he said, grounding his umbrella. 'Not, I'm afraid, that anything I can tell you is likely to be of the slightest use. . . .'

I thanked him and we sat. His eye a bored inquisitor's, he said: 'You know, at any rate, what you're *supposed* to be?'

Simply, I answered: 'I am the newly appointed Assistant Welfare Officer of the Colonial Department.'

He closed his eyes. 'I don't know—forgive me—how you got the job. But may I enquire if you know anything about our colonial peoples?'

'I once spent a most agreeable holiday in Malta. . . .

'Quite so. A heroic spot. But I mean Negroes. Do you happen to know anything about them?'

'Nothing.'

'Nothing whatever?'

'No.'

He emitted a thin smile. 'In that case, may I say I think you're going to have quite a lot of fun?'

'I sincerely hope so. . . . I have certain vague impressions about

Negroes, of course. I rather admire their sleek, loose-limbed appearance. . . .'

'Yes, yes. So very engaging.'

'And their elegant flamboyant style of dress is not without its charm. . . .'

'Ah, that far, personally, I cannot follow you.'

'On the other hand, for their dismal spirituals and their idiotic calypso, I have the most marked distaste.'

'I'm with you there, Pew, I'd glad to say. The European passion for these sad and silly songs has always baffled me. Though their jazz, in so far as it is theirs, is perhaps another matter.'

He had risen once again. I saw he had made up his mind I was beyond hope.

'And what do I do with our coloured cousins?' I asked him, rising too.

'Yours is a wide assignment, limitless almost as the sea. You must be their unpaid lawyer, estate agent, wet-nurse and, in a word, their bloody guardian angel.'

The note of disdain, even though coming from a professional civil servant to an amateur, had become increasingly displeasing to me. I said with dignity: 'Nothing, I suppose, could be more delightful and meritorious.'

He had now closed his eyes; and stood, at the door, a Whitehall Machiavelli.

'Some might say,' he told me softly, that your duty is to help them to corrupt our country.'

Up went my brows.

'So some might say . . . their irruption among us has not been an unmixed blessing. Thousands, you see, have come here in the last few years from Africa and the Caribbean, and given us what we never had before—a colour problem.'

His eyes opened slowly in a slit. 'Could it not be,' I said, 'that we have given them just that in their own countries?'

'My dear Pew! Could it be that I positively find myself in the presence of a *liberal*?'

'My dear boy, of course you do! What else can one comfortably be in these monolithic days?'

He smiled with every tooth.

'A liberal, Pew, in relation to the colour question, is a person who feels an irresponsible sympathy for what he calls oppressed peoples on whom, along with the staunchest Tory, he's quite willing to go on being a parasite.'

Though I sensed it was a phrase he'd used before, I bowed my bleeding head.

'I own,' I told him mildly, 'that I *am* one of those futile, persistent, middle-class Englishmen whom it takes a whole empire, albeit a declining one, to sustain. . . . Remove the imperial shreds, and I'd be destitute as a coolie, I confess. . . .'

This pleased him. 'To use the vulgar phrase,' he said, 'you must learn to know which side your bread is buttered on.'

But this excursion from the concrete into the abstract seemed to me unhelpful in so far as learning my new job was concerned. I made my last desperate appeal. 'You haven't told me, though . . .'

'Please study your dossiers Pew: the instructions are pasted inside each of their covers. Look:

Government Hostels;
Landlords taking non-Europeans;
Facilities for Recreation and Study;
Bad Company and Places to Avoid;
Relations with Commonwealth Co-citizens of the Mother Country.

And so on and so forth, dear man. And may I advise you' (he looked at his watch) 'to hurry up and read them? Because your clients will be turning up for interviews within the hour. Meanwhile I shall say goodbye to you and wish you the good fortune that I fear you'll so much need.'

'Might I enquire,' I said, reluctant even now to see him go, 'to what fresh colonial pastures you yourself are now proceeding?'

A look of mild triumph overspread his face.

'Before the month is out,' he answered, 'I shall be at my new post in one of our Protectorates within the Union of South Africa.'

'South Africa? Good heavens! Won't you find, as a British colonial official, that the atmosphere there's just a little difficult?'

In statesmanlike tones he answered: 'South Africa, Pew, is a country much maligned. Perhaps they have found a logical solution for race relations there. That is the conclusion to which I've rather reluctantly come. Because if my year in the Department has taught me anything, it's that the Negro's still, deep down inside, a savage. Not his fault, no doubt, but just his nature.' (He stood there erect, eyes imperiously agleam.) 'Remember that, Pew, at your Welfare Officer's desk. Under his gaberdine suit and his mission school-veneer, there still lurk the impulses of the primitive man.'

He waved—as if an assegai—his umbrella, I waved more wanly, and lo! he was gone out of my life for ever.

Alone, I picked up the dossiers, crossed out his name, and wrote in its place my own: Montgomery Pew. Then, like a lion (or monkey, possibly?) new to its cage, I walked round my unsumptuous office examining the numerous framed photographs of *worthy* Africans and West Indians, staring out at me with enigmatic faces, whose white grins belied, it seemed to me, the inner silences of the dark pools of their eyes.

2

Johnny Macdonald Fortune takes up the tale

MY FIRST ACTION on reaching the English capital was to perform what I've always promised my sister Peach I would. Namely, leaving my luggages at the Government hostel, to go straight out by taxi (oh, so slow, compared with our sleek Lagos limousines!) to the famous central Piccadilly tube station where I took a one-stop ticket, went down on the escalator, and then *ran up the same steps in the wrong direction.* It was quite easy to reach the top, and our elder brother Christmas was wrong to warn it would be impossible to me. Naturally, the ticket official had his word to say, but I explained it was my promise to my brother Christmas and my sister Peach ever since in our childhood, and he yielded up.

'You boys are all the same,' he said.

'What does that mean, mister?'

'Mad as March hares, if you ask me.'

He looked so sad when he said it, that how could I take offence? 'Maybe you right,' I told him. 'We like living out our lives.'

'And we like peace and quiet. Run along, son,' this official told me.

Not a bad man really, I suppose, so after a smile at him I climbed up towards the free outer air. For I had this morning to keep my appointment at the Colonial Department Welfare Office to hear what plans have been arranged there for the pursuit of my further studies.

In the Circus overhead I looked round more closely at my new city. And I must say at first it was a bad disappointment: so small, poky, dirty, not magnificent! Red buses, like shown to us on the cinema, certainly, and greater scurrying of the population than at home. But people with glum clothes and shut-in faces. Of course, I have not seen yet the Parliament Houses, or many historic palaces, or where Dad lived in Maida Vale when he was here thirty years ago before he met our Mum. . . .

And that also is to be one of my first occupations: to visit this house of his to see if I can recover any news of his former landlady —if dead, or alive, or in what other circumstances. Because my Dad, at the party on the night I sailed right out of Lagos, he took me on one side and said, 'Macdonald,' (he never calls me John or Johnny—always Macdonald) 'Macdonald, you're a man now. You're eighteen.'

'Yes, Dad . . .' I said, wondering what.

'You're a man enough to share a man's secret with your father?'

'If you want to share one with me, Dad.'

'Well, listen, son. You know I went to England as a boy, just like you're doing. . . .'

'Yes, Dad, of course I do. . . .'

'And I had a young landlady there who was very kind and good to me, unusually so for white ladies in those days. So I'd like you to go and get news of her for me if you ever can, because we've never corresponded all these many years.'

'I'll get it for you, Dad, of course.'

Then my Dad lowered his voice and both his eyes.

'But your mother, Macdonald. I don't very much want your mother to know. It was a long while ago that I met this lady out in Maida Vale.'

Here Dad gave me an equal look like he'd never given me in his life before.

'I respect your mother, you understand me, son,' he said.

'I know you do, Dad, and so do Christmas and Peach and me.'

'We all love her, and for that I'd like you to send me the news not here but to my office in a way that she won't know or be disturbed by.'

'I understand, Dad,' I told him. 'I shall be most discreet in my letters about anything I may hear of your past in England when a very young man.'

'Then let's have a drink on that, Macdonald, son,' he said.

So we drank whisky to my year of studying here in England.

'And mind you work hard,' Dad told me. 'We've found two hundred pounds to send you there, and when you return we want you to be thoroughly an expert in meteorology.'

'I will be it, Dad,' I promised.

'Of course, I know you'll drink, have fun with girls, and gamble, like I did myself. . . . But mind you don't do these enjoyments too excessively.'

'No, Dad, no.'

'If your money all gets spent, we can't send out any more for you. You'd have to find your own way home by working on a ship.'

'I'll be reasonable, Dad. I'm not a child. You trust me.'

And afterwards, it was Peach clustering over me with too much kisses and foolish demands for gowns and hats and underclothes from London, to impress her chorus of surrounding giggling girls. I told her all these things were to be bought much cheaper there in Lagos.

And to my brother Christmas, I said, 'Oh, Christmas, why don't you come with me too? I admire your ambition, but surely to see the world and study before fixing your nose to the Lands Office grindstone would be more to your pleasure and advantage?'

'I want to get married quickly, Johnny, as you know,' my serious elder brother said. 'For that I must save, not spend.'

'Well, each man to his own idea of himself,' I told him.

And my mother! Would you believe it, she'd guessed that some secret talk had passed between Dad and me that evening? In her eyes I could see it, but she said nothing special to me except to fondle me like a child in front of all the guests, though not shedding any tears.

And when they all accompanied us to the waterfront, dancing, singing and beating drums, suddenly, as the ship came into view, she stopped and seized me and lifted me up, though quite a grown man now, and carried me as far as the gangway of the boat upon her shoulders.

'Write to me, Johnny,' she said. 'Good news or bad, keep writing.'

Then was more farewell drinking and dancing on the ship until, when visitors had to leave, I saw that my Mum had taken away my jacket (though leaving its valuable contents behind with me, of course). And she stood hugging it to her body on the quay as that big boat pulled out into the Gulf of Guinea sea.

3

The meeting of Jumble and Spade

PRIMED BY MY BRIEF STUDY of the welfare dossiers, I awaited, in my office, the arrival of the first colonials. With some trepidation; because for one who, like myself, has always felt great need of sober counsel, to offer it to others—and to strangers, and to such exotic strangers—seemed intimidating. Perhaps I should add, too, that I'm not quite so old as I think I look: only twenty-six, Heaven be praised; and certainly not so self-assured as my dry, drained, rarely perturbable countenance might suggest.

Picture my mild alarm, then, when there was a first polite knock upon my door. Opening it, I beheld a handsomely ugly face, animal and engaging, with beetling brow, squashed nose and full and generous lips, surmounted by a thatch of thick curly hair cut to a high rising peak in front: a face wearing (it seemed to me) a sly, morose, secretive look, until suddenly its mouth split open into a candid ivory and coral smile.

'I'm Fortune,' said this creature, beaming as though his name was his very nature. 'Johnny Macdonald, Christian names, out of Lagos, checking to see what classes in meteorology you've fixed for me.'

'My name is Pew—Montgomery. Please do come over to these rather less uncomfortable leather chairs.'

I observed that he was attired in a white crocheted sweater with two crimson horizontal stripes, and with gold safety-pins stuck on the tips of each point of the emerging collar of a nylon shirt; in a sky-blue gaberdine jacket zipped down the front; and in even lighter blue linen slacks, full at the hips, tapering to the ankle, and falling delicately one half-inch above a pair of pale brown plaited casual shoes.

'Your curriculum,' I said, handing him a drab buff envelope, 'is outlined here. You begin next week, but it would be well to register within the next few days. Meanwhile I trust you're satisfied with your accommodation at the hostel?'

'Man, you should ask!'

'I beg your pardon?'

He gave me a repeat performance of the grin. 'It's like back in mission school at home. I shall make every haste to leave it as soon as I find myself a room.'

'In that case,' I said, departmentally severe, 'the rent would be appreciably higher.'

'I have loot—I can afford,' he told me. 'Have *you* ever lived inside that hostel, you yourself?'

'No.'

'Well, then!'

The interview was not taking the turn I thought appropriate. Equality between races—yes! But not between officials and the public.

'I should perhaps warn you at this juncture,' I informed him, 'that to secure outside accommodation sometimes presents certain difficulties.'

'You mean for an African to get a room?'

'Yes. . . . We have however here a list of amiable landladies. . . .'

'Why should it be difficult for an African to get a room?'

'There is, unfortunately, in certain cases, prejudice.'

'They fear we dirty the sheets with our dark skins?'

'Not precisely.'

'Then what? In Lagos, anyone will let *you* a room if you have good manners, and the necessary loot. . . .'

'It's kind of them, and I don't doubt your word. Here in England, though, some landladies have had unfortunate experiences.'

'Such as . . ?'

'Well, for one thing—noise.'

'It's true we are not mice.'

'And introducing *friends*. . . .'

'Why not?'

'I mean to sleep—to live. Landladies don't wish three tenants for the price of one.'

'So long as the room is paid, what does it matter?'

'Ah—paid. Failure to pay is another chief complaint.'

'Don't Jumbles never skip their rent as well as Spades?'

'I *beg* your pardon once again?'

'Don't Jumbles ...'

'Jumbles?'

'You're a Jumble, man.'

'I?'

'Yes. That's what we call you. You don't mind?'

'I hope I don't.... It's not, I trust, an impolite expression?'

'You mean like nigger?'

I rose up.

'Now, please! This is the Colonial Department Welfare Office. That word is absolutely forbidden within these walls.'

'It should be outside them, too.'

'No doubt. I too deplore its use.'

'Well, relax, please, Mr Pew. And don't be so scared of Jumble. It's cheeky, perhaps, but not so very insulting.'

'May I enquire how it is spelt?'

'J-o-h-n-b-u-l-l.'

'Ah! But pronounced as you pronounce it?'

'Yes: Jumble.'

It struck me the ancient symbol, thus distorted, was strangely appropriate to the confusion of my mind.

'I see. And ...' (I hesitated) '... Spade?'

'Is us.'

'And that is not an objectionable term?'

'Is cheeky, too, of course, but not offending. In Lagos, on the waterfront, the boys sometimes called me the Ace of Spades.'

'Ah ...'

He offered me, from an American pack, an extravagantly long fag.

'Let's not us worry, Mr Pew,' he said, 'about bad names. My Dad has taught me that in England some foolish man may call me sambo, darkie, boot or munt or nigger, even. Well, if he does—my fists!' (He clenched them: they were like knees.) 'Or,' he went on, 'as Dad would say, "First try rebuke by tongue, then fists".'

'Well, Mr Fortune,' I said to him, when he had at last unclenched them to rehitch the knife edge of his blue linen tapering slacks, 'I think with one of these good women on our list you'll have no trouble....'

'If I take lodgings, mister,' he replied, 'they must be Liberty Hall.

No questions from the landlady, please. And me, when I give my rent, I'll have the politeness not to ask her what she spends it on.'

'That, my dear fellow, even for an Englishman, is *very* difficult to find in our sad country.'

'I'll find it.' He beetled at me, then, leaning forward, said, 'And do you know why I think your landladies are scared of us?'

'I can but imagine . . .'

'Because of any brown babies that might appear.'

'In the nature of things,' I said, 'that may indeed well be.'

'An arrival of white babies they can somehow explain away. But if their daughter has a brown one, then neighbouring fingers all start pointing.'

I silently shook my head.

'But why,' he cried, 'why not box up together, Jumble and Spade, like we let your folk do back home?'

I rose once more.

'Really, Mr Fortune. You cannot expect me to discuss these complex problems. I am—consider—an official.'

'Oh, yes. . . . You have to earn your money, I suppose.

I found this, of course, offensive. And moving with dignity to my desk, I took up the Warning Folder of People and Places to Avoid.

'Another little duty for which I'm *paid*,' I said to him, 'is to warn our newcomers against . . . well, to be frank, bad elements among their fellow countrymen.'

'Oh, yes, man. Shoot.'

'And,' I continued, looking at my list, 'particularly against visiting the Moorhen public house, the Cosmopolitan dance hall, or the Moonbeam club.'

'Just say those names again.

To my horror, I saw he was jotting them on the back page of his passport.

'To visit these places,' I went on, reading aloud from the mimeographed sheet I held, 'has been, for many, the first step that leads to the shadow of the police courts.'

'Why? What goes in in them?'

I didn't, perhaps fortunately, yet know. 'I'm not at liberty to divulge it,' I replied.

'Ah well . . .'

He pocketed his passport, and took me by the hand.

'Have you any further questions?' I enquired.

'Yes, Mr Pew. Excuse my familiar asking: but where can I get a shirt like that?'

'Like this?'

'Yes. It's hep. Jumble style, but hep.

He reached out a long, long hand and fingered it.

'In Jermyn Street,' I said with some self-satisfaction, but asperity.

'Number?'

I told him.

'Thanks so very much,' said Johnny Macdonald Fortune. 'And now I must be on my way to Maida Vale.'

I watched him go out with an unexpected pang. And moving to the window, soon saw him walk across the courtyard and stop for a moment speaking to some others there. In the sunlight, his nylon shirt shone all the whiter against the smooth brown of his skin. His frame, from this distance, seemed shorter than it was, because of his broad shoulders—flat, though composed of two mounds of muscle arching from his spine. His buttocks sprang optimistically high up from the small of his back, and his long legs—a little bandy and with something of a backward curve—were supported by two very effective splayed-out feet; on which, just now, as he spoke, gesticulating too, he was executing a tracery of tentative dance steps to some soft inaudible music.

4

A pilgrimage to Maida Vale

THIS MAIDA VALE is noteworthy for all the buildings looking similar and making the search for Dad's old lodging-house so more difficult. But by careful enquiry and eliminations, I hit on one house in Nightingale Road all crumbling down and dirty as being the most probable, and as there was no bell or lock and the door open, I walked right in and called up the stairs, 'Is Mrs Hancock there?' but getting no reply, climbed further to the next floor. There was a brown door facing me, so I drummed on it, when immediately it opened and a Jumble lady stood there to confront me: wrung out like a dish-rag, with her body everywhere collapsing, and when she saw me a red flush of fury on her face.

'Get out! I don't want your kind here.'

'I have to speak to Mrs Hancock.'

At these words of mine her colour changed to white like a coconut you bite into.

'Hancock!' she called out. 'My name's Macpherson. Why do you call me Hancock?'

'I don't, lady,' I told her. 'I merely say I wanted to speak to a lady of that name.'

'Why?'

'To bring her my Dad's greetings—Mr David Macdonald Fortune out of Lagos, Nigeria. I'm his son Johnny.'

By the way she eyed me, peering at me, measuring me from top to toes, I was sure now this *was* the lady of Dad's story. And I can't say, at that moment, I quite admired my Dad in his own choice. Though naturally it was years ago when possibly this woman was in better preservation.

Then she said: 'You've brought nothing ever to me but misery and disgrace.'

'But lady, you and I've not met before.'

'Your father, then. Your race.'

'So you *are* Mrs Hancock, please?'

'I used to be.'

'Well, I bring my Dad's greetings to you. He asks you please for news.'

'His *greetings*,' she said, twisting up her mouth into a mess. 'His greetings—is that all?'

I was giving her all this time my biggest smile, and I saw its effect began to melt her just a little. (When I smile at a woman, I relax all my body and seem eager.)

'Your father's a bad man,' she said.

'Oh, no!'

'You look like him, though. He might have spat you out.'

'I should look like him, Mrs Macpherson. I'm legitimate, I hope.'

This didn't please her a bit. She stared white-red at me again till I thought she'd strike me, and I got ready to duck or, if need be, slap back.

'So you've heard!' she shouted out. 'Then why's your father never done anything for Arthur?'

'Arthur, lady?'

'For your brother, if you want to know. Your elder brother.'

Clearly she didn't mean my brother Christmas. Then who? I began to realize.

'I've got a half-brother called Arthur, then?' I said, trying to act as if I felt delighted. 'Well! Can't I meet him?'

'No!'

'Oh, no!'

'No! You certainly can not.'

At this very moment, there glided up beside her a little Jumble girl, quite pretty, seventeen or so I'd say, who I noticed had a glove on one hand only.

'Don't shout, Mother,' she said. 'You'd better ask him in.'

'Oh, very well,' this Mrs Macpherson said, coming over all weary and looking even ten years older.

Their room was quite tidy, with assorted furniture, but poor. I do *hate* poor rooms.

'I suppose I'd better go and make some tea,' the old lady told us both.

(These Jumbles and their tea in every crisis!)

The little girl held out her hand—the hand that didn't wear the glove. 'I'm Muriel,' she said. 'I'm Arthur's sister, and Mum's second daughter.'

'But Miss Muriel,' I said to her, 'I can guess by your skin's complexion that you're not Arthur's true sister.'

'I'm his half-sister, Mr Fortune. Me and my sister Dorothy are Macphersons, Mum's proper children after she got married.'

'And your father?'

'Dad's dead. They caught him in the war.'

'I'm sorry . . .'

'Arthur, you see . . .' (she looked modest as she spoke, though I wasn't sure if it was felt or acted) '. . . Arthur was Mum's mistake before she met our Dad.'

'And Arthur: where is he?'

'In jail.'

'Ah!'

'He's always in and out of jail.'

'Oh. For what?'

'Thieving and suchlike.'

She stood and fiddled with the table-cloth frillings, then said to me: 'And didn't *your* father know about Arthur, and all the trouble Mum's had with him for more than twenty years?'

'I'm sure he didn't.'

But I began to wonder.

After a polite and careful pause, I said, 'Then Muriel, you and me are almost relatives, I'd say. We're half-half-brother and sister, or something of that kind.'

She laughed at this. 'We're not real relations, Johnny. But Arthur is a link between us, I suppose. . . .' Then she looked up at me and said, 'But do be careful what you say to Mother. She hates all coloured people now.'

'On account of my Dad and Arthur?'

'Not only that. There's Dorothy—my elder sister, Dorothy.'

'Yes?'

'She lives with a coloured boy. He's taken her away.'

'To marry?'

'No. . . . He's a Gambian.'

'Oh, those Gambians! Nigerians, of course, are friendly folks, and

Gold Coast boys respectable often, too. But Gambians! Don't judge us, please, by them. . . .'

'This one's a devil, anyway,' she told me. 'Billy Whispers is his name, and he's bad, bad, a thoroughly bad man.'

And now the old lady she came shuffling back. It was clear that she'd been thinking, and maybe refreshing herself a bit as well.

'Is your Dad rich?' she said at once.

'He's reasonably loaded.'

'In business now?'

'Export and import—he has his ups and downs.'

She stood right in front of me, nose to chest.

'Well, in return for his *greetings*, will you ask him please to make me some small return for his running away and leaving me to rear his son?'

'I could write to him, Mrs Macpherson. . . .'

'Can you imagine what it was to rear a coloured child in London twenty years ago? Can you imagine what it's like for an English girl to marry when she's got' (I saw it coming) 'a bastard nigger child?'

I made no reply whatever.

'Mother!' cried Muriel. 'That's no way to talk.'

'He'd best know what I think! I could have done better than your father, Muriel, if it hadn't been for that.'

'Mother!'

'And your sister Dorothy's going the same way.'

'Oh, Mother!'

'I was a pretty girl when I was young. . . . I could have been rich and happy. . . .'

And here—as I could see must happen—the lady broke down into her tears. I understood the way she felt, indeed I did, yet why do these women always blame the man? I'm sure Dad didn't rape her, and however young she was, she must have known a number of the facts of life. . . .

Little Muriel was easing her off into a bedroom. When she came out again, I said to her, 'Well, perhaps I should go away just now, Muriel. I'll write to my Dad much as your Mum requests. . . .'

'Stay and drink up your tea, Johnny.'

We sat there sipping on the dregs, till I said, 'What do you do for a living, Muriel?'

'I work in a tailor's, Johnny. East End, they're Jews. Cutting up shirts. . . .'

'You like that occupation?'

'No. . . . But it helps out.'

'Don't you have fun sometimes? Go dancing?'

'Not often. . . .'

And here I saw she looked down at her hand.

'You hurt yourself?' I said.

She looked up and shook her head.

'We must go out together one day, if you like to come with me,' I said to her.

She smiled.

'Next Saturday, say? Before I start out on my studies?'

She shook her head once more.

'Now listen, Muriel. *You've* got no colour prejudice, I hope. . . .'

'No, no, Johnny. Not at all. But you'd be dull with me. I don't dance, you see.'

'Don't dance? Is there *any* little girl don't dance? Well, I will teach you.'

'Yes?'

'Of course I will, Muriel. I'll teach you the basic foundations in one evening. Real bop steps, and jive, and all.'

Here she surprised me, this shy rather skinny little chick, by reaching out quite easily and giving me a full kiss on the cheek.

'Johnny,' she said. 'There's one thing you could do for me. . . . Which is to get me news of my sister Dorothy. Because she hasn't been here or written for over a month, and I don't like to go out and see her south side of the Thames in Brixton, on account of that Billy Whispers.'

'Just give me the address, and I'll go see.'

'It's a house full of coloured men and English girls.'

'Just give me the address, will you, Muriel, and I'll go out that way immediately. I want to get to know the various areas of this city, if it's going to be my own.'

5

Encounter with Billy Whispers

THIS BRIXTON HOUSE stood all by itself among ruins of what I suppose was wartime damages, much like one tooth left sticking in an old man's jaw.

Now what was curious to me was this. As I approached it, I could clearly see persons standing by the upper windows, and even hear voices and the sound of a radiogram. But when I knocked on the front door of it, no one came down however long I continued on. So I walked all round this building and looked over the very broken garden wall.

There I saw a quite surprising sight: which was a tall Spade—very tall—standing in a broken greenhouse, watering plants. Now Spades do garden—it wasn't that—but not ones dressed up like he was, fit to kill: pink slacks, tartan silk outside-hanging shirt, all freshly pressed and laundered.

'What say, man?' I called out to him. 'Do you know Billy Whispers?'

Here he spun round.

'Who you?'

'Fortune from Lagos, mister. A friend of Mr Whispers' lady's family.'

As this man came out of the greenhouse, wiping his hands, I saw by the weaving, sliding way he walked towards me that he was a boxer. Round about his neck he wore a silver chain, another on each wrist, and his face had a 'better be careful or I slap you down' expression.

I waited smiling for him.

'Mr Whispers,' he said, 'is not at home to strangers.'

'His lady is?'

'What's she mean to you?'

'I have a message for her.'

At this I vaulted, like in gymnasium, over the wall, and went leisurely across to meet him.

'Haven't I seen,' I said to him, 'your photo in the newspapers?'

Now he looked proud and pleased, and said to me, 'I'm Jimmy Cannibal.'

'I thought you was. Light-heavy champion till they stole your legitimate title just a year ago?' (But as is well known, this Jimmy Cannibal lost it on a foul.)

'That's me.'

'You growing tomatoes?' I asked him, pointing to his greenhouse.

But he looked fierce again and shook his head.

'What, then?' and I started over.

He gripped me by my shoulder and spun me round. But not before I'd seen what plant it was in flower-pots inside there.

'Keep your nose out, Mr Nigeria,' he said.

So strong was he, I saw I'd better fight him with my brains.

'It's smoking weed,' I said. 'You give me some perhaps?'

'You blow your top too much, Mr Stranger.'

We stood there on the very edge of combat. But just then I heard a window scraping and, looking up, I saw a face there staring down at us: a mask of ebony, it seemed to me from there. This face talked to Jimmy Cannibal in some Gambian tongue, and then said to me, 'You may come up.'

As we both climbed the stairs (this Cannibal behind me breathing hot upon my neck), I got the feeling of every room was occupied by hearing voices, men's and women's, and sometimes the click of dice.

On a landing Cannibal edged past me, put his head round the door, then waved me in. He didn't come inside himself, but stood out there on the landing, lurking.

This Billy Whispers was a short man with broad shoulders and longer arms than even is usual with us. Elegantly dressed but quite respectable, as if on Sundays, and with a cool, cold face that gazed at me without fear or favour.

'You come inside?' he said. 'Or do you prefer to stand there encouraging draughts?'

'I'm Fortune,' I said, 'from Lagos.'

'I know a lot of Lagos boys.'

'You're Gambian, they tell me. Bathurst?'

He nodded at me and said, 'My friend was telling me of your interest in my greenhouse.'

'I saw you grew charge out there . . .'

'You want to smoke some?'

'Well, I don't mind. I used up all I had on the trip over. . . .'

'I'll roll you a stick,' this Billy Whispers said.

I sat on the bed, feeling pleased at the chance of blowing hay once more. For much as I care for alcoholic drinks of many kinds, my greatest enjoyment, ever since when a boy, is in charging with weed. Because without it, however good I feel, I'm never really on the top of my inspiration.

Meanwhile this Billy took out two cigarette-papers, and joined them together by the tongue. He peeled and broke down a piece of the ordinary fag he held between his lips, and then, from a brown-paper pack in a jar above the fireplace (a large pack, I noticed), he sprinkled a generous dose of the weed in the papers and began rolling and licking, easing the two ends of the stick into position with a match.

'But tell me,' I said, 'if it's not enquiring. You didn't grow all that hemp you have from outside in your greenhouse?'

'No, no. Is an experiment I'm making, to grow it myself from seed.'

'Otherwise you buy it?'

He nodded.

'You can get that stuff easy here?'

'It can be got. . . . Most things can be got in London when you know your way around.'

He gave the weed a final tender lick and roll, and handed it me by the thin inhaling end.

'And the Law,' I said. 'What do they have to say about consuming weed?'

'What they say is fifteen- or twenty-pound fine if you're caught. Jail on the second occasion.'

'Man! Why, these Jumbles have no pity!'

At which I lit up, took a deep drag, well down past the throat, holding the smoke in my lungs with little sharp sniffs to stop the valuable gust escaping. When I blew out, after a heavy interval, I said to him, 'Good stuff. And what do they make you pay for a stick here?'

'Retail, in small sticks, half a crown.'

'And wholesale?'

'Wholesale? For that you have to find your own supplier and make your personal arrangement.'

I took one more deep drag.

'You know such a supplier?' I enquired.

'Of course. . . . I know of several. . . .'

'You don't deal in this stuff personal, by any possible chance?'

Here Billy Whispers joined his two hands, wearing on each one a big coloured jewel.

'Mister,' he said, 'I think these are questions that you don't ask on so early an acquaintance.'

Which was true, so I smiled at him and handed him over the weed for his turn to take his drag on it.

He did this, and after some time in silence he blew on the smouldering end of the weed and said to me, 'And what is it, Fortune, I can do for you here?'

'I'm Dorothy's half-half-brother.'

'What say?'

'Arthur, her brother, is my brother too.' And I explained.

'But Dorothy she not know you,' he said to me. 'Never she's spoken to me about you.'

Then I explained some more.

'If that old lady or her sister's worried about Dorothy,' he said at last, 'just tell them to stop worrying because she's happy here with me, and will do just what I tell her.'

'Could I speak with her, perhaps?'

'No, man. You could not.'

At this state of our interview, the door was opened and into the room came a short little fattish boy, all smiles and gesticulation, of a type that beats my time: that is, the Spade who's always acting Spadish, so as to make the Jumbles think we're more cool crazy than we are, but usually for some darker purpose to deceive them. But why play this game of his with me?

'Hullo, hullo, man,' he cried to me, grasping at both my hands. 'I ain't seen you around before. . . . Shake hands with me, my name is Mr Ronson Lighter.' And he let off his silly sambo laugh.

I said, 'What say?' unsmilingly, and freed my hands. 'What say,

Mr Ronson Lighter. Did your own mother give you that peculiar name?'

He giggled like a crazy girl.

'No, no, no, mister, is my London name, on account of my well-known strong desire to own these things.'

And out of each side coat pocket he took a lighter, and sparkled the pair of them underneath my eyes.

Still not smiling, I got up on my feet.

And as I did—smack! Up in my head I got a very powerful kick from that hot weed which I'd been smoking. A kick like you get from superior Congo stuff, that takes your brain and wraps it up and throws it all away, and yet leaves your thoughts inside it sharp and clear: that makes all your legs and arms and body seem like if jet propelled without any tiring effort whatsoever.

But I watched these two, Billy Whispers and this Mr Ronson Lighter, as they talked in their barbarian Gambian language. I didn't understand no word, but sometimes I heard the name of 'Dorothy.'

So I broke in.

'I'd like to speak to her, Billy, just a moment, if you really wouldn't mind.'

They both looked up, and this Mr Ronson Lighter came dancing across and laid his hand upon my head.

'Mister,' he said, 'that's a real Bushman hair-style that you've got. Right out of the Africa jungle.'

'You got any suggestions for improving it?' I said, not moving much.

'Why, yes. Why don't you have it beautifully cut like mine?'

His own was brushed flat and low across his forehead, sticking out far in front of his eyes as if it was a cap that he had on.

'I'll tell you of my own personal hairdresser,' he said. 'The only man in town who cuts our fine hair quite properly. He'll take off your Bushman's head-dress,' and he messed up my hair again.

'But possibly *your* hair's so elegant because you wear a wig,' I said to him. And taking two handfuls of his hair, I lifted him one foot off the floor.

He yelled, and in came Jimmy Cannibal, making a sandwich of me between the two of them.

'Mr Whispers,' I said, easing out as best I could, 'I don't like familiarity from strangers. Can you tell that, please, to these two countrymen of yours?'

Billy was smiling for the first time. He had some broad gaps between all his short teeth, I saw, and pale blue gums.

I was planning perhaps to leap out through the window when the door opened yet once more, and there stood a girl that by her body's shape and looks was quite likely to be Muriel's sister. But what a difference from the little chick! Smart clothes—or what she thought was smart—bleached hair, and a look on her face like a bar-fly seeking everywhere hard for trade.

'What's all the commotion?' she enquired.

'Get out to work, Dorothy,' said Billy Whispers.

'Oh, I'm going, Billy.'

'Then move.'

She leaned on one hip, and held out her crimson hand.

'I want a taxi fare,' she said. 'And money to buy some you-know-whats.'

Whispers threw her a folded note and said, 'Now go.'

Still she stood looking what she thought was glamorous, and it's true that, in a way, it was. And me still between these two body-guards, both of them waiting to eliminate me.

'You're a nice boy,' she said to me. 'Where you from—Gambia too?'

Billy got up, strolled over and slapped her. She screamed out louder than the blow was worth, and he slapped her again harder, so she stopped. 'Now go,' he said to her again. 'And see that your evening's profitable.'

She disappeared out with a high-heel clatter. I slipped away from among the two bad boys and took Mr Billy by the arm.

'Billy Whispers,' I said, 'do you want a scene with me too here in your bedroom?'

He looked at my eyes and through beyond them, adding up, I suppose, what damage I'd do to any life, limb or furniture, before I was myself destroyed.

'Is not necessary,' he said, 'unless you think it is.

'By nature I'm peaceable. I like my life.'

'Then shoot off, Mr Fortune, now. . . .'

The two started muttering and limbering, but he frowned at them only, and they heaved away from me.

'Goodbye, Mr Whispers,' I said. 'I dare say we'll meet soon once again, when I'll offer you some hospitality of mine at that future time.'

'Is always possible, man,' he answered, 'that you and I might cross our paths some more in this big city.'

6

Montgomery sallies forth

MY FLAT (two odd rooms and a 'kitchenette', most miscellaneously furnished) is perched on the top floor of a high, narrow house near Regent's Park with a view on the Zoological Gardens, so that lions, or seals, it may be, awake me sometimes in the dawn. Beneath me are echoing layers of floor and corridors, empty now except for Theodora Pace.

When the house used to be filled with tenants, I rarely spoke to Theodora. Such a rude, hard, determined girl, packed with ability and innocent of charm, repelled me: so clearly was she my superior in the struggle for life, so plainly did she let me see she knew it. She made it so cruelly clear she thought the world would not have been in any way a different place if I had not been born.

But circumstances threw us together.

A year ago, the property changed hands, and notices to quit were served on all the tenants. All flew to their lawyers, who thought, but weren't quite sure (they never are, until the court gives judgment), that the Rent Acts protected us. A cold war began. The new landlord refused to accept our rents, some tenants lost heart and departed, and others removed themselves, enriched by sumptuous bribes. When only Theodora and I remained, the landlords sued us for trespass. We prepared for battle but, before the case came into court, the landlords withdrew the charge, paid costs, left us like twin birds in an abandoned dovecote, and sat waiting, I suppose, in their fur-lined Mayfair offices, for our deaths—or for some gross indiscretion by which they could eject us.

Throughout this crisis, Theodora behaved with Roman resolution. Uncertain how to manœuvre against anyone so powerful as a landlord, I clung steadfastly to her chariot wheels, and she dragged me with her to victory. Small wonder that the B.B.C. should pay so talented a woman a large salary for doing I never could discover what.

Thenceforth, Theodora became my counsellor: sternly offering me advice in the manner always of one casting precious pearls before some pig. (Her advice was so useful that I overcame a strong inclination to insult her.) It was through Theodora, as a matter of fact, that I'd got the job in the Colonial Department.

So on the evening of my first encounter with Johnny Fortune, I returned to my eyrie, washed off the pretences of the Welfare Office in cool water, and went down to knock on Theodora's door. She shouted, 'Come in,' but went on typing for several minutes before raising her rimless eyes and saying, 'Well? How did it go? Are you going to hold down the job this time?'

'I don't see why not, Theodora. . . .'

'It's pretty well your last chance. If you don't make good there, you'd better emigrate.'

'Don't turn the knife in the wound. I know I was a failure at the British Council, but I did quite well there before the unfortunate happening.'

'You were never the British Council type.'

'Perhaps, after all, that's just as well.'

'And until you learn to control yourself in such matters as drink, sex and extravagance, you'll never get yourself anywhere.'

'I'm learning fast, Theodora. Be merciful.'

'Let's hope so. Would you care for a gin?'

Though she'd rebuke me for tippling, Theodora was herself a considerable boozer. But liquor only made her mind more diamond sharp.

'Cheerio. What you need, Montgomery, is a wife.'

'So you have often told me.'

'You should look around.'

'I shall.'

'Meanwhile, what is it you have to *do* in that place?'

I told her about the Welfare dossiers.

'It all sounds a lot of nonsense to me,' she said, 'though I dare say it's worth twelve pounds a week for them to keep you. The chief thing for you to remember, though, is that it's just a job like any other, so don't get involved in politics, race problems, and such inessentials.'

'No.'

'To do a job well, and get on, you must never become involved in it emotionally.'

'Theodora, do tell me! What *is* it you do yourself within the B.B.C.?'

'You wouldn't understand,' she said, 'even if I told you.'

I looked round at the bookshelves, packed to the ceiling with the kind of volume that would make this library, in thirty years' time, a vintage period piece.

'I thought,' I said, 'I might go down and investigate that hostel this evening.'

'Why? Is it your business?'

'To tell you the whole truth, I'm not sure what my business is. My predecessor hadn't the time or inclination to tell me much, and my chief's away on holiday for another week. It's an awkward time for me to take over.'

'Then leave well alone. Just do the obvious things till he gets back.'

'But I've heard such complaints about our hostel. One student in particular, called Fortune, said it's quite dreadful there.'

'It probably is. All hostels are. They're meant to be.'

She started typing again.

'I'll leave you then, Theodora.'

'Very well. And do learn to use your time and get on with a bit of work. Your biography of John Knox—how many words have you written this last month?'

'Very few. I'm beginning to dislike my hero so much he's even losing his horrid fascination.'

'Persevere.'

'I shall. May I have another gin?'

'You can take the bottle with you, if you can't resist it.'

'Thank you. And what are *you* writing, Theodora?'

'A report.'

'Might I ask on what?'

'You may, but I shan't tell you.'

'Good evening, then.'

I went upstairs sadly, and changed into my suit of Barcelona blue: a dazzling affair that makes me look like an Ealing Studio gangster, and which I'd ordered when drunk in that grim city, thereby, thank goodness, abbreviating my holiday in it by one week. As I drank heavily into Theodora's gin, the notion came to me that *I* should visit these haunts against which it was my duty to warn others: the Moorhen, the Cosmopolitan dance hall, and perhaps the Moonbeam club. But first of all, I decided, adjusting the knot of my vulgarest bow tie (for I like to mix Jermyn Street, when I can afford it, with the Mile End Road), it was a more imperative duty to inspect the Welfare hostel. So down I went by the abandoned stairs and corridors, and hailed a taxi just outside the Zoo.

It carried me across two dark green parks to that S.W.1 region of our city which, since its wartime occupation by soldiers' messes and dubious embassies, has never yet recovered its dull dignity. Outside an ill-lit peeling portico the taxi halted, and I alighted to the strains of a faint calypso:

'I can't wait eternally
For my just race equality.
If Mr England voter don't toe the line,
Then maybe I will seek some other new combine'

somebody was ungratefully singing to the twang of a guitar.

I gazed up, and saw dark forms, in white singlets, hanging comfortably out of windows: surely *not* what the architect had intended.

I walked in.

There I was met by three men of a type as yet new to me: bespectacled, their curly hair parted by an effort on one side, wearing tweed suits of a debased gentlemanly cut, and hideous university ties. (*Why* do so many universities favour purple?) They carried menacing-looking volumes.

'Can I be of assistance to you?' said one to me.

'I should like to speak to the warden.'

'Warden? There is no such person here by nights.'

'We control the hostel ourselves, sir, by committee,' said another. 'I, as a matter of fact, am the present secretary.'

And he looked it.

'Oh,' I said, 'is Mr Fortune possibly in? A Lagos gentleman.'

'You could find that for yourself, sir, also his room number, by consulting the tenancy agenda on the public information board.'

He pointed a large helpful finger at some baize in the recess of the dark hall. I gave him a cold official smile, ignored the baize board, and walked upstairs to examine the common rooms and empty cubicles.

This Colonial Department hostel smelt high, I soon decided, with the odour of good intentions. The communal rooms were like those on ships—to be drifted in and out of, then abandoned. The bedrooms (cubicles!), of which I inspected one or two, though lacking no necessary piece of furniture, yet had the 'furnished' look of a domestic interior exhibited in a shop window. And over the whole building there hung an aura of pared Welfare budgets, of tact restraining antipathies, and of a late attempt to right centuries of still unadmitted wrongs.

And all this time the nasal calypso permeated the lino-laden passages. As I approached the bright light from a distant open door, I heard:

> 'English politician he say, "Wait and see,"
> Moscow politician he say, "Come with me."
> But whichever white employer tells those little white lies,
> I stop my ears and hold my nose and close my eyes.'

I peered in.

Sitting on the bed, dressed in a pair of underpants decorated with palm leaves, was a stocky youth topped by an immense gollywog fuzz of hair. He grimaced pleasantly at me, humming the air till he had completed the guitar improvisation. Whereupon he slapped the instrument (as one might a child's behind) and said, 'What say, man? You like a glass of rum?'

'I'm looking,' I told him, 'for Mr J. M. Fortune.'

'Oh, that little jungle cannibal. That bongo-banging Bushman.'

'I take it,' I said, accepting some rum in a discoloured tooth-glass, 'that you yourself are not from Africa?'

'Please be to God, no, man. I'm a civilized respectable Trinidadian.'

'The Africans, then, aren't civilized?'

'They have their own tribal customs, mister, but it was because of their primitive barbarity that our ancestors fled from that country some centuries ago.'

This was accompanied by a knowing leer.

'And the song,' I asked. 'It is of your own composition?'

'Yes, man. In my island I'm noted for my celebrated performance. It's your pleasure to meet this evening no less a one than Mr Lord Alexander in person.'

And he held out a ring-encrusted hand with an immensely long, polished, little-finger nail.

'Perhaps, though,' he went on, 'as I'm seeking to make my way in *this* country, you could help me into radio or television or into some well-loaded night-spot?'

'Alas!' I told him, 'I have no contacts in those glowing worlds.'

'Then at least please speak well of me,' he said, 'and make my reputation known among your friends.'

'Willingly. Though I have to tell you that I don't care for calypso. . . .'

'Man, that's not possible!' He stood up in his flowered pants aghast. 'Surely all educated Englishmen like our scintillating music?'

'Many, yes, but not I.'

'Now, why?'

'Your lines don't scan, you accentuate the words incorrectly, and the thoughts you express are meagre and without wit.'

'But our leg-inspiring rhythm?'

'Oh, that you have, of course. . . .'

'Mr Gentleman, you disappoint me,' he said. And taking a deep draught from the rum bottle, he strolled sadly to the window, leaned out, and sang into the opulent wastes of S.W.1:

> 'This English gentleman he say to me
> He do not appreciate calypso melody.
> But I answer that calypso has supremacy
> To the Light Programme music of the B.B.C.

I made my getaway.

Prying along an adjacent marble landing (affording a vertiginous perspective of a downward-winding statue-flanked white stair), I saw a door on which was written: 'J. Macdonald Fortune, Lagos. Enter without knocking.' I did so, turned on the light, and saw a scene of agreeable confusion. Valises up-ended disgorging the bright clothes one would so wish to wear, shirts, ties and socks predominating—*none* of them fit for an English afternoon. Bundles of coconuts.

A thick stick of bananas. Bottles, half empty. Rather surprising—a pile of biographies and novels. And pinned on the walls photographs of black grinning faces, all teeth, the eyes screwed closed to the glare of a sudden magnesium flare. A recurring group was evidently a family one: Johnny; a substantial rotund African gentleman with the same air of frank villainy as was the junior Mr Fortune's; his immense wife, swathed in striped native dress; a tall serious youth beside a motor-bicycle; and a vivacious girl with a smile like that of an amiable lynx.

On the table, I noticed an unfinished letter in a swift clerical hand. I didn't disturb it, but . . .

'Dear Peach,

'How it would be great if I could show you all the strange sights of the English capital, both comical and splendid! This morning I had my interview at the Welfare Office with—well, do you remember Reverend Simpson? Our tall English minister who used to walk as if his legs did not belong to him? And spoke to us like a telephone? Well, that was the appearance of the young Mr Pew who interviewed me, preaching and pointing his hands at me as if I was to him a menacing infant. . . .'

Ah!

'. . . I have made visits, too, this afternoon, both of which will interest Dad—tell him I'm writing more about them, but don't please tell our dearest Mum or Christmas that I give you this message. Just now I have returned here to my miserable hostel (hovel!—which soon I shall be leaving permanently) to change to fresh clothes and go out in the town when it's alight.

'And Peach! It's true about the famous escalator! It can be done, early this morning I made the two-way expedition, easily dashing up again until . . .'

Should I turn over the sheet? No, no, not that. . . .

I closed the door softly and walked down the chipped ceremonial stair. At its foot, the secretary waylaid me.

'And did you then discover Mr Fortune?' he enquired.

'No.'

'Will it be necessary for me to convey to him some message of your visit?'

'No.'

He frowned.

'As secretary of the hostel committee, may I ask of your business on our premises?'

I gave him a Palmerstonian glare, but he met it with such a look of dignified solemnity that I wilted and said, 'I am the new Assistant Welfare Officer. My name is Montgomery Pew.'

'And mine, sir, is Mr Karl Marx Bo. I am from Freetown, Sierra Leone.'

We shook hands.

'I hope, sir,' he said, 'you have not the same miserable opinion of our qualities as he who previously held down your job?'

'Oh, you mustn't think that. Come, come.'

'May I offer you a cup of canteen coffee?'

'I'd love it, but really, I'm in somewhat of a hurry. . . .'

I moved towards the massive door. Mr Bo walked beside me, radiating unaffected self-righteousness.

'Here in London, I am studying law,' he told me.

'That means, I suppose, that you'll be going into politics?'

'Inevitably. We must make the most of our learning here in London. Emancipation, sir, is our ultimate objective. I predict that in the next ten years, or less, the whole of West Africa will be a completely emancipated federation.'

'Won't the Nigerians gobble you up? Or Dr Nkrumah?'

'No, sir. Such politicians clearly understand that national differences of that nature are a pure creation of colonialism. Once we have federation, such regional distinctions will all fade rapidly away.'

'Well, jolly good luck to you.

'Oh, yes! You say so! But like all Englishmen, I conceive you view with reluctance the prospect of our freedom?'

'Oh, but we give you the education to get it.'

'Not give, sir. I pay for my university through profits my family have made in the sale of cocoa.'

'A dreadful drink, if I may say so.'

He tolerantly smiled. 'You must come, sir, if you wish, to take part in one of our discussions with us, or debates.'

'Nothing would delight me more, but alas, as an official, I am debarred from expressing any personal opinion, even had I one. And now, for the present, you really must excuse me.'

And before he could recover his potential Dominion status, I was out of the door and stepping rapidly up the moonlit road. 'To the Moorhen public house,' I told a taxi driver.

He was of that kind who believe in the London cabby's reputation for dry wit.

'Better keep your hands on your pockets, Guv,' he said, 'if I take you there.'

7

Montgomery at the Moorhen

THOUGH FOND OF BARS and boozing in hotels, I'm not a lover of that gloomiest of English institutions—the public house. There is a legend of the gaiety, the heart-warming homeliness of these 'friendly inns'—a legend unshakeable; but all a dispassionate eye can see in them is the grim spectacle of 'regulars' at their belching back-slapping beside the counter or, as is more often, sitting morosely eyeing one another, in private silence, before their half-drained gassy pints. (There is also, of course, that game called darts.)

It wasn't, then, with high eagerness that I prepared to visit the Moorhen. Nor was I more encouraged when the driver, with a knowing grimace, decanted me on a corner near the complex of North London railway termini. The pub, from outside, was of a dispirited baroque. And lurking about its doors, in groups, or half invisible in the gloom, were Negroes of equivocal appearance. One of these detached himself from a wall as I stood hesitating, and approached.

'What say, mister?' he began. 'Maybe you want somesings or others?'

'Not that I'm aware of,' I replied.

'Oh, no?'

'No. . . .'

'Not this?'

Cupped in the hollow of his hand he held a little brown-paper packet two inches long or so.

'And what might that be?'

'Come now, man,' he said with a grin of understanding and positively digging me in the ribs. 'Is weed, man.'

'*Weed?* What on earth should I want with weed? Now if you had seedlings, or even the cuttings of a rose . . .'

'I see you's a humourisk,' he said.

As a matter of fact, I wasn't quite so ignorant, for I had read my Sunday papers. But this was the first time I'd seen the stuff.

'All sames,' he went on, closing his fingers over the little packet, 'if you need some charge later in your evenings, come to me. Mr Peter Pay Paul is what's my name.'

I thanked him remotely, and pushed open the door of the Moorhen's saloon.

Within, where dark skins outnumbered white by something like twenty to one, there was a prodigious bubble and clatter of sound, and what is rare in purely English gatherings—a constant movement of person to person, and group to group, as though some great invisible spoon were perpetually stirring a hot human soup. Struggling, then propelled, towards the bar, I won myself a large whisky, and moved, with the instinct of minorities, to the only other white face I could see who was not either serving behind the bar, or a whore, of whom there were a great many there, or a person of appearance so macabre as scarcely to be believed. The man whom I addressed was one of those vanishing London characters, the elderly music-hall comical, modelled perhaps on Wilkie Bard, all nose, blear eyes, greased clothes and tufts of hair. 'Cheerio!' I said to him.

He eyed me.

'Crowded tonight.'

'Yus.' (He really said 'Yus'.) 'More's the pity.'

'Oh, you think so? You don't care for crowds?'

'Course I do—when they're rispectable. But not when they're darkies like what's here and all their rubbish.'

'Rubbish?'

He gazed all round the room like a malevolent searchlight and said, 'Jus' look for yourself. And to think a year or so ago this was the cosiest little boozer for arf a mile.'

'But if,' I said, 'you don't like it, why do you come here?'

'Ho! They won't drive me out! They drove out me pals, but they won't drive me.'

'Drove them?'

'They left. Didn't care for it as it got to be ever since the Cosmopolitan opened opposyte.'

'That's the dance hall?'

'Yus. They let those darkies overrun the dance hall, but they haven't got a licence there. So what did they do? Came trooping over the road for drinks like an invasion, and turned this place into an Indian jungle.'

'And the landlord let them?'

'He can't refuse. At least he did try to for the sake of his regulars, but when he saw all the coin they dropped on to his counters, he gave up the fight, and me pals all had to move on. But not me. This is my pub and I'm staying in it till something happens and they all get thrown out again.' And this outpost of empire stared at me with neurotic, baleful zeal.

A juke-box that had been blaring out strident threepennyworths now stopped. I edged my way over to an argumentative group around it, one of whom, a hefty, vivid-looking Negro, was shouting out what sounded rather like:

'Ooso, man. See molo keneeowo p'kolosoma nyamo Ella Fitzgerald, not that other woman. See kynyomo esoloo that is my preference.'

The speaker was wearing pink trousers, a tartan silk shirt bedecked with Parker pens, and a broad-brimmed hat ironed up fore and aft like a felt helmet. A watch of gold, and silver chains, dangled on his gesticulating wrists.

A smaller man beside him, an ally apparently, turned to the others and said, 'Is best let Mr Cannibal have his own choice of record if someone will please give him a threepence bit.'

No one offered, and I ventured to hand the giant a coin.

'Oh, this is nice,' said the smaller man. 'Here is this nice personality who gives Mr Cannibal his tune!' He took the coin from me with two delicate fingers, put it in the juke-box, then said smiling wide, 'So I offer you a cigarette? And then maybe you offer me a light in your own turn?'

I took the Pall Mall, and held out my Ronson to his own. His fingers encircled it as if to guard the flame when, hey presto! the lighter was flicked from my hand, and this person had scurried through the throng towards a farther corner.

I looked about me and saw amiable laughing faces whose eyes dropped politely when mine caught theirs. I began to make my way through them towards the robber and found that, while not exactly stopping me by standing full in my tracks, they presented hard shoulders that made progress difficult.

When at last I reached the corner, I saw an ancient hair-stuffed sofa tottering against the wall. On it were seated Mr Cannibal, the little nuisance who'd taken my lighter, and a third man who wasn't talking, only listening. He was small, tightly built into his suit, at ease, alert, alarming, and compact. He glanced up at me: our eyes locked: his glare had such depth that my own sank into his, and while for two seconds I stood riveted, this stare seemed to drain away my soul.

I blinked, hemmed in behind a wall of dark faces and drape suits. Abruptly, I shook my brain, moved a pace towards the thief, and said to him: 'Can I have my lighter?'

The gabbling conversation in jungle tones went on until the third time of asking. Then the little thief looked up and said, 'What is this stranger? You ask for some light from me, or what?'

It was a shock to see how with this race, even more than with our own, an expression of great amiability can be replaced, on the same face, within seconds, by one of cold indifference and menace.

'No,' I said, enwrapping myself with draped togas of torn Union Jacks. 'Not a *light*, but the *lighter*.'

He took it out of his pocket and tossed it up and down in his hand.

'You wish to *buy* this?' he asked.

'No. Merely to have it back.'

'You mean you say that this my lighter is *your* lighter?'

'Well, my dear chap, you know it is.'

The giant got up, and so did the lighter-lifter, but not the third man, who sat looking at eternity through his lashes.

'Then what I ask,' said the culprit, 'is if your words mean that you call me now a thief?'

The giant stood looking like the Black Peril. The third man now glanced up at me again. When his eyes fixed once more on mine, I felt myself absorbed into a promiscuity of souls closer even than that which can bind, and then dissolve, two animal bodies in each other.

'No,' I said, faltering. 'Keep it.' And as I moved off: 'I hope it brings you luck.'

Rage and disgust filled my heart. 'That idiot at the Welfare Office was right!' I cried out to myself, as I heaved back through the crowd. 'Disgusting creatures! Bring back the lash, the slave trade! Long live Dr Malan!'

Standing in the doorway was a figure different from the gaudy elegants inside—one dressed in dungarees, half shaven, with anthropoid jaws and baby ears, more startling even than alarming. He gave me a great meaningless grin, held out a detaining hand and said (this is the rough equivalent), 'You want some Mexican cigaleks?'

'No, no.'

'At sree sillins for twentik, misters. . . .'

'Oh, really? Well, yes, then.'

He slipped them to me discreetly. Lighting up, awaiting for the return of my shattered poise, I asked him, 'How do you get these, then?'

Conspiratorially, he replied: 'From him G.I.s who sells me in cartoons wisouts no legal dutiks. So you better keep him secrix.'

'They sell them to you here?'

'No, out in him streek, because of Law and his narks that put the eye insides. Anysing from G.I. stores you wants I gess you: sirts, soss, ties, jackix, nylons, overcoats, socolates or any osser foots . . .'

'You make a good profit?'

He looked bland.

'I muss have profix for my risks. That is my bisnick.'

'Do other boys here have things to sell?'

'Oh, misters! Here is him big Londons Spadiss markik place! Better than Ossford Streek hisself!' And he roared out laughing loud, doubling himself up and slapping himself all over. Then he looked coyly discreet. 'Those bad boys,' he said, 'they relieves you of somesink?'

'Yes. You saw? They stole my lighter.'

'A Ronsons?'

'Yes.'

'Of course. Was Mr Ronson Lighter who took it. That is his professins: when he sees Ronson lighter, he muss steal him.'

'And who are his friends?'

'The Billy Whispers peoples. Gambian boys, real bad. Billy hisself, and Jimmies Cannibals and Mister Ronson Lighter, this that robs you.'

'What do they do for a living?'

'Prey!'

His eyes gleamed sympathetically and, I thought, with envy. Then he went on:

'That is their seats over in him corners. This is the seats of all bad Asfrican boys where they go gather makin' deals. No Asfrican boy who is not top London hustler go near their corners, and no Wess Indians dare go by never. Mister, if you have loot, or goods, or wishes they can prey on, please keep clear of him Billy Whispers and all his surrounding mens.'

He told me this as one who reveals a precious, precarious State secret. Then he looked severe.

'Those boys they sink I stupit—"Boos-a-man" [Bushman] they call me, becos I come out from my home in him interiors, not city folks like those wikit waterfronk boys. . . .' He ruminated, flashing his eyes about. 'They sink I stupit because of no educasons. But [crescendo] my blood better than their blood! My father sieftan [chieftain]!'

'Yes?'

'Yes. I sief's son.'

Diffidence but enormous pride: as if making a huge joke that was no joke, as if calling on me to recognize a splendid truth even if incredible.

'Then why do you leave your people and come here to England?'

'I? Oh, to see these sights. To live. Also, to learn my instrumink.'

'Your . . .'

'My sassofone. I work stoke in him governmik boiler-room by nights, to get loot for lessons for my instrumink. Then, when my time come, I go home to fashinate my cousins with my tunes.'

'And how are your studies progressing?'

'Whass say?'

'Are you mastering your instrument?'

'Man, up till now is my instrumink who is most times mastering me. Ah! But lissen!'

And we heard:

'You leave your mother and your brother too,
You leave the pretty wife you're never faithful to,

You cross the sea to find those streets that's paved with
gold,
And all you find is Brixton cell that's oh! so cold.'

'Thass Lord Alissander! He always come playing here evening, hopin' for sillins and publicitix.'

He plucked at my arm and led me out to the corner of the street. Mr Lord Alexander was leaning against the pub wall, strumming and singing in the middle of a softly humming circle.

'Give us some bad song now, man!'

'Some little evil tune, Lord Alexander!'

'Oh, no! No, no, not me in this respectable country....

'This little Miss Commercial Road she say to me,
"I can't spend much more time in your society.
I know you keep me warmer than my white boy can do,
But my mother fears her grandson may be black as you."'

There was laughter; but on the far side of the street, standing against the brick fence that lined the bombed-out site, were two figures in mackintoshes who were now joined by a tall police Inspector with the shape of an expectant mother. The Bushman took my arm:

'Lissen, man,' he whispered, 'I soot off now, that look to me like him Law be making his customary visicts. Come! We soot off to him Cosmikpolitan dansings, and find whass cookings there....'

Looking back, we saw the three coppers sweeping on the group, which scattered; and then Lord Alexander being led off, the uniformed Inspector carrying the guitar as if it was a truncheon.

8

A raid at the Cosmopolitan

THIS COSMOPOLITAN DANCE HALL is the nearest proximity I've seen yet in London to the gaiety and happiness back home.

For the very moment I walked down the carpet stair, I could see, I could hear, I could smell the overflowing joys of all my people far below. And when I first got a spectacle of the crowded ballroom, oh, what a sight to make me glad! Everywhere us, with silly little white girls, hopping and skipping fit to die! Africans, West Indians, and coloured G.I.s all boxed up together with the cream of this London female rubbish!

A weed peddler came up to me. 'Hullo, hullo, man, you're new,' this too much smiling man said.

I gave him my frown. 'And what you want?' I said.

'Is what *you* want,' he answered, and showed me his packet. 'I'm the surest sure man in the business. You can call me Mr Peter Pay Paul.'

I took it, opened it, eyed it, sniffed it. 'If this is weed,' I said, 'I'm Sugar Ray Robinson.'

His face looked full of pain. 'Then you's dissatisfied?' and he tried to snatch the little packet back.

I held it far. 'What is your foolish game, Mr Peter Pay Paul? What is this evil stuff you peddle to poor strangers?'

He glared at me hard; then smiling again, said, 'Well, I see you's a smart fellow, not rich in ignorance. So I tell you secretly. Is asthma cure I peddle to G.I.s.'

'Tell me some more.'

'This asthma cure, you see, is much like the weed to look at, but naturally is cheaper and of no effect. But G.I.s are so ignorant and anyway so high with liquor, that they buy it from me in large quantities.'

'Well, I'm no G.I., mister, nor ignorant, you'll understand.' And I pushed past him towards the edge of the dancing floor.

And there, wearing dark glasses, and standing among the awaiting pouncers, who should I see but my dearest friend of schooldays in Lagos—Hamilton! 'Hamilton!' I cried out. 'Hamilton Ashinowo, baddest bad boy of the whole mission school!'

Round about he spun, peered, took off his dark glasses (Wow! how that man had been charging, his eyes closed up almost shut), then called out: 'No! No! Is Johnny! Johnny, since when you arrive, my little boy?' And he seized me and gabbled at me in our private tribal tongue.

Hamilton, my dear friend at the mission school, had left it by expulsion two years before I came away when he was found by the Reverend Simpson selling palm wine at profitable prices from a canvas bag he kept hidden underneath his dormitory bed. Hamilton was the love and mock of all of us at school. Mock for his tall wobbling figure, his huge teeth in his pale pink gums, his arms that hung down to his knees like a chimpanzee, and for the celebrated frenzy dance of all his body when excited, that caused him to leap and break out in sharp cries of gasping joy. But loved by us all for his everywhere good nature to everyone, even those not at all deserving of it from him.

'Villainous Hamilton!' I cried out. 'Let's have a drink to celebrate this reunion.'

'Man, in this Cosmopolitan is only coffees, ciders and Coca-Colas, but if you like we can cross the road over to the Moorhen.'

'No, no, stay here and tell me all your activities since we meet. How did you get here, and what is your full present position?'

'I came here, Johnny, on a merchant ship.'

'As passenger? As crew?'

'As stowaway. Then one month in their English jail, and I'm a free British citizen again.'

'And how do you live on what?'

'Ah, now, that . . .' He smiled and wobbled. 'Well, man, I hustle If you ain't got no loot from home, and you don't like the work in the Jumble post office, or railways, for six pounds less taxes and insurances, then, man, you must hustle.'

'And what is your particular hustling?'

'Oh, Johnny, you ask such private questions! Tell me of you, now. You been here long?'

'Some few day now.'

'And you think you like this city?'

'I think yes I do, but not my lodging. I'm in that Welfare hostel.'

'Oh, no! That underpaid paradise! You enjoy it?'

'Mister, I'm moving out before the week is ended. Are rooms in town so very hard to find?'

'They can be found, yes, though Jumbles that take Spade will rob you in their charge of rent....'

'Aren't there no Spades here that have houses?'

'Oh, yes. They rob you even better, but they leave you free. I live in one such house myself.'

'And that house is where?'

'By Holloway. I live out there at times.'

'At times?'

'Man, I have *several* addresses. I keep them for various private reasons of convenience.'

'Hamilton, all this is so mysterious to me.

'I tell you more later, man, far from these overhanging ears. Meantime if you leave your hostel, will you come and live with me if you prefer? The landlord is Mr Cole, an Ibo man. I pay two pounds the week which you can share.'

'Immediately, Hamilton. I move into your house tonight.'

By this time the Cosmopolitan was getting hotted hotter up. And I was struck to notice that though the band was only Jumble imitation of our style, it was quite a hep combination, with some feel of the beat, not like those dreadful records of the English bands I'd heard back home which never can play slow, and never can play easy to the limbs. Out on the floor our boys were acting cool and crazy, letting their little girls do all the work as they twisted them around; or if any of our boys did break in a quick shuffle, the chicks were left gasping tied in hopeless knots. The English boys, of which a few were out there on the floor, all leaped around their partners like some bouncing peanuts, supposing they would show these easy Spades the genuine hot footwork of the jungle. To ask for partner, as I saw, all you must do was just walk up and grab. Though I did notice some polite student boys with spectacles who bowed and enquired, in Jumble style, for which they got refusal.

Then I saw Billy Whispers' Dorothy. She danced with a G.I., dressed up sharp, with vaseline in his hair and graceful.

'Hamilton,' I said, 'do you know a Bathurst boy called Whispers?'

'That Billy? Who doesn't know of him? Now heaven help that poor G.I. if Dorothy take him home.'

'Is that Billy Whispers' racket?'

'One that he has, with robbery and violence, assisted by Ronson Lighter and by Jimmy Cannibal.'

'Why they call that boxer that? He eat his mother?'

'I expect not yet. But he tell his Jumble victims he was fed up on boiled missionary in his village. This news impress them, see, and wins their unlucky trust.'

'Hamilton, hold my cigarette, I'm going to dance with her.'

'Look after yourself then, Johnny, and don't lose me from your view.'

Dorothy's G.I. was not a bit pleased to see me, but she cut all the ground out under his long feet by saying to me, with her English idea of the speech of a tough Brooklyn chick, 'Why, hullo, feller. Never thought I'd see *you* again so soon.'

'I'm like that bad penny, Dorothy. I always keep turning myself up.'

'Aren't you going to ask me to dance?'

'Come on, then, I'll spin you round a while.'

But soon we circled far off to the quiet corner where the partners were wedged up close.

'Does Billy know you're here?' she asked me.

'Can't say. Why? You belong to that man?'

'I don't belong to nobody, see?' (This came out in her natural Brixton language—no more Brooklyn.) 'I live with Billy Whispers, yes. But only so long as I want to. Me, I walk out just when I like.'

'That's not what I thought from how he acted to you there this afternoon. It seemed like he had you all wrapped up.'

'Oh, did it!'

'I'm glad it's not so, Dorothy. Because Muriel and your mother's getting worried about the influence of Billy on you.'

She stopped dancing.

'Oh, is she! My mother—that old cow: yes, I said "cow"! And Muriel, my good little sister! Do you know why she's so good,

Johnny? Because she's deformed! She can't do any better for herself. Didn't you see her hand?'

'I saw she had the glove on it. . . .'

'She's only got three fingers on that hand.'

'She had some accident?'

'No. She was deformed from birth.'

'Which fingers has she missing?'

'The end ones. I tell her it means she'll never get married, if she can't wear a wedding ring. . . .'

'Fingers aren't everything on a body, Dorothy.'

'No, but they come in handy, don't they?'

'She's got a pretty figure, and a happier smile than you.'

'Muriel? She's never been known to smile since she was born.'

She put her arms round my neck and hung on me.

'What about your brother Arthur, Dorothy? When is he coming out?'

'It was six months he got, so it should be any time now, with the remission. But me, I don't have anything to do with him. I don't like these half white, half Africans.'

'You might have one yourself, the way you're living.'

'Are you kidding? I'd get rid of it. Anyway, I'm going to have my ovaries removed.'

'That'll be nice and comfortable.'

We circled round a bit, and I held her off from taking any too great liberty. But she pressed up close and said to me, 'Why don't you ask me out to tea one day, Johnny?'

'Oh, I drink coffee.'

'You know what I mean.'

'Don't rush me off my feet, now, Dorothy. Why you not wait until I make the offer?'

'Oh, if that's how you feel . . .' And she walked straight out of my arms. I watched her fine figure, which certainly gave you the appetite, as she vanished from my view.

As I was strolling back to look for Hamilton, who should I see, sitting at a table, but this unusual couple: a rough-looking jungle boy, who I thought by his cheek-marks might be of the Munshi tribe, and with him who else but the Welfare Office gentleman, Mr Montgomery Pew. Oh-ho! I thought. What can this be?

His long body was wrapped all round the table legs, his hungry face held up by both his hands, and his sad eyes were shooting round the room like trying to find something they could rest on with any comfort.

'Why, Mr Pew!' I said to him. 'You visiting this wicked spot to see if I obey your wise advice to me?'

'Why, Mr Fortune!' he cried back, 'do come and have a glass of this disgusting lemonade. Here is a friend of mine—Mr Bushman, I much regret I don't know your full name.'

I said a few words to this Bushman in his own Munshi tongue, which is one of the four African languages I know fluently. I said I had business to discuss with Mr Pew, and as for him, would he please cut out and hunt some crocodiles? But he answered me in his terrible style of English.

'If you spiks to me insolting,' he said, 'be very careful or I soot you.'

'What you shoot me with, man?'

This puzzled him one moment, but he said, 'I will soot you with my amonisions.'

I laughed at the Bushman's face.

'This gentleman,' said Mr Pew, 'is a chieftain's son, and as such must be treated with respect. Besides which he's been most kind and obliging to me in all manner of ways.'

I saw Mr Pew was high—real gone.

'Blow now, you chieftain's son,' I said to him. 'Chief means no nothing now to any educated Africa man.'

'Wash out for youself,' the Bushman said to me, 'or one day I take an' soot you.' But he got up, and slowly he slide away.

Mr Pew waved after him, then turned to me and said, 'A delightful personality. To tell you the truth, I find this place quite gripping. An Elizabethan fragment come to life in our regimented world.'

No sense in that bit, so I said to him, 'Don't tell me this is *your* first visit here.'

'My dear Fortune, yes, it is. Believe it or not, I've only been attached to the Welfare Office a few days.'

'And already you give good advice to Africans! Well, well. How like an Englishman, if I may say.'

'But it's my job, my duty, Mr Fortune!'

'This "Mr Fortune"! Can't you call me Johnny like the whole world do?'

'And I'm Montgomery.' He held out his hand. 'But not, please, ever "Monty", under any circumstances.'

'If you say so, Montgomery. And now you'll be looking after colonial people's welfare?'

'In my small way, I hope so. I know nothing about you all, Johnny, but I like your people. . . .'

'We never trust a man who tells us that.'

'Oh, no? No?'

'We know in five seconds if you like us without you say so. Those who *say* they like us most usually do not.'

This Montgomery now grasped my arm in the most serious way. 'Well, even if I mustn't say I like you, I *do*,' he told me.

'Oh, that's all right, then.' And I smiled my best high-grade smile.

It was fortunate for us that Hamilton came over at this moment to warn me that some trouble was expected.

'Johnny, you must come with me, there's plain-clothes Law mustering up outside.' And then in our language: 'Who is this white?'

'Not dangerous, I think. What's cooking?'

'G.I.s have stated that their overcoats have been robbed them from the cloakroom. Naturally, our boys like those nice long blue nylon weatherproofs, and do these Americans expect their entertainment here for nothing? Always causing argument and disturbances. I not surprised those Yankee whites will string them up on trees.'

'Now, Hamilton.'

'If they keep on with their foolish agitations, this nice place will soon be closed by public opinion. Come, now. Let we buy some V.P. wine before the closing, and me I'll take you to an Indian restaurant called Fakir for rice and clean cooked chicken, not like that Jumble food, all grease.'

But just then some twenty Law appeared at the entrance steps, the band stopped, and a large cop went over to the mike and shouted: 'All stay where you are for questioning. No one moves.'

'Johnny,' said Hamilton in our speech again. 'You got weed on you? If yes, do slip it in that white man's pocket while he doesn't look.'

'No, he's my friend, I think. But I'll take care. Don't you worry, Hamilton, for me.'

'If they trouble you, say you're a G.I., and ask they hand you over to the U.S. patrol. They don't know your face, so they'll release you, I expect. Me, I have little business I must do, and I go hide.'

'We scatter then, Hamilton, and all meet at this Fakir, if you give me the address. Come please, Montgomery. We make our way slowly to the exit.'

Little packs of weed were falling like leaves upon the floor. Some boys were edging over to the back ways out, but others were mostly standing still with faces innocent and proud. Six silly high G.I.s were pointing the finger at some persons they said had taken away their coats.

As we got near the stairs, we were stopped by three Law in plain clothes that made them look even more like Law.

'Just a minute, you two. Stand on one side.'

'But, mister,' I said, 'I'm a student and must be back at my residential hostel by closing time, ten-thirty.'

'And who are you?'

'My name,' Montgomery tell them, 'is Jerusalem, Lew Jerusalem, I'm here on professional duty as editor of the *Bebop Guardian*.'

Silly.

'Stand on one side, the Inspector will talk to you,' they say to him.

'But me, mister,' I said. 'Look, here is my passport, proving I've just landed in this country, and here also are my student's papers concerning my meteorological studies.'

I spoke so humble and eager, and papers are often of much assistance with the Law. But this time they didn't make their magic.

'Stand on one side as well.'

The Law was now filtering all over the big hall, picking up here a boy, there a tough or frightened chick. I could see no sign of Hamilton, and hoped he'd melted.

Our three Law were busy now questioning others, so I decided on a dash. But at the top of the stairs two more sprang out and grabbed me, and led me to their car. And that worried me, because in my coat pocket I still had some sticks of weed that I'd not wished to lose like others did by dropping them on that floor. . . .

9

Introduction to the Law

WHEN JOHNNY RAN UP THE STAIRS I felt he'd deserted me: it was clear he didn't yet regard me as a friend; and this regret first showed me I already thought of him as one. There I was, left among a herd of suspect colonials, too dispirited to mind much when we were shepherded up the steps, and surrounded by a posse of constables who escorted us down the street with careful eyes, like a crocodile of wicked juveniles. The cool air smacked my brain, and I walked with dignity, slightly apart, in the manner of a distinguished stranger, until we reached a squat, square, windowless building, and were elbowed in.

In the hall we were kept waiting quite a while, next separated into bands and taken into smaller rooms. There, to my delight, I saw Johnny, and also, among others, Mr Peter Pay Paul.

A plain-clothes officer came up to me. 'May I have your name?' This time I gave it. 'And your address? Your age? Your occupation?' All in a little notebook. The occupation particularly interested him.

Then, fixing me with that *double* look that sits in coppers' eyes ('I say this, but I don't mean it, and you know I don't, and I know you know . . .' Or, 'Yes, I'm evil too, but, you see, my evil's licensed to discover yours'), he said, 'You won't mind if we ask you to submit to a search?'

'Of course not. But why?'

'You were found in the company of persons who are suspected of smoking hemp.'

'Is this search voluntary?'

'Oh of course.' (A tight-skinned smile.)

Johnny, from his bench across the room, said in a loud voice, 'Mr Pew, if you are searched voluntary, I suggest you ask for a non-police witness to be present also.'

'Shut your trap, you,' said the Law.

'Why, Johnny?'

'The Law, when it searches, sometimes finds things on a person that the person didn't have before the search began.'

'Keep quiet.'

'Mister. Am I arrested? If so, tell me, and for what. Then you can make your search, of course, but also you must make a charge and see it sticks. But if I am not arrested, please let me speak out my mind as a free man.'

I was in admiration at such audacity. 'You know this man?' the officer said to me.

'Certainly. He's a friend of mine.'

'So much a friend, Montgomery, that will you please give me some matches for my cigarette?'

I handed Johnny the box I'd bought to replace my lighter. As he took it, the officer grabbed it from him and opened it eagerly, scrabbling among the matches. While he did this, I saw Johnny quickly put his hand up to his mouth and swallow.

'Perhaps now you give me my friend's match-box?' he said to the vexed cops.

'We'll begin this search,' the officer replied. 'Unless anyone thinks they've any further objections.'

A uniformed man came in, dashed at me first, turned my pockets vigorously out, then poked and patted around my clothing. Curious how even innocent objects, like handkerchiefs and rings of keys, look suspect on a station table.

Johnny meanwhile had emptied his own pockets on to it. 'Would you like me to undress to naked?' he enquired.

In silence, they dashed at him as well. Evidently this bull-rush, this mock assault, was part of their technique.

Nothing.

Then Mr Peter Pay Paul. They found on him six little packets. 'Is asthma cure,' he said, grinning proudly.

'You're for the cells,' said the Law.

'But no! Why? This is not weed. Is National Health medicine, I swear it on my mother's life!'

'We'll see what the magistrate says to that,' the Law replied, and dragged him off.

'Poor foolish boy,' said Johnny softly. 'This asthma trick is one he play once too much. And surely when he appears in court, the evidence by then will be real weed and not this asthma cure.'

'You mean they'd switch that stuff for something real?'

'That is their usual way back home, where their stores of impounded stocks are used for such a purpose.'

'But this is England, Johnny. Our coppers don't do that.'

He looked at me blandly. 'Oh, is that so? Then I have much to learn of England. . . .'

The Law now returned. 'We won't keep you much longer,' it said to me, 'but perhaps you'd step into the next room a minute?'

I waited for fifteen. Then the plain-clothes man came in and offered me a cigarette.

'Of course, you'll understand, Mr Pew, why we had to search you too. We know a man in your position wouldn't probably be mixed up in anything dubious, but there it is.'

'There is what?'

'We have to take precautions. And also, of course, we don't want to be accused of discrimination, do we.' He gave me an oh, so friendly smile. 'As a matter of fact, Mr Pew, I was wondering if a man with your connections mightn't be willing to do us a good turn now and then.'

I looked blank.

'You see, between you and me, this colour problem's becoming quite a problem for us, too. Particularly in the matter of dope. Of course, these boys, it doesn't do them much harm, I don't suppose, they're used to it, even though it's not within the law. But the girls, Mr Pew, the younger girls they give it to! It's corrupting them. Yes, corrupting them and making them serve these black men's evil ends.'

His eyes shone, like some fake cleric's, with a slightly mad, holy zeal.

'What has all this to do with me, officer?'

He leaned forward at my face. 'I'll ask you. Mr Pew, if in your position you don't think it your duty to pass on any information that may come your way about the sources of this drug traffic.'

I got up.

'Officer, I have no such information. And if I had, frankly . . .'

'Yes?' (A monosyllable heavy with malice and with menace.)

'I'd not at all feel it my duty to pass it on to you.

'Oh, would you not.'

He slapped his hands on his knees, smiled most unpleasantly, and rose. 'I only mentioned it, sir, because sometimes we coppers can do a good turn in return for one that's done to us. And a friend in need can sometimes be a friend indeed.'

'Yes, I see your point.'

He opened the door. 'At any rate, remember what I say, in case you might find you'd better change your mind. Just ask for the Detective-Inspector of the C.I.D.—the Vice Inspector,' he added with taut official grin.

In the corridor outside his office, I caught a glimpse of a Negro loitering. Who was it? Yes! The boxer Cannibal who'd helped steal my lighter at the Moorhen. When he saw me, he turned hurriedly away.

Johnny was waiting in the street outside. 'What keep you so long?' he asked—suspiciously, I thought.

'That Vice Inspector tried to sign me up as a nark.'

'And you accepted the offer of this Mr Purity?'

'My dear Fortune!'

I was quite offended, and we walked two blocks in silence.

'It seems to me, Johnny,' I said at last, 'that you're very well informed about the police force and their habits.'

'I should be. I'm a policeman's son.'

'But you told me your father was in business.'

'He serve one time when a younger man in the force back home. I know the Law—I know it both sides round. In Lagos, as anyone will tell you, I was something of a bad boy in my way. What they call one of the waterfront boys . . . up to various tricks, and often encountering my own Dad's former friends. . . .' He stopped and rubbed his stomach. 'Oh, heavens, I don't like the taste of that brown paper I have to swallow down when I eat those sticks of charge I had about my person.'

'I thought that might be it. I wish I had your nerve. . . .'

Another coloured man was lurking at the next corner: haunting the city thoroughfare as if poised with a spear in the deep bush. His face to me was quite invisible, but Johnny said, 'Is Hamilton,' and they began a deep conversation in a voluble, staccato rumbling tongue.

'Hamilton,' Johnny told me with admiration, 'escaped the Law's attention by crouching on top of the lavatory doors. Then he could return, when all invaders left, to pick up the weed he find undetected on the floor.'

'Come now,' said Hamilton. 'I have some V.P. wine. We go to the Fakir for some necessary eat and drink.'

We walked through the warm night, with a wide white blaze on the city sky where the summer sun refused to set.

'Johnny,' I said. 'You talk to Hamilton in African. But to others you talk in English. Why?'

'I do not speak with Hamilton in African. I speak to him in the language of our tribe. There is no "African", but many, many tribal languages.'

'How many?'

'More than one hundred in Nigeria. Some I know, like Yoruba, Hausa, Munshi and my own. But others I do not, so I speak English.'

'So you speak five languages. Bravo!'

'I teach you some Africa words one day—words of my tribe. Say "*Madu*".'

'*Madu*. What have I said?'

'"My friend." Come, we go eat. You like this Indian food?'

'No. About Indian food, there's a great mystery: how can a race so ancient and so civilized have devised anything so repellent? It always seems predigested and regurgitated. And the handkerchiefs it ruins!'

'Oh? You like that fish-and-chip stuff better? Come, we go in.'

The Indians were, as is usual, a family, and they welcomed my friends with the aloof professional deference that scarcely veils indifference and contempt. Johnny and Hamilton chose a distant corner beside an ash-tray made of an elephant's foot, and began their surreptitious chemistry with cigarette papers and little packets. After puffs, inhalations and exchange of butts, Johnny handed me the cigarette. 'It give you appetite,' he said.

'No, thanks.'

'You never smoked this stuff?'

'As a matter of fact, once, yes. In Egypt. But from a hubble-bubble.'

'And you liked it?'

'It had no effect whatever.'

'Oh-ho! Listen to this experienced Jumble man! Then either, Montgomery, your hubble-bubble contained rubbish, or you took a very feeble drag.'

'You'll have to be careful, smoking that stuff here.'

'Oh, these Indians don't mind,' said Hamilton.

'I mean here in England. Remember Inspector Purity.'

'Man,' Johnny said, 'wherever there are Spades there will be weed.'

'You smoked a lot at home?'

'In Africa, with due discretion, you can smoke in even public places.'

'Not in the main street, naturally,' Hamilton explained, 'or underneath the copper's nose, as that is useless provocation.'

'Even as babies, we may meet it,' Johnny said. 'A mother, to soothe our cries, may ease us to comfort with a gentle loving puff. Later, as boys, we make the experiment as you do here with your tobacco.'

'And do not forget,' said Hamilton, waving his hand, 'that many of us are Mahometans and cannot indulge in liquor. Weed is to us what liquor is to you.'

'But stronger, surely.'

'Depending on the quantity you partake.'

'Liquor,' said Johnny, 'opens you outwards and gives you a foolish love of fellow men, the wish to chatter to them in a cheerful, not selective way. But weed, you see, turns you happily inward to sit silent in the greater enjoyment of your personality. Try some?' And he held out the stick again.

'But it's habit-forming.'

'No,' they both said. And Johnny added, 'Charging is different from popping as liquor is.'

'Popping?'

'With needles. White stuff—man, that's danger! But not this—just you try it.'

'No, thanks. No, not for me.'

In came great piles of the predigested food, and Hamilton uncorked the V.P. wine.

Looking past his shoulder, I saw a huge shapeless man, but one with eyes a-glint, come lumbering light-toed through the door. Customers, when they saw him, lowered their eyes and talked a little louder. He had on a thick overcoat, despite the summer, and a large felt hat which he did not remove.

'Say nothing to this person,' Hamilton told me. 'He's Johnson: Johnson the tapper.'

'What's a tapper?'

'Man, you'll see.'

The huge man drew up a chair, smiled lippily at us all and reached out fat fingers to take food. Hamilton lifted the plates out of his reach. The stranger snatched up a glass of V.P. wine and drank it. 'Cigarettes?' he said to me.

I was getting some out, but felt Johnny's hand upon my wrist.

'Then give me one pound or else ten shillings,' said the intruder.

'But why?'

He stroked my arm and looked at me sideways. 'Come now, come now, come now,' he kept on saying.

The Africans ate on, taking no notice of him whatsoever.

'Come, little white friend,' said the tapper, in a soft, gentle, stupid, persistent voice. 'Give me some sustenance.' And he began patting me on the back—gently at first, then harder.

'Go away,' I said, half rising.

'Ignore him, please,' said Johnny. 'He will shoot off in time.'

'How can I ignore him?'

But sure enough, the tapper slowly stopped his patting, sat huddled a while in silence in his chair, then shambled to another table.

'It is useless,' said Johnny, 'to instruct a tapper. If you resist, he will create some foolish disturbance. If you play cool, he will lose interest of his profit, and fade away.'

'To be a tapper is a profession,' Hamilton explained to me. 'A horrible one, of course, but these people cannot be dismissed.'

'They are unfortunate, and must not be subject to humiliation, Johnny said. 'Come: do we take some coffee? You, Montgomery?'

'All right.'

'Black?'

'Yes, black.'

'I shall drink white in compliment to you. Then Hamilton will take us to the Moonbeam club, and show us the delights of London's wicked mysteries. How about chicks to dance with, Hamilton? Are they to be found upon those premises?'

'That G.I.s' rendezvous is loaded up with chicks. Chicks of all activities and descriptions, some trading, and other voluntary companions full of hope.'

'There's a little girl in Maida Vale I'd like to ask—I wonder if she'd come?'

'You know a girl already, Johnny? Speedy!'

'A family friend, Hamilton, that I must see. I have some news for her about her sister. What say we go along and pick her up?'

'We could walk out that way, this Moonbeam's open until when the dawn . . . But first, Johnny, I more like you come over and see your future home with me.'

I had a sudden inspiration. I know,' I said, 'a very nice woman to make up the party . . . a most engaging English girl, called Theodora. I'm sure she'd like to come. Let's go to my place and ask her. We could have another drink there too, I think and hope.'

We walked out through the Indians' vague bows into the star-skied town, and hailed a cab. It was the hour at which all honest Londoners have hurried to their beds and wisdom, and when the night owls, brave spirits in this nightless city, emerge to gather in the suspect cellars that nourish the resistance movement to the day.

'Why have I done this?' I reflected, as we drove home between rotting Georgian terraces, and the ominous green of the thick trees in Regent's Park which, when night falls, are reclaimed from man by a jealous, antique Nature. 'Theodora won't be in the least bit interested, and no more will these wild Africans be in her.'

We crept stealthily up through the echoing floors of my grim house. There was a light under Theodora's door. Asking my friends to wait, I knocked, and she bade me enter in her bold, emotionless tones.

It is a curiosity of Theodora's austere and purposeful nature that she wears intimate clothes of a sensual and frivolous kind. There she was, still typing away, but dressed now in a gown and nightdress made for a suppler, more yielding body.

'You were a long time at that hostel,' she said. 'Did you enjoy yourself?'

'Theodora. Would you care to go out dancing?'

'You've been drinking again, Montgomery.'

'Of course I have. Would you like to come into a world where you've never set foot before, even though it's always existed underneath your nose?'

She flipped out the sheet she was typing, and held it on her lap. 'Go on,' she said.

'I have two delightful friends outside most keen to meet you. Would you be willing to receive them, even if in your off-duty dress?'

'Negroes?'

I nodded.

Theodora took off her spectacles (which suit her), eyed me reflecting, then said, 'Bring them in.'

The Africans stood looking at Theodora with frank curiosity, an amiable show of modesty, and complete self-assurance. I introduced them.

'A nice place you have here,' said Johnny Fortune. 'You're an eager reader of literature, too, as I can see.'

'Miss Pace,' I said, 'is a doctor of some branch of learning—economics, I believe.'

'Letters,' said Theodora. 'Montgomery, please go upstairs and fetch back my bottle of gin.'

When I returned, I was disconcerted to hear Theodora say: 'This legend of Negro virility everyone believes in. Is there anything in it, would you say?'

'Lady,' Johnny answered, 'the way to find that out is surely by personal experiment.'

'And is it true,' the rash girl continued, unabashed, 'that coloured men are attracted by white women?'

'I'd say that often is the case, Miss Pace, and likewise also in the opposite direction.'

I hastened to pour out gin. I did not like my friend Theodora treating them in this clinical manner.

'Mr Fortune,' I said, 'has come here to study the movement of the isobars.'

'With what object?' Theodora asked.

'Because back home, my studies over, I'll get a good job upon the airfield.'

'I see. And you, Mr Ashinowo, as I think it was. What do you do?'

'Lady,' said Hamilton, 'at one time I pressed suits by day and worked in the Post Office by night.'

'Doing what?'

'As switchboard relief operator. But I was sacked, you see, for gossiping, they said, with some subscribers.'

'And you did?'

'I tried to make friends that way when nice voices called me up for numbers. But this, I was told, was not my duties, and they sacked me.'

'And now?'

'I live on hope mostly, and charity from the splendid National Insurance system.'

I broke in impatiently on all this. 'The point really is, Theodora, would you care to step out with us, for time is getting on.'

But politely, though quite firmly, she replied, 'No, I don't think so, thank you, Montgomery. I'm sure you gentlemen will excuse me, but I have work to do.'

'Do change your mind,' said Johnny to her. 'Even a serious lady like yourself must at times relax herself.'

She smiled and shook her head. My two friends knocked back their gins, told me they would be calling home a moment, and gave me directions where to meet them in an hour. I saw them to the door and, like two innocent conspirators, they set off loping and prowling up the street.

Theodora was typing again when I returned. 'I think I'm in danger,' I told her, 'of becoming what Americans call a nigger-lover.'

' "Negro-worshipper" is the polite phrase, I believe. You spent the whole evening with those people?'

'Yes. And I say, thank goodness they've come into our midst.'

'Why?'

'Because they bring an element of joy and fantasy and violence into our cautious, ordered lives.'

'Indeed. Isn't there another side to the coin?'

'There must be, but I haven't found it yet. Unless it is that they live too much for the day. . . .'

Theodora got up and fiddled with her documents. 'It's always a danger,' she said, 'to fall in love with another race. It makes you dissatisfied with your own.' She tucked typed sheets away in little files. 'Most races seem marvellous,' she continued, 'when one meets them for the first time. It may surprise you, Montgomery, but once I was enamoured of the Irish. Yes, think of it!' (She shuddered.) 'I loved them for what I hadn't got. But I'm damned if I love what I found out that they had.'

'You're swearing, Theodora. It's unlike you.'

'You'd better go to bed.'

I drained the gin. 'You're not coming to this ball with me, then? Those boys will certainly put it down to colour prejudice.'

'Don't be so cunning, Montgomery. It's too transparent. Your friend Fortune wouldn't think so, anyway. He's too intelligent.' Theodora tightened the gown around her waist, smoothed meditatively her lean, albeit shapely, thighs, then turned round and said to me, 'All right, very well—I'll come.'

I gazed at her awestruck. 'Might I ask, Theodora, why you've changed your inflexible mind?'

There was a pause; then: 'It will be an opportunity to study conditions.'

'What does that mean, my dear?'

'Conditions of coloured people living in London.'

'But why? Why you?'

'The Corporation might put on a series of talks. It's a topical and unusual theme.'

I drew breath. 'Theodora! I shall not be party to such a plot! If you come out with my friends, it is to come out with them, and not to ferret raw material for impartial radio programmes.'

There was a silence.

'Very well,' she said at last. 'I accept your condition. I'll get dressed.'

10

Hamilton's sad secret

HAMILTON AND I rejected possibilities of a late tube or bus, and instead sought a taxi among the endless streets that led in the direction of his Holloway home. I cannot tell you what a joy it was to see Hamilton again, just as in youth, and to know of a sure friend in this after all very unknown city. I put my arm through his, and said to him (just near a huge, empty railway station), 'Oh, Hamilton, one day we'll return together to set alight to that dreadful mission school.'

'If ever I get home, Johnny, yes, we shall.'

'But surely, Hamilton, you will go back to Lagos in the due course of time?'

'I don't know. Many things keep me here.'

'What, Hamilton? You love this country?'

'No, no, but I have means to live here in better comfort than I could hope for back home. . . .'

'What means?'

'I tell you this in a bit later time.'

He'd looked at me with an alarmed expression, quite unlike him.

'That Jumble,' he said, 'that Mr Pew. Is he to be trusted, in your opinion?'

'Why not, until he proves us otherwise?'

'I have been here two years, and still I have no Jumble friends.'

'You do not seek for them, perhaps? Whites are all right if you are proud and strong with them.'

'Friendship between us is not possible, Johnny. Their interest is to keep us washing dishes, and in their kindest words are always hidden secret double thoughts.'

'Hamilton, you know, if our people has one bad weakness, it is our jealousy always, and suspicion.'

'Suspicion of Jumbles? Jealousy of them? Why not so?'

'Even for ourselves, our people have that bad feeling. You know it, Hamilton. If one man rises up, the others try all to pull him down—even when there is no advantage to them.'

'That may be true,' said Hamilton. 'And certainly these Jumbles are more faithful to each other than we are to our own kind. When the trouble comes, they stick: our people scatter.'

A taxi cruised by, he hailed it, and gave to the driver no fixed address, but the name of the corner of two streets. Then closing the glass panel, he said to me, 'Never let your own private addresses be known in this Jumble city, especially to such as taxi drivers who make their report on passengers they carry to the Law.'

We walked from the taxi stop round several blocks, Hamilton glancing sometimes back along the streets behind, then dived in the basement of a silent house. Hamilton opened, and turned on the lights with a great smile. 'Welcome to my place,' he said, 'which is also to be from now your home.'

It certainly was a most delightful residence: with carpets and divans, and shaded lamps and a big radiogram and comfort. He turned on the sound which gave out first Lena Horne. 'She! One of my favourites,' I told him.

'Then listen to her, man, while I go change my shirt.'

Up on his walls, Hamilton had stuck many photographs: like Billy Daniels, and Dr Nkrumah, and Joe Louis in his prime, and Sugar Ray; and also Hamilton's acquaintances, all sharply dressed and grinning—rocking high with charge, I'd say, when these snaps of them were taken.

'Hamilton,' I called out, 'who's this little girl?'

He didn't answer, so I walked through the door into the kitchen. He was standing over the sink injecting his arm with a syringe.

'Hamilton!' I cried, and tried to seize it away.

'You stand back, man, from me!'

I never saw Hamilton so ferocious. His face looked at my face I thought with hatred.

He popped, then locked his syringe into a drawer.

'Come back in the big room, Johnny. You should not have left it without my invitation.'

I was silent, and in a short while he was smiling.

'Hamilton,' I said, 'how long you been on that needle?'

'One year now, I think.'

'Hamilton!'

'I'm licensed now, Johnny—no trouble with the Law. I buy my allotment, but sell half of it. That's one of my ways to live.'

'Is that the only way possible to live, old friend?'

'Don't be too hard with me, Johnny. You're new to London, and your Dad has loot to send you, don't forget. Wait till you're skinned like I was, and then see.'

'I wish it was not this, Hamilton.'

We sat for a while with only the radiogram breaking silence: then there was a soft knock, and in came a short man wearing some Jumble clerk's striped trousers, and slippers, and braces over a grease-smeared vest, and a face to match it all—quite uninviting.

'Oh, Johnny,' said Hamilton, 'this is my landlord, Mr Cole, who we call "Nat King" in honour of his great namesake. This is Johnny Fortune, Mr Cole, who'll be staying with me here from now.'

'Very pleased,' said Mr Cole. Then handed Hamilton a little sheet of paper.

'Papers are not necessary, Mr Cole. I know I owe you all of three weeks' rent.'

'Some five it is, Hamilton Ashinowo.'

'Four by next Friday.'

'How much is it, Hamilton?' I said. 'I can advance you any sum that's necessary.'

The notes passed to Hamilton and then to Mr Cole. 'A Lagos boy?' he said to me in his horrible Ibo accent.

'Yes.'

'Newcomer to town?'

'Yes.'

'Student boy, perhaps?'

'Yes, Mr Cole. I see you soon be familiar with my personal history.'

He looked at me with no smile at all, and said, 'I have to be acquainted with the residents of my house. You a gambler?'

'I might perhaps be one.'

'We must play cards some day.'

'If you say so, sir.'

'Friends come most nights into my room upstairs. You'll understand this is no common gamble-house like you may find down in the town, but serious.' He stopped by the door. 'Do your studies include a knowledge of trigonometry?' he asked me.

'Oh, I'm not that far up.'

'I'm learning it for my hobby. I thought perhaps you'd help me with the problems. But never mind, so long as you can gamble.'

He went away with his valuable pound notes.

'A mean man,' said Hamilton, 'that "Nat King" Cole. Watch out for him.'

'Mean in what way?'

'Treacherous. Nothing is meaner, Johnny, than we are when we go sour. I tell you, man, I know the London landlords. Even a white is not so mean as our race can be to us. . . .'

Hamilton was lying back now on the divan, and I saw that his two eyes slowly began to close. 'Wake up, we're going to that club,' I cried to him; but his drug worked its effect, and when I'd removed his shoes and loosened up his clothing, and stood looking sadly at him for a while, I went out once more into the London night.

It was difficult for me to find the home of Muriel and her mother, as I had forgotten the street name and number, and had only the force of instinct to guide me there. Another thought also began to strike me: this was not Lagos, where we never slumber, but a city which after midnight seemed like the Land of Deads. Would I be welcomed by those Macphersons at so late an hour?

But though the street, when I found it, was all in blackness, I was happy to see lights blazing on the Macpherson floor. This time the front door was locked shut, so I stood underneath and called up Muriel's name; and then, when no answer came, threw little blocks of earth from the outside garden at the window-panes.

With a screech one flew open, and out on to the balcony there stepped Mrs Hancock, or Macpherson. Even I was alarmed at her wild and strange appearance. She was naked except for a short nightdress, her grey hair hung down like ghost upon her shoulders, and in her hand she carried a huge book which she held upwards, like a club.

'Who is it,' she cried, 'that disturbs the Lord's servants at their midnight prayers?'

'Good evening, Mrs Macpherson,' I called up. 'Is me, Johnny Fortune, your young friend.'

'What?' she shrieked out. And to my disgust, I saw she'd snatched away her nightgown to the thigh, which shone all blue and gristly, like a meat carcass, in the electric light.

'I too,' she cried out shrill, 'I too could be evil if I wanted to, like you wicked men.'

At that she hurled the book down on my head. I picked it up: it was a black-bound hymnal. The window shut swiftly with a clatter.

Then the door opened, and out came little Muriel. 'Mum's got hysteria,' she said. 'Arthur's come back. He's been released.'

'He's in there too?'

'No. Mum refused to let him stay, so he's gone off to the Moonbeam to find some friend he can stop with.'

'That's funny, Muriel, because I came here to ask you out with me to just that place—to dance and hear about your sister Dorothy and what I have discovered.'

'Oh, I don't want to go to the Moonbeam. . . .'

'But, Muriel, I must meet Arthur, to see if I can help him. And how will I know him without you there to point him out?'

She looked upstairs. 'Mum's so hysterical,' she kept on saying.

'Well, give her back her religious volume and leave her make her prayers and singing. Who is it she's praying for—for Arthur?'

'No. For suffering humanity.'

'Oh, come along now, Muriel. I'll look after you in any place we go.'

'All right, Johnny,' she said. 'I'll get my keys.' And taking the hymnal from me, she disappeared into the madhouse up the stairs.

11

The Moonbeam club

STRANGE GIRL, THEODORA! When I'd taken a quick bath and changed once more (sober dark grey, this time) I came downstairs to find she was resplendently got up: she looked like a lively rector's daughter's notion of a sinner.

'Theodora!'

'Well?'

'You look bewitching, but bizarre.'

'You've seen me in evening dress before.'

'But this! Where did you get it?'

Though I'd not thought she had it in her, her chiselled face now looked almost demure. 'In Italy, last holidays,' she said.

'You continually amaze me.'

'Come!' she said determinedly, and took me by the arm. I trembled, and we walked out once again into the unpredictable London night.

Soon we reached the outskirts of Soho; and being already, as I imagined, one of the freemasonry of the secret coloured underground, I did not hesitate to ask the way to the Moonbeam club from any dark face I saw. Apparently some recognized me, for they gave knowing grins and said they'd seen me earlier at the Moorhen. But I, as yet, could hardly distinguish their faces one from another, and even less whether the brown eyes were baleful or benevolent. Thereby I gave offence to the Bushman, who waylaid me quite close to our final destination.

'Yous no mo' remembers me, then, mister?' he said. 'Earlier time I sell you cigaleks.'

'Oh, but of course. How are you and your instrument, my dear chap? And can you show me to the Moonbeam?'

'You dunno that ways? Come, and your lady too.' He led us down a street where, curiously enough, I'd often visited a little Italian restaurant that wasn't. But never had I thought that the bombed site across the way contained, by night, in its entrails, the Moonbeam club.

The whole street was transformed: the horrid little restaurant was dark and shuttered, and the bombed site alive with awnings, naked lights, and throngs of coloured men. Cars were parked thick outside.

'What you does,' said the Bushman, 'is spik with Mr Bumper Woodman about how he makes you a members. But take care! All those Moonbeam owners is not Asfricans, like me, but is Wess Indians.'

I thanked him, and we crossed and joined a queue of trollops and G.I.s

Mr Bumper Woodman was a coloured giant in a belted mackintosh, somewhat run to seed. His chest protruded even farther than his belly, and his face wore an impersonal scowl. He asked my name, and who had recommended me. I said Johnny Fortune had.

'Is no such man a member here.'

On the impulse of the moment I said, 'Mr Billy Whispers, then.'

'He is inside,' said Mr Woodman. 'Please now you wait, I go see.'

We watched the G.I.s streaming in, all gracefully dressed like chorus boys in a coloured revue. They moved slowly, but persistently, as men of a race which knows that, come what may, it will go on for ever.

Billy Whispers came upstairs with Mr Woodman and a third coloured man of oriental appearance.

'I am Mr Cochrane,' this third man said, in singsong Jamaican, falsetto and lilting, so like transatlantic Welsh. 'I am the resident manager of this establishment, and will wish to know your qualifications for entering, since Mr Whispers tells me your identity is quite unknown to him.'

'Good evening, Mr Whispers,' I said. 'I expect you remember me from the Moorhen earlier on.'

The African looked at me coolly, and made no reply.

'I'm to meet Johnny Fortune here, I don't know if he's turned up yet, so I thought you'd kindly sign us in.'

'You know Johnny Fortune?'

'I should say I do.'

'He's new arrived in this country.'

'I met him only this morning, but we're already quite great friends.'

'Yes? Is it? Then I shall sign you in till Johnny come, and check with him later on about you.'

'Now just a minute,' said Mr Cochrane. 'If there's a doubt about the sponsorship of this gentleman and lady, nothing can be determined that would prejudice the issue.'

'How beautifully you speak,' said Theodora, with conviction. 'You must have gone to a university like me.'

'Though not college trained, lady, I have a pretty reasonable acquaintance with general knowledge of all descriptions.'

'You sign him in, man, like I say,' said Billy, and he turned and went downstairs.

Mr Cochrane opened a huge ledger, and charged us ten shillings each. 'Our club rules are strict about introducing liquor,' he said, 'and Mr Woodman must examine you for any portable bottles.'

Mr Woodman frisked me, and asked to see in Theodora's handbag.

'You must have been a policeman once,' I said.

'Not so, man. Me boxer. Me once fight Joe Louis, but me did not altogether defeat him.'

Then we were allowed downstairs—two long floors down (can London be so deep?), past coloured photographs of American Negro singers and white starlets, all blonde hair and breasts, till we reached a little entrance hall. Nobody was about, but there was a public call-box to the outside world, embossed with a thousand pencilled phone numbers. The sound of throbbing music came from beyond the door.

'Should I dial for ambulance or fire, Theodora?'

'They always come when they're needed,' she said, and opened the Moonbeam club's inner door.

It was a long low room like the hold of a ship, no windows and only walls. At one end, in front of a huge portrait of the rising moon, was a seven-piece orchestra, only whose eyes, teeth and shirt fronts were visible at this distance. At the other, just behind us, was a soft-drink bar, with Coca-Cola advertisements and packets of assorted nuts, where teas and coffees were also being served. Among the square columns that held up the low roof were tables, some set in sombre alcoves. And between them a small floor where couples jived gently, turning continually like water-beetles making changing patterns on a pond.

By the bar, I saw Mr Karl Marx Bo. 'You're taking time off from your studies?' I asked him.

'Man, even the greatest brains must occasionally relax.'

'Please meet my friend Theodora Pace. Theodora, Mr Karl Marx Bo.'

'Good early morning to you, lady. You like I find you a table? But the drinks is much more expensive when you sit.'

He led us, without waiting for a reply, to a little gallery I hadn't seen: up six steps, and overlooking the larger trough of the dancers and the tight-packed tables.

'Theodora,' I said, 'is, like you, a student of social phenomena.'

'Is that why you bring her to this interesting G.I. knock-shop?'

'Is that what happens here, then?'

'Everything happens here, lady. But mostly it is a spot where fine young American coloureds can destroy themselves with female white trash peddled to them by West Indians and by my fellow countrymen, who collect these women's earnings and usually the G.I.'s pocket-book as well.'

'Then why do you come here, Mr Bo?' said Theodora.

'Lady, it is a weakness, but serious individual as I am, I cannot always resist the lure of a little imitation joy.'

'You found more joy in your own homeland?'

'Oh, naturally. We Africans, you see, are not a people who deposit our days in a savings bank, like you do. Our notion is that the life is given us to be enjoyed.'

Theodora fixed him firmly with her spectacles. 'But one must build,' she said. 'To build a civilization requires effort, sacrifice. If you find the English mournful, it is because we turn the easy joys into parliaments, and penicillin.' I began to think Theodora had also been at the gin. 'You will find that out,' she continued, 'when you put on shoes and come out of the easy jungle. The new African nations will have to learn to sing less, smile less, and work.'

'Theodora, you're being priggish, tactless and a bore.'

'Is all right, Mr Pew. I have no objection to this lady's open personal statements.'

'Thank you, Karl Marx,' said Theodora. 'Well, then. If your countrymen find life so enjoyable at home, why do they flock here to England?'

'Always these white people who ask us why we come here! Do we ever ask you, lady, why your people came to our country long ago?'

'Don't be so *sensitive*, Mr Bo. I'm not saying you oughtn't to come here . . .'

'Oh, thank you, thank you.'

'. . . but only asking *why* you do.'

'I came here to study, as you know.'

'You, yes. But all the others. All the hundred thousand others, or whatever the figure is, because nobody knows.'

'Your statistics are illogical, lady, if you speak of Africans. Most of that number are West Indians, and you know very well why they come here—it is to eat. Their little islands will not hold their bursting populations, and America, where they wish much more to travel, has denied them the open door. So they come here.'

Theodora leaned forward and tapped the table four times with her finger.

'Please don't be so elusive, Mr Bo,' she said. 'Do stick to the point. West Africa is prosperous, expanding, filled with opportunity. Why come here?'

'To study: law, and nursing, and et cetera . . .'

'Yes, yes, you said so.'

'Or in show business. You like the wild illusion of our African drummers.'

'Nonsense. How many Africans are there in show business in London? Fifty at most? And anyway, you know you can't compete in that with American Negroes, or even with West Indians, because your music isn't entertainment as we understand it. In fact, it's not "show business" at all.'

'Oh, no? Not entertaining to you?'

'You know very well, Mr Bo, that African music is too real, too obsessive, too wonderfully monotonous, too religious, for Europeans ever to put up with it. We like something much less authentic.'

'I see you are a serious student of our art.'

'Of course I am. I don't speak of what I don't know about.'

'Theodora, your conceit's repulsive.'

'Be quiet, Montgomery. Go on, Mr Bo. Why do you all come here?'

Beneath her fierce onslaught, Mr Bo looked dreamy, seeming to retire within himself. 'Some boys are afraid of curses,' he said softly.

'Of spells? Of witchcraft?'

'I see you smile, Miss Pace. You should not smile. I could show to you boys here, even scientific students, who believe that family of theirs have died from spells, and fear the same themselves if they return.'

'And you: you surely don't believe such nonsense yourself?'

'Anything many people believe is not exactly nonsense, Miss Theodora. You are, of course, superior to such superstitions, but then perhaps you have no wonderful sense of magic and mystery any more.'

A shrewd thrust, I thought, and Theodora clearly didn't like it. She hitched her Italian gown, and returned to the attack. 'That might account for a few dozen who stay here,' she said, 'but not for thousands.'

Mr Bo looked at her through veiled eyes, ironically. 'Others,' he said, 'come here to flee their families' great love. A family in Africa, you see, is not like here. Our whole life and business belong to every second cousin. A family only loves you and gives you some peace when you let it eat you.' Mr Bo chuckled warmly, and flung up his hands. 'Some boys are here who wish to escape those circumstances. Here you can live out your own life, even if it is miserably.'

Theodora, in the realm of the mind, is like a huntress who's not satisfied until she's bagged her lion. 'That can't be the only reason,' she said, stabbing her coffee cup with a spoon quite viciously.

Mr Bo lit two cigarettes in his lips, and passed her one.

'You seem so obstinately inclined,' he said, 'that I shall tell you the real reason for your satisfaction. It is this.' He gazed at her, and said: 'The world has broken suddenly into my country: and we are determined to break out equally into the world.'

'Go on.'

'At home there is reasonable happiness, yes, and comfort. But when in a cinema we see the London streets shining, gleaming and beckoning, we stop and think, "Here am I, shut in my prison, cut out from where there is creation, and riches, and power in the modern world. There, in that distant place, the life is bigger, wider, more significant. That is something I must see, and show I can be master of it." So we come wandering here, like the country boys back home who dream to visit the big town.'

Theodora gazed back, visibly entranced. 'All right,' she said, 'you all come here. And what do you find?'

'Find almost always great deception. Hard times, or else, like these children you see in this club here, living prosperously for a while with little crimes. In either case, it is failure for us here.'

'Then why don't you go back?'

'Because of shame. The country boy can't go back home from the city until he makes some fortune. But opportunity for this is denied to us by you.'

'Because there's a colour bar, you mean?'

'Is there a colour bar in England, Miss Theodora?'

'You know there is.'

'If you say so, then, I say it too. Universal politeness, and universal coldness. Few love us, few hate us, but everybody wish we are not here, and shows this to us by the correct, stand-away behaviour that is your great English secret of public action.'

'And you resent it.'

'No, I do not resent it. Me, I laugh. For very soon this colour bar will die away.'

'You think so?'

'I do. When we have African prime minister, who will say: "Mr England, I have a million pounds to spend in Birmingham with you, but perhaps I go spend them in Germany, or in Tokyo, Japan." This speech by our prime minister will change more hearts of yours in half a day than nice-thinking people among you fail to do in all these years. All else is useless propaganda: I mean all statements of clergymen about brothers under the skin, all efforts you make to banish your shame at ancient conduct to us by being kind to us, and condescensious.'

'I am never condescending, and not particularly kind.'

'No, lady. Perhaps you are just civilized. But if you wish for an intelligence test of your true persuasions, answer please truthfully these two questions. You also, Mr Pew.'

He pointed a finger at her, then one at me. Theodora smiled (her nose twitching, however, slightly).

'Number one. Do you agree to total political freedom for coloured races without any restrictions whatever? Miss Theodora?'

'No.'

'Mr Pew?'

'Yes.'

'Second question. Would you yourself marry a coloured man—or woman?'

'Yes,' said Theodora; and added, 'If I loved him, of course.'

'No,' I said.

'Why not, Mr Pew?'

'For the child's sake.'

'It would be racially degenerate?'

'It would be miserable.'

'Subject to social pressures? Excluded by both races?'

'Yes.'

Mr Bo glared at us.

'That is the familiar argument. But why should such a half-caste race not serve as spearhead for enlightenment? Be necessary victims in the victorious struggle?'

'Perhaps,' I could not forbear to say, 'you should ask the half-caste child what he thinks of that.'

The band stopped, and we all sipped coffee in the silence of misunderstanding. Mr Karl Marx Bo, suddenly, looked bitter.

'Well,' he said, 'you are both nice people, I am sure, but I think you also are what we despise even more than we do those who hate us—you are full-time professional admirers of the coloured peoples, who like us as you like pet animals. Miss Theodora, do you wish to dance?'

'Alas, Mr Bo! My friend Theodora is unable to.'

'Speak for yourself, Montgomery. Karl Marx, shall we take the floor?'

And she did, and twirled with him quite creditably. Admirable Theodora!

I looked round the cavern, which had a warm coloured fug and stuffiness—sticky, promiscuous and cloying, a hot grass hut in the centre of our town. The men lounged and watched, languid and attentive, the white girls sat up chattering, playing hard to get. How sad there were no coloured girls there of equal dignity and beauty to the men.

Mr Ronson Lighter came over. He handed me my Ronson lighter. He looked very cross.

'Oh, thank you,' I said.

'Billy say I to give you that.'

'Much obliged.'

'Also that you come over to speak with him.'

'I'm here with a friend.'

'That you bring her over too. He offers you both coffee.'

Billy was sitting among his henchmen in so dark a corner as to be doubly invisible. He reached up a hand, took mine, and pulled me gently down.

'Johnny, he still not come here yet?' he said.

'No. What can have happened to him?'

'Perhaps he change his mind. He was with Hamilton Ashinowo?'

'Yes.'

'Then perhaps Hamilton will offer him some special entertainment. So he change his mind and stay back home.' Mr Whispers softly laughed.

This was mysterious. So, 'Good evening, Mr Cannibal,' I said. 'I hope you had no trouble at the police station.'

There was a loud silence.

'You were in police station tonight, Jimmy?' Billy Whispers asked him.

'No.'

Billy looked at me. So did Mr Cannibal: he seemed angry and alarmed.

I said: 'Perhaps I made a mistake.'

'I hope you do,' said Billy Whispers.

The silence continued till the coffee came. 'You get this your lighter?' Whispers said to me.

'Yes. Thank you.'

'Accidents do happen. My boy did not know you was a friend of Johnny Fortune's. He is a nice boy, Johnny. Too nice for this city, I expect. I hope he may soon go back home.' He turned to a half-caste girl upon the bench. 'This is Barbara,' he said. 'She likes to dance with you.'

'I don't dance.'

'She teach you. Barbara, go with this man on to the floor.'

We went. The girl said, 'Why did you tell him you saw Jimmy at the station?'

'Why not? Wasn't he caught up in that raid like everybody else?'

'He can't have told Billy he was there. . . . I can see Billy suspects him of something. It looks like trouble to me.'

'But Mr Cannibal's his friend.'

'Cannibal's slippery. We all know that.'

She spoke with a Cardiff accent. It came oddly out of her half-African face, the sound so ill assorted with a physical beauty that had reached her from thousands of miles away.

'You come here often?' I said.

'I'm a hostess here.'

'You work for the management?'

'No. For Billy Whispers. He controls most of the hostesses here.'

'The management let him?'

'These West Indians are frightened of the Africans. They don't interfere. Can't you dance any better than that?'

'No. You were going to teach me.'

'Just hold on to me, then. Bring your body close and don't think of your feet. You like coloured girls?'

'I think so.'

'You ever been with one?'

'No.'

Barbara glanced up at me with mild surprise. We passed Theodora and Mr Karl Marx Bo. 'Come and sit down,' I said to Barbara, 'and meet my friend Theodora.'

'That fish-face woman? Isn't she a copper?'

'Not to my knowledge.'

'Are you one, by the way?'

'Heaven forfend.'

'Eh?'

'What difference does it make what I say, Barbara? Just think what you like about us. Time alone will show.'

'Tell your friends to come to Billy's table, then. I have to get back to him.' She stepped across the floor, professionally swinging her magnificent bottom.

I said to Theodora as we followed, 'Where *did* you learn to dance so well? You're a perpetual revelation.'

Lowering her voice, she said, 'I was at one time in the Wrens, and lived a rather rackety life. It's a period I prefer to forget about, and I'll thank you not to refer to it again.'

Billy waved us into his corner with a comprehensive smile. With him now there was an enormous coloured G.I., and holding both the G.I.'s hands a lovely, harsh-faced white girl.

'Is Dorothy,' said Billy, 'and her good friend Larry.'

'Hi, man. You American or British?' Larry asked me.

'British.'

'Oh, that's all right, then.'

'Larry doesn't like Americans,' Dorothy explained.

'But isn't he one?'

'Oh, yes, but not an *American*, if you see what I mean.'

She hugged him, then let out a sudden shriek. 'Look there!' she cried. 'It's my brother Arthur!'

A tall gold-skinned boy came gangling gracefully across the floor, grinning with imbecile guile, his lower lip pendent, his eyes flashing dubious charm. He kissed Dorothy, shook hands with everyone, sat down and put his arms round several shoulders.

'I come out this morning,' he told everybody. 'An' hitch-hiked up to town. An' I called at back home and found Muriel. An' she told me about our new brother Johnny. Have you seen him, Dorothy?'

'Johnny? Yes, I seen him. He's a fresh boy, just like you.'

'Ma wouldn't take me in, I've no place I can go, and I'd like to ask my new brother Johnny to help me with some loot until I can get settled. Unless you can help me, Billy, or you, Dorothy, or someone.'

He gazed lazily around, exuding animal magnetism and anxiety.

'Larry,' said Dorothy, 'you won't mind if I have this dance with my little brother?'

But Mr Cochrane, the resident manager, who'd been standing by like a janizary, stepped up. 'I'm sorry, gentlemen, and ladies too,' he said, 'but I cannot permit your wife, Billy, to take the floor in slacks.'

Billy said nothing. Larry the G.I. took Mr Cochrane's arm.

'Listen man,' he said. 'Let me instruct you about clothing. All you West Indians go about dressed in zoot-suit styles we've thrown away ten years ago, and we don't complain about you.'

'It is not a question of styles, but of being costumed respectably for my club.'

'This girl, man, is smart as any film star. They all of them wear slacks in their off-duty hours.'

'Flim star or no flim star,' said Mr Cochrane (and he did say 'flim'), 'she must please attire herself in a proper skirt.'

'Oh, blow, man,' said Ronson Lighter. 'Twist now—you dig?'

Mr Cochrane stood his ground. 'I refuse all permission. I shall stop the orchestra.'

Mr Bumper Woodman arrived with several companions. All the men stood up. I saw Theodora reaching for her handbag.

'Why, oh why,' said Mr Karl Marx Bo to Mr Cochrane, 'do you stir up trouble with your African cousins? If you want to make some trouble, why you not go and fight with Dr Malan?'

'Me tell you insults is quite ineffectual, Mr Student,' said Mr Woodman.

'Oh-ho! Listen to this veteran Caribbean pugilist!'

'Listen to these Ras Tafaris, all long hair and dirty finger-nails.'

'These sugar-cane suckers! These calypso-singing slaves.'

'Slave? My ancestor had the wisdom to leave your jungle country.'

'You ancestor was so no good, my ancestor he go sell him to Jumble slave-ship.'

'You ras-clot man—you's wasted.'

'These bumble-clot men—these pussy-clots.'

'Come to your home in Africa, man, and we teach you some good behaviour.'

At this moment of clenched fists and hands slipping inside pockets, a very tall slim man, with a piece bitten out of one ear, approached. 'Now come,' he said. 'Come, come, come, come, come.'

'Mr Jasper!' cried Dorothy. 'Are you the boss here, or aren't you? Tell your men to see reason!'

Mr Jasper listened to several explanations, then said in a high, smooth voice, 'Miss Dorothy, I lend you a skirt from out of our cabaret costumes. I hope you will accept this solution, Mr Whispers.'

'No.'

'Yes, man.'

'No, man, no.'

'Come,' I whispered to Theodora. 'This is our cue to leave.'

12

Foo-foo in the small, late hours

WHEN I ARRIVED with Muriel outside this Moonbeam club (which every Spade we met seemed heading for, like night beasts to their water-hole), I saw at once, from very much past experience, that trouble was going on inside. People were peering down the entrance stairs and jabbering, and noise of shouts and crashings floated up. I drew Muriel far into a doorway, as I expected any moment the intrusion of the Law.

Then customers came scurrying up too. Among them I see Montgomery, and with him his Miss Theodora. I said to Muriel to wait, and went across to them.

'Oh, Mr Fortune,' Theodora cried. 'There's fighting going on downstairs.'

'Your brother Arthur,' said Montgomery, 'and Billy and his friends are battling with some wild West Indians.'

Well, I suppose our African troubles aren't his business, but all the same, has he not a pair of fists to stay and help my friends?

I'd seen there were two quite old American saloon cars with drivers that seemed Africans to me. I went over quickly and asked were they for hire? They were.

'What is a place to meet not far from here?' I asked Miss Theodora.

She said the big radio building of the B.B.C.

'Get in,' I told her, 'with Montgomery. Muriel,' I shouted, 'come over here! Go quickly where this lady says,' I told the two drivers, putting pound notes in their hands, 'and all of you wait for me there till I arrive.'

Then I plunged down the Moonbeam stairs.

At the bottom, by the entrance door, I saw Dorothy and Cannibal and various other friends all torn and tattered. The West Indians had expelled them out. I told them where to scatter at the place I'd sent the cars.

'But, Johnny!' Dorothy cried out. 'Billy's still in there, and Ronson and your brother Arthur.'

'Do as I tell you, Dorothy, I am always best alone. Cannibal, now, blow with these people to the big radio building. I bring all the others soon whether dead or else alive.'

I heaved and pushed open the club door. The band was still playing, all now up upon their feet. Chicks were standing on the chairs, laughing and screaming, and G.I.s cheering and acting with no responsibility at all. On the dance floor I saw Billy with Ronson and one other, who were murdering, and being murdered, by the West Indians.

I climbed over the bar counter, and started smashing crates of Coca-Cola by heaving them with loud crashes on the floor. The band stopped and faces began to turn round in my direction. 'Look, Mr Jasper!' a tall West Indian cried. 'Your valuable stock is being depleted.'

I picked up four bottles, and burst through to the dance floor. I grabbed up the microphone, which lay there overturned, and cried out: 'Billy, we cut out! The Law will soon be intruding! Here, Billy, catch this bottle!'

We battered our way towards the door. The customers were generally friendly, and seemed to regret the ending of this silly mess. Come on, Bumper Woodman,' they kept crying to a huge West Indian. 'Show us how you beat Joe Louis to his knees.'

But it was Ronson Lighter he was fighting now, and that crooked boy, even despite his dirty blows, looked like getting massacred by the big West Indian's bulkiness, till Billy Whispers snatched the microphone from my hands and cracked this Woodman on the skull with a cruel smack. We all beat it up the stairs.

'Come on, let's run,' said Ronson Lighter. 'I smell the coming of the Law.' And we saw two beetle cars come sweeping round the distant corner.

'Not run, no,' I said, 'is better stroll rapidly like serious gentlemen.'

'Thank you,' said Billy, 'for your interference.' He wiped blood from both his hands.

'Who is this third boy?' I asked him. 'Can this be my brother Arthur?'

For I'd seen him fighting also on the Moonbeam floor, and his certain strong resemblance to my Dad, and doing him great credit with his vigorous blows; but as I walked beside him now, and he turned smiling to me, smoothing his knuckles, I also caught his mother's crazy glance in both his eyes.

'What say?' said Arthur, as we turned two swift corners. 'Bless you, my brother—you're my boy!' He put his arm around me and said softly, 'You'll help me with some loot now, Johnny, won't you.'

'We see about this, Arthur. We talk about all those things.'

By twisting around in zigzag circles, we had now arrived outside a big white block building standing on its own. Our friends were by the cars in a cluster on the street, laughing and chattering in this silent London early dawn.

Billy introduced me round. 'Come!' I cried out. 'What's needed is to celebrate our survival from these dangers. We all of us go now to my friend Hamilton's and eat some foo-foo.'

'*Foo-foo?*' said Miss Theodora, needlessly wrinkling up her nose.

'Is a standard African dish, lady, like your English shepherd pie, but I think nicer.'

This English lady smiled and shook her head.

'Then let us drop you off, Miss Theodora,' I said, 'at your house, or any other convenient point of your selection. Billy, you take Montgomery and some of us in this one car, and Miss Theodora and we here will travel in the other.'

Of course Billy understood what I intended, and our cars shot ahead through the dark, wide thoroughfares. When Miss Theodora saw we were not going near her house at all, she turned to me and said, 'Am I being kidnapped?'

I said, 'No, lady, just forcibly invited. And you have your good friend Montgomery to take care of you as well as me.'

I felt Miss Theodora next to me relax.

At my new Holloway home, I found that Hamilton had partly returned to life, and was wandering about, holding a coffee cup, with just some slacks on, and talking to Mr Cole, who was in striped pyjamas. I told them to make themselves suitable to welcome all my guests, and I took Mr Cole upon one side.

'These are good friends,' I said, 'and perhaps you could fix some liquor at a reasonable price for their entertainment that will do honour to your house.'

'You have the loot for that now?'

I gave him more pound notes, and he looked dignified, and blew.

Billy asked for the necessary meat and semolina to make foo-foo, and Hamilton took him and Cannibal and Ronson Lighter to the kitchen. Arthur all this time was following me about, his eyes with a look of admiration, and his arm always on my shoulder. 'There you go, man!' he kept saying to me. 'There you go!'

'Take it easy, bra,' I said to him. 'I see you straight tomorrow morning.'

'Tell me about my Dad. Is he a rich man? Is he loaded?'

'He's a fine man, our Dad.'

He looked at me hideous all at once. Even I was just a little scared.

'Then why's he left me skinned in hopeless destitution?'

I took no notice of this foolishness, and put some Billy Eckstine on to Hamilton's radiogram. Soon Mr Cole appeared with armfuls of Merrydown cider and Guinness stout and V.P. wine. All the while I saw that this companion of Montgomery's, this Miss Pace, examined me as if I was a zoological exhibit. I went and sat down beside her on the collapsible settee.

'So you are in the employment of the B.B.C., Miss Theodora,' I said to her. 'That's a real serious occupation.'

'I'd thought,' she said rather rapidly, 'of putting on a series of talks in which colonial citizens would relate their experiences when they arrive here.'

She looked at me. I said nothing.

'Though I'm wondering if, to tell anything like the truth, these talks might perhaps reveal more than our listeners would stand for.'

Now I can tell as well as any when a chick has been reduced by my physical appearance, and behind this white girl's word I read a positive design to drag me between sheets before too long. But this was most unattractive to me in her case, particularly as little Muriel, who was much more to my liking and intention, was standing by.

'Oh, yes, Miss Theodora?' I said, playing cool.

'"Theodora,"' she told me, 'please, no "Miss". If I do decide to go ahead with the talks, would you consider taking part?'

I told her politely it would no doubt be a pleasure; and thinking I'd done my duties as the host, I was leaving her for Muriel when she shook my hand and said, 'Then won't you dance with me?' Someone had now swept Muriel away, so I smiled at this not so tempting girl and took her hands.

But even above the high cry of Billy Eckstine we all heard a wild scream, and there was Hamilton, still half naked in his slacks in spite of what I tell him, standing stiffly by his empty bed, pointing and gazing down at it and crying, 'This poor little boy is dead!'

'Hamilton!' I ran over and held his shaking shoulders. 'What little boy?'

'Me, Johnny! Look! There I am—dead!'

'Man, you're still high! Sit down now, and act serious. There's company present all around you.'

'I'm not dead then, Johnny?'

'Oh, Hamilton!'

He began to sob.

'Come with me in the kitchen and cool down, man. You'll find they're making foo-foo there. Eat some, it will calm you. Really, my dear friend Hamilton,' I said when I'd got him past the door, 'you must get off that needle—it will kill you dead.'

'You'll have to help me, Johnny.'

But out in the kitchen, though the pots and pans were simmering, there were no Billy, Cannibal or Mr Ronson Lighter. I sat Hamilton down, gave him a cigarette, and went and looked out through the back door to the garden.

There, in the early light, I saw Billy and Ronson Lighter beating Jimmy Cannibal. This man was a boxer, yes, but Billy, I could see, was a little killer, and Ronson grabbing at Cannibal in evil places.

I opened the door and shouted: 'What is it, Billy?'

Cannibal broke free and scrambled over the garden wall.

'What for you mix in this?' cried Billy. He raised up his hands against me, then he said, 'Oh, well . . .' smoothed down his clothes, and came to the kitchen door. There was blood on Ronson Lighter's coat, and I led him to the tap.

'That Cannibal has been making a friendship with the Law,' said Billy.

'How you know that?'

'That Jumble friend of yours saw him talking with coppers in the station.'

'Montgomery tell you that? But I was there with him too.'

'You were? All the time with him?'

'No, not all the time.... Why didn't that foolish man tell *me* about he see Cannibal?'

'Is that Jumble to be trusted?'

'I think so.'

'He'd better be.'

'Billy,' I said, 'if Cannibal was with the Law, how do you know they didn't just pull him in for something? What make you think he's blowing off his top?'

'He tell us, when we ask him, he was not in there at all. So if he was, it must be for some evil purpose. I finished with that man, and if he's said a word against me... Well, if ever the Law puts the hand on me, that boy had better leave town.

'Billy, you get so excited. And your foo-foo will all be burning.'

He came over to the stove and dished it out on the big plate. 'You can't trust even your own people in this country,' he said. 'This country turns men bad.'

'Well, Billy, you was never one big angel yourself, were you?'

He gave me a sideways smile. 'Maybe I not, but I not shop my friends like Cannibal.'

Mr Cole came through the kitchen door. 'Did I hear fighting noises? I must have no fighting on my premises.'

'Play cool, man. There'll be no more battle.'

'This Hamilton,' said Mr Cole. 'He must control his conduct.'

'Who sells him this bad stuff?' I said. 'He can't get all that bad on just his legal ration.'

I caught the glance of Billy and of Cole, who looked at each other.

'Whoever sells my friend that stuff,' I said, with a hard stare at each of them, 'is going to find himself an enemy of mine. And you, Hamilton, you'd better change your habits of life unless you wish to die when still quite young.'

We all drank some ruby wine in silence; then carried the dishes in among the dancers of the bigger room.

We passed round the water to wash, and everyone sat down upon the floor: even the Jumbles, who we showed how you crouch around the dish, and take up your wad of semolina, dip it in the red peppery gravy, and scoop up your piece of meat. They did it quite free and nicely, though burning painfully in the mouth, and with sometimes the unnecessary dribbles.

'And how is recent developments in Africa?' said Mr Cole to me.

'Oh,' I told him, 'it looks like in one or two years' time we have our freedom.'

'What you need in Africa, Africa man,' said Arthur, 'is a blow-everyone-up party, including your own crooked Africa politicians.'

'This man is talking ignorant and foolish,' said Mr Karl Marx Bo. 'What's needed is more education, and more honesty.'

'They'll never let you govern yourselves, man,' said Larry the G.I.

'They will, because we'll make them,' said Mr Bo. 'And then we Africans come across and free our poor American brothers, who all they do is sit on their seats and sing their spirituals.'

Little Barbara thought this so funny, and let out a cheap laugh.

'If we don't get this freedom soon, we take it, like the Mau Mau do,' said Mr Ronson Lighter.

'Mau Mau haven't managed to take much,' said Miss Theodora, in a sharp way, 'except a lot of African lives.'

'Oh, stop all your politics,' cried Dorothy, 'while we're eating food.'

'We shoot you like Mau Mau, man,' said Ronson Lighter, pointing a pepper-pot with an evil grin upon my friend Montgomery.

'If you was in Kenya, Mr Montgomery,' said Billy Whispers, 'what side would you be?'

'My own people's, of course,' Montgomery replied. 'When trouble comes, you must go with your own tribe.'

'Oh-ho! And if I take you prisoner, you know what I do?' said Ronson Lighter to him.

I broke in. 'If I take my friend Montgomery prisoner,' I said, 'I grab away his weapon, yes, but maybe himself, I turn him loose.'

Muriel smiled up at me, and move much closer.

Hamilton jumped up. 'This man's an African!' he cried, taking Montgomery round his neck. 'I know my brother, because I see he is an African.'

'No, no, not me.'

'Yes, man! You's an African! And I prove it to you now! I give you a present, a great gift.'

Hamilton went to his cupboard, and pulled off a hanger the dress of our dear tribe. 'Come, man, you put this on!' he cried.

'I couldn't accept,' Montgomery said.

'You are my guest,' Hamilton told him severely.

'Yes, put it on,' said his friend Theodora. 'I'm sure it'll suit you to perfection.'

Hamilton pulled it on over Montgomery, and tied the cloth round his head. He looked really quite strange in it, but he stood there quite clearly filled with flattery and pleasure. He took my friend Hamilton's hand. 'I do appreciate it,' he said. 'Thank you very, very much.'

Now Billy Whispers and Ronson Lighter were starting to roll weed, in company with Hamilton and Mr 'Nat King' Cole: which I'd rather they'd practised in private in the kitchen, instead of in this public way in front of strangers. They passed the sticks round, and Dorothy was eager, and little Barbara, and my brother Arthur, as I of course expected of him.

But Muriel wouldn't touch the stuff, and our other English visiting friends, though Billy Whispers tried to press them to it, which he shouldn't do, really, because weed is something it's best not to handle unless you have the mastery of its action from experience since an earlier age. In this refusal, they had the support of Larry the G.I. and Karl Marx Bo.

'All you get out of that,' said Mr Bo, 'is crazy antics and then ruin. That rubbish is the ruin of my people.'

'Many good men,' said Larry, 'have lived inside penitentiaries on account of that goddamned ganga.'

'Just listen to this Yank,' said Dorothy, all tough and daring. 'Man, ain't you never raved nor rocked in your career?'

'With this I forget my troubles,' Arthur said, soft and silly. 'And of troubles, I say that I have plenty.'

'It'll give you plenty more,' said Muriel. 'It'll send you right back inside where you came out of.'

'Let Arthur be,' said Dorothy. 'Is he telling *you* what you should do?'

'Why let him be?' cried Karl Marx Bo. 'She's right, this chick.

Weed kills your conscience, don't we all know it? It opens the door to what is violent inside of you, and cruel, and no good sense, and full of fear.'

'It don't make you silly like this liquor does,' said Mr Cole. 'It may slow you up, your bodily movement, but it leaves you with a better control and perfect speech.'

'Perfect speech to say some rubbish like you do,' said Larry the G.I.

Little Barbara laughed. 'Why you all so serious about it, anyway?' she said. 'Isn't life hard enough without it?'

Miss Theodora, she was listening closely. She seemed a little troubled with anxiety, and also by her unusual ignorance of this subject. Though this did not stop her now from saying her word.

'But you, Mr Bo,' she asked him. 'If you know so much about it, surely you must have smoked it once yourself?'

'Who hasn't, lady!' cried this legal student. 'But some, when they burn their fingers in the fire, can learn, and others not. What this man Cole here says is true. It leaves your mind clear, yes, but only half of it, the half that has the proud and the darker thoughts. You think that the world is you, is yours, you think it is you that make the laws of all creation. Off goes your personality, you lose control of it, and in walks the dark spirit to take over. And all the time, under that stuff you say to yourself: "How can anyone as wonderful as me be wrong?" Then you go off and rob a bank, or kill your grandmother.'

The weed-smokers laughed at this serious fellow countryman. Myself, I thought the mistake was to mix up the smokers with the others. These arguments often come up when those who smoke hemp sit down with those who don't. . . .

So I got up and put on discs, and asked Muriel to dance with me. But this was the time, I could clearly see, when the party came near its death, because the light outside the curtains grew stronger than the electricity inside, and everyone was losing pleasure in the other's company. The two boys waiting with their cars outside came knocking to ask for instructions, or else they'd shoot off, and wanted more money for waiting, anyway. So Larry the G.I. went off with Dorothy, and Billy told Ronson Lighter to see little Barbara home. And in the other car, Montgomery went with Theodora and serious Mr Karl Marx Bo. I saw them off there in the already daylight street.

Dorothy leaned out and snatched a kiss I hadn't offered. 'I'll see you again soon, my man,' she said.

At the other car I shook hands in a more steady manner.

'Keep in touch, Johnny,' said Montgomery, sitting like an emir in his native dress. 'You know my telephone number.'

'And don't forget,' said Theodora, gripping my hand, 'I rely on you for my colonial programme.'

'Yes, yes, yes, yes,' I answered, and told the drivers in the Yoruba tongue to hurry them all off.

Back in the room, I found Hamilton in a deep slumber, and Cole inviting Billy and my brother Arthur to a game of dice. 'You will come too?' he said. I wished this badly, for dice are in my blood, but first there was the question of my Muriel. So they went upstairs without me, after Arthur had borrowed from me three pounds which was all that I had left.

Muriel was sitting by the radiogram. I kissed her quite freely, and she came up easily into my arms.

'Stay with me now, Muriel,' I said.

'No, Johnny, no, not here. . . .'

'Then where? This is my home, and Hamilton will sleep soundly for six hours. . . .'

'No, Johnny, not till I know you better.'

That woman's phrase! Which means, as all men know, 'Not till *I* ask you!' And why did she not go with all the others in the cars, if her real purpose was not to stay? If I had not been fond of this little child, and tired too, to tell the truth, and longing for my sleep, she would not have escaped me by her feeble answers.

So I said, 'Very well, Muriel, get all your things, and I shall go out to find your cab.'

She got up slowly, but by the door she stopped and clung and kissed me. 'Africans' skins are soft,' she said to me.

FIRST INTERLUDE

Idyll of miscegenation on the river

A PLEASURE STEAMER put out on the river, and seated in its prow alone were Muriel Macpherson and Johnny Macdonald Fortune. His left hand clasped her right, he held both on her lap, the white and brown fingers interlocking.

'It takes us an hour to reach the palace down the stream,' she told him.

'Well, I see they have beer on board, so that don't matter.'

Beside the helmsman, on the open bridge behind, a hybrid character—nautical in peaked cap and jacket of dark blue, but landlubber from the waist down with grey slacks and sandals—had taken his stance before a microphone. Crackling through amplifiers dispersed about the ship, his voice described, in accents part Cockney, part bogus North American, part the pedantic patronizing of the lecturer, the points of interest on either shore, disturbing the peace and contemplation of the few, but delighting the docile many, who swung their heads, as if spectators at a tennis match, towards the curiosities whose histories he recounted.

Muriel said: 'Do you have rivers in your country, Johnny?'

'Of course we have rivers: that's why we're called Nigeria.'

'Did you swim in them—like those boys there? You can swim, Johnny, can't you?'

He leapt, climbed on the railings of the boat, and made as if to dive. Muriel let out a scream, and clutched his ankles. He swayed. Passengers, distracted from the amplifiers, turned, frowned and laughed.

He slipped down on the deck into her arms, and held her tight a moment. 'You're a madman, Johnny Fortune! I can't trust you a split second. I must never let you out of my sight in future.' Not to be surprised again, when they sat down this time she held him closely round the shoulder.

He said: 'You're like my sister Peach. That's what she says to me as well—ah, women!'

The loud-speaker blared: 'And opposyte the old St Paul's—turn your heads this way, please' (the heads switched south) '—is the Bankside power station, a controversial electrification project, and there—the small yellow edifice is the one I'm alluding to—the former residence of Sir Christopher himself, from whence he watched across the river the lofty pile of his cathedral rising up, and then, just adjacent, in the district known previously as the "Stews"—with its bear-gardens, and colony of Dutch and Flemish women of easy virtue, as they were called (now all cleaned up, of course)—the site of the old Globe theatre, erected by the brothers Burbage in 1598 for the smash-hits of their mate Bill Shakespeare, who acted there himself in what he termed affectionately his "wooden O" . . .'

'What is Peach like?' asked Muriel.

'Peach? She is like all our women. The more she loves you, the more she tries to grasp you and take charge of you.'

'Your women are like that, out there in Africa?'

Johnny frowned.

'You know something, now? Is a secret I'm telling you, so open up the ears and close the lips. One chief reason why our boys get settled often with your white girls here is that our own back home are such big bosses. They do everything for you, yes, much more than any white girl would, and cook so well, and work, but in exchange for this, they try to gain possession of your private person.'

Muriel mused. 'But is it true' (she paused) 'that some of your boys really prefer us more?' He didn't answer, and looked downstream ahead. 'I mean,' she went on, 'like us better just because we're white?'

He turned towards her. 'That's what they say, isn't it? That's what the white newspapers all say in their Sunday editions. That all we want is rape some innocent white lady?'

'You're not being serious, Johnny.'

'As if there was any need to rape!'

'Don't flatter yourself: you're all so conceited.'

He preened himself, and looked it.

'Now on our left,' the amplifier intoned, 'we have the Billingsgate fish market and wharves, so named after Belin, legendary monarch of the Britons in their primitive era, and best known now, of course, for the fish porters' highly coloured language, of which I will attempt an imitation. Why, Gorblimey, you . . .' (the loud-speakers emitted only deafening crackles) '. . . sorry, ladies and gents, but I've been censored. Beneath us at the moment—that is, beneath the boat and underneath the river bed—is the oldest of the numerous Thames tunnels, now disused, constructed between 1825 and 1843 by Sir Marc Isambard Brunel, the Frenchman. And now, my friends and folks, arising in historic splendour on the northern bank is the ancient Tower of London, celebrated alike for its Traitors' Gate, Crown Jewels, scaffold, dungeons, ravens, Beefeaters, Bloody Tower and instruments of torture. . . .'

Johnny and Muriel barely glanced, and gazed ahead at castellated Tower Bridge, the last gate before the river becomes the ocean that weds the city to the outer world. She pressed his shoulder down a bit, and laid her head on it. 'You didn't answer me properly, though,' she said. 'Do you really like us better?'

'Does who like who?'

'You boys like us white girls.'

'Some of us do, perhaps.'

'Only some, Johnny?'

'Oh, you cannot judge by England, Muriel. There's so few of our own girls here, it has to be a white chick or else nothing. And can you imagine us with nothing?'

They kissed discreetly, with a slight grin of complicity.

'But if you had a free choice,' Muriel persisted, 'would you choose one of us? Choose us because we're different? Or because, if you marry one of us, it's easier to fit in and make a living?'

'What is this, Muriel! You make me some proposition of matrimony? Don't be so speedy, woman—we've only met up just one month. It's the man's supposed to make that invitation, didn't you know?' (She looked demure.) 'I tell you something, though, and don't forget it. If ever one of our boys does marry one of you, there's no doubt who we think is being done the favour.'

Muriel reflected, vexed, then half understanding. 'It's true,' she said, 'your boys are often better class than girls they marry here. . . .'

'Is not class I mean. Even when class and wealth is equal, is we who do the favour!'

The boat passed underneath the bridge, and faces suddenly grew darker. Muriel watched her native city as the boat chugged on between Venetian façades of eyeless warehouses, dropping into ancient Roman mud, where barges lay scattered derelicts under lattices of insect cranes. This was her first sight of Dockland, shut off from inquisitive view on land by Brobdingnagian brick walls. Missing familiar pavements and shop windows, Muriel saw her city as a place quite unfamiliar, and wondered what it might do to her, and Johnny Fortune.

'It's queer to think,' she said, 'how close we are, we two, and yet so far.'

'We're close enough.'

'Don't choke me, Johnny. No, no, I mean sharing Arthur as a brother, and yet no one drop of the same blood in our veins. . . .'

'Our blood's the same colour, Muriel, is all that matters. Everything that comes out of all human body is the same colour—did you think of that?'

She did: 'Johnny, don't be disgusting.'

Undaunted by the absence, in these lower reaches of the river, of interesting monuments, and remembering the hat he'd pass round before the journey ended, the resourceful guide still bludgeoned the passengers' defenceless ears: '. . . Wapping Old Stairs, where the bloodthirsty Judge Jeffreys was arrested in 1688, while attempting to flee the vengeance of the populace in the disguise of a sailor, and just there the former Execution Dock, where Captain Kidd and other notorious pirates were hanged in public in 1701 . . .'

Johnny tried to light a cigarette, but the breeze was too powerful, and he stubbed it out. 'You white chicks,' he said, 'are all so maidenhood and pure. You're badly brought up, you know.'

'We're not!'

'You are. And that's why you have no manners. And why you have no manners is that you let your kids run wild.'

'Didn't you run wild once?'

'I did, yes, but I also was closely instructed in excellent manners to older people and to strangers, unlike here: to say good morning and good afternoon, and always be respectful to the other man until he gave good reason to act different.'

'But Africans deceive strangers sometimes, don't they?'

'We do. We do, but we do not rub the man's face in the dirt. We may kill and rob him, yes, but we do not make him a shame to himself, like you. Kill a man, and his spirit will forgive you, but make him ashamed, and he will never so.'

Muriel just saw what he meant. She looked round at her fellow countrymen and women, and asked herself if they would. But all were now engrossed in the guide's tales of opium dens among the non-existent Chinese population of Limehouse Reach.

'I've learned a lot,' she said, 'from Arthur and his friends about how to treat you boys.'

'You speak as if we were some cattle or baboons. Respect us, that is all.'

'Oh, yes, you must be polite to coloured boys, always very polite—good manners seem to mean so much to you. But that's not all. You have to be very patient, too.'

'Are we so slow?'

'You're quick in your minds, but you mustn't ever be hurried. I can't say "Hullo—goodbye" to one of you like I can to one of our boys, without you get offended. It seems you think time's no object. . . .'

'Time is to be used. When I meet a countryman on the path back home, I talk for five minutes at least before I pass on my way.'

'That's what I mean.'

The boat swung south, and sailed down past the Isle of Dogs.

'What matters most of all,' said Muriel, softly as if to herself, 'is that you must never be afraid of a coloured man. If he bluffs you, you must say, "All right, do what you like, I'm not afraid of you,"—and you must mean it.'

Johnny Fortune laughed at her. 'I see you make a careful study of our peculiarities.'

'I've made no study, Johnny. I think you understand a man you love, that's all.'

Even to her embarrassment, he wrapped her in his arms and gave her, in full view of the passengers, a sexy squeeze. Losing interest in the guide, the tourists had taken increasing notice of the couple in the prow. They beamed at the embrace: this was how they expected a coloured man to act.

'I tell you one thing,' said Johnny, hugging her to death. 'What little white girls like most of all is force.'

'Oh, do they!'

'They do. All the boys say so.'

'Not the nice girls, they don't.'

'Oh-ho!' Johnny glared at her like a witch-doctor, and spoke in a throaty whisper. 'If you touch them gently, they just scream. So what you do? You take them to some little room up in some empty house, far off from ears, and say to them, "Scream now, lady! Scream!"'

'I wouldn't come.'

'You would. Oh, yes, you would!'

'I mean you wouldn't have to do that with me.... If I love a boy, I love him. If I didn't, I'd never be alone with him.'

'So you are an African! Tell me, then, Africa woman! Truthfully, now, Muriel. Why do you love us so?'

'I don't love you all—I love you.'

'Why so?'

'Because of what you said: those lovely manners you all have. And because you're all so beautiful to look at.'

'You think our ugly faces are so beautiful?'

'Not just your faces—it's the way you move. When you walk, you walk from the top of your head right down to the very tip of your toes.... You step out as if you owned the world....'

Fortune grew bored by this. Why praise a beauty that was evident to all?

'And then,' she went on, as he turned to gaze at the liquor bar and moistened his full lips, 'you're such fun to be with. If you say, "Let's do this, or that," to a coloured boy, his first answer isn't, "No." He's ready to fall in with any bright idea.' (Johnny was no longer listening.) 'Of course, sometimes your boys get sad and gloomy, all of a sudden for no reason.... And often those lovely smiles of yours don't mean a thing....'

Johnny was looking at a merchant ship, sailing stern first towards them down the river to the open sea. 'Come!' he said. 'Let us get ourselves some glass of lager beer.'

The little bar amidships smelt of heat, and airlessness, and stale ale. The boy serving was an undersized lad with a Tony Curtis hairdo, who slopped the lager in the glasses with amateur abandon. He eyed Johnny Fortune with enthusiasm.

'And for you what?' Johnny asked the boy. 'Some orange juice or Coke?'

'Ta, Guv, I'll have a Pepsi. You're not a boxer, are you?'

'Me? No. I box, though.'

'Of course you do. But I thought you could maybe get me Sugar's autograph.'

'I know boys who visit at his camp. Give me your name, and I shall get you this signature of Mr Robinson.'

'I'm Norman, the captain's son. Care of the boat will find me. Good 'ealth. I drink beer for choice, but Dad won't let me on his boat, I'm under age.'

The huge ship passed, and the craft rocked in its wash. Johnny looked through the port-hole, flattening his face. 'Perhaps she sail out to Africa,' he said.

'She's British,' said Muriel, squeezing up beside him. 'What a lot of ships we have.'

'So many. So old and battered.'

'We're a rich country, Johnny.'

'You? England is quite wasted, Muriel.'

'Wasted? It's not!'

'I tell you. The lands of opportunity are America, and China, and Africa, specially Nigeria.'

'Yes? Who cares, though!' She kissed him as he was still talking. 'It's hot, Johnny. Can't we get this port-hole open?'

'Hot! You call this heat? Nigeria would melt you.' He rubbed a sweaty nose against her own.

'Wait till the cold comes. Then you'll see something you don't know about.'

'Snowballs, you mean?'

'Not snow—just *cold*. You'd better buy yourself a duffel.'

'You, Muriel, will keep me warm.'

The boy came and wiped the table needlessly. He held Johnny by the arm, delicately feeling his biceps.

'You coloured boys,' he said, 'are wonderful fighters. You're the tops.' The blue eyes in his pimply face gazed at Johnny's own with rapture.

'We also have intelligent citizens, you know. There are African students who fully understand atomic energy.'

'Oh, so long as they can fight! You're brave!'

Johnny smiled with condescension, rubbed the boy's back, and pushed him gently off.

'They all love you, Johnny,' Muriel said.

'So long as you do.'

'I do. Oh yes, I do.' She stared at him, and clutched as if she feared he'd disappear. 'I'd do anything for you,' she said.

'Anything! Big words.'

'If you want to stay with me, you can. If you wanted to get married ever, you just say. If you want a child, I'll give you one—a boy: we'll call it Johnny-number-two. I'd work for you, Johnny—any work. I'd go to jail for you—do anything.'

'Muriel! Muriel! What sad thoughts you speak of.'

'You mean getting married?'

'I mean all these things that you imagine. You are my girl—it is enough. What else is there?'

'I love you, Johnny. Once we get into each other's blood, your race and mine, we never can cut free. All that matters to me is that you're brave, and beautiful, and you've got brains, so I can be proud of you. Nothing else matters to me at all.'

The boy came back. 'We're nearing Greenwich Palace now. Do you want to have a look on deck?'

Up in the sun, beneath a pink-blue sky, they watched the stately architectural rhetoric slide into view. 'I smell the sea,' said Fortune, sniffing. When Inigo Jones's splendid white cube appeared between Sir Christopher Wren's gesticulations, Muriel cried out, 'That one's for us! That's where we'll live—the little one.' They stood hand in hand by the railings to be first off at the pier, as the boat swung round the river in a circle. No one else followed them; and when the boat headed back up the river, they saw it wasn't stopping at the palaces.

Muriel called out to the helmsman. 'Can't we get off?'

'Get off, miss? No, we don't stop.

'But it said it was an excursion to Greenwich Palace.

'This is the excursion, miss. We take you there and back, to see it, but you get off where you came from in the City.'

PART II

Johnny Fortune, and his casual days

1

Pew becomes a free-lance

An autumn day, some three months later, found me sitting in a coffee shop frequented by B.B.C. executives, face to face with Theodora and profoundly dejected.

'You're out?' she said.

'Sacked. My interview was a disaster.'

And it had been.

My chief was one of those who think it best to be kind to be cruel. With the air of sharing a great joke, he said to me, 'Well, Pew, the blow's falling, I dare say you expected it,' and gave me a ghastly grin.

'Sir?'

'We're not taking up our option on you, Pew. I expect you'd like some reasons. I'll give you three. The police have been making enquiries about you, and we don't like that. You've visited our hostel frequently without authority and behaved oddly, so it seems. And then, Pew, in a general way, we think you've been a little too familiar with the coloured races. Oh, don't interrupt, I know we're the Welfare Office, and we're in duty bound to help these people in their hour of need. But remote control's the best, we've found. Not matiness. Not going native, if I may so express myself.'

'May *I* make an observation, chief?' I said, when I saw the game was lost.

'You may indeed, if it will ease your feelings.'

'I'm not surprised the coloured races hate us.'

He wasn't a bit disconcerted.

'But they don't, Pew, that's where you make your second big mistake. They don't like us, certainly, but they don't hate us. They just accept us as, I suppose, a necessary evil.'

Determined to have the last word, I said: 'Nothing could be worse than to be neither loved nor hated. It puts one on a level with the Swiss.'

Theodora didn't congratulate me on this rejoinder. 'It's always best,' she said, 'in tricky interviews, to say one word for every six the other person says.'

'But did I in fact say more! And, anyway, my dear Theodora, you yourself have not always been, of recent months, a model of discretion.'

'Oh, have I not?' she said, glancing round at the coffee-swilling executives.

'This series of talks of yours on the colour question has seemed to call for an awful lot of planning.'

'All B.B.C. series must be meticulously planned for months ahead.'

'No doubt, though I can't think why. But I mean you've been bringing Johnny Fortune and his pals against their wills into your flat on far too many occasions.'

'Against their wills? They've been delighted.'

'They're so polite.'

'In any case, I've not seen Johnny now for a month.'

'Nor I. He's disappeared mysteriously from his usual haunts.'

The waitress disgustedly put down the check. I reached for it. 'No,' said Theodora. 'You must economize.'

'I have in my pocket a month's salary in lieu of notice.'

'And then?'

'Then? Only Australia remains.'

Theodora snatched the check away. 'Perhaps you could free-lance for the Corporation,' she said. 'So many mediocrities get away with it.'

'Thanks, Theodora,' I said quite bitterly, and arose. She called me back, but not until I was half-way down the stairs. Her face, from that distance, looked agonized and proud. I crossly returned, and she said in a throaty whisper, 'Find him, Montgomery!' Then swirled to some raw-boned feminine executives at the adjacent table.

I went out bemused into the chilly morning and, passing despondently by one of the many dilapidated subsidiary buildings near Portland Place that house the detritus of the B.B.C., who should I see emerging but a resplendent figure whose fortunes, it seemed, had risen as my own had fallen: none other than Mr Lord Alexander in a rose suit—yes, rose—and carrying a guitar case. I hailed him, and was mortified that at first he didn't recognize me.

'You sang for me,' I reminded him, 'at the hostel some months ago.'

'Oh yes—oh yes, indeed, man. Before my unfortunate arrest, which luckily ended only in seven days.'

'And since then, my lord, since then?'

'Well, man, I've swum into the glory. Radio programmes and cabaret work, and even a number of gramophone recordings.'

'Congratulations, my dear chap. You've written some good new songs?'

'*All* my songs is good, but specially enjoyed are those on British institutions: "Toad-in-hole and Guinness stout", and "Please, Mr Attlee, don't steal my majority", and "Why do I thirst between three and five?" . . .'

'Let us thirst no more, Lord Alexander. The pub's nearby.'

'Me, I will buy you something.'

Over two light ales, I asked him if he had news of Johnny Fortune. He lowered his voice. 'They say,' he told me, 'that little boy has turned out not too good.'

'But where is he? I've been up to Holloway, I've been round all the bars, and he's nowhere to be found.'

'The boy's moved down East End, they tell me, which is a bad, bad sign.'

'Why so?'

'There's East End Spades and West End Spades. West End are perhaps wickeder, but more prosperous and reliable.'

'Do you know where I can find him in the East End?'

'Myself I don't know, but anyone would tell you at Mahomed's café in the Immigration Road. That is a central spot for all East End activities.'

I bought Alexander a return drink, thanked him heartily, and leapt into a cab.

2

Misfortunes of Johnny Fortune

'TROUBLES,' I SAID TO HAMILTON, 'do not come singly.'

'No, Johnny.'

'Never would I think I could be so very foolish.'

'No, Johnny, no.'

'Sometimes I even think I must eat up my pride and return to my Dad in Lagos like the prodigal son.'

We were sitting in my miserable room, a former sweet-shop on the ground floor of the Immigration Road. Muriel, thank goodness, was out now at her work. But Hamilton and I had little joy in our male company, for we were both quite skinned and destitute.

'You tell me to use a needle is bad,' said Hamilton, 'but to gamble away your wealth—is that not a greater injury? Two hundred pounds fly off, Johnny, in three short happy months.'

'They rose once to nearly four hundred pounds with all my profits.'

'But tumbled again to two times zero afterwards.'

I got up and combed my hair, for there was little else to do. 'Not even a fire, Hamilton. Not even a cigarette. And do you know, my greatest sorrow is the total neglect of my meteorological studies?'

'Your greatest sorrow is not that—it is that you are boxed up with this Muriel.'

And what could I say to that? At first I had been fond of that little girl, and she had given me some excellent physical satisfactions. But when all my loot was gone, and the only serious work that I could find, in the building industry, was too poor paid and degradation, she had begun to support me with her pitiful wages from the shirt factory where she was employed.

'Johnny,' said Hamilton. 'You're quite sure this little girl of yours does work in that shirt shop?'

'Of course. Now why?'

'You're positive she's not hustling?'

'Muriel, Hamilton, is no harlot like her sister Dorothy.'

'Be sure of that. Because to live on the immoral earnings of a woman is considered a serious crime in this serious country.'

'Muriel is too honest and too simple.'

'No chick is simple.'

'That is true. . . .'

'This child of hers she says is one day to be yours. You believe her story, Johnny?'

'How can I tell? It could be so. . . .'

'You will let her have it, Johnny?'

'Hamilton! I am no infant murderer.'

Hamilton stretched his long body out.

'Perhaps not,' he said. 'But if she has it, and you refuse her marriage, as I expect you to, she can then weep before the magistrate until he grants her an affiliation order. This will oblige you to support her till the infant is sixteen years of age.'

'Man, I shall skip the country if that happens.'

I looked at my dear friend's eyes. More sunken away than when first I discovered him again, and his whole body shrivelling up with that evil drug, it seemed to me that only wicked thoughts came now into his mind.

'Hamilton,' I said. 'Let's go into the street and take the air. Sitting here leaguing all the day in idleness is just a nightmare.'

'Walking gives me only a hopeless appetite.'

'When do you draw your drug ration, Hamilton?'

'Not till tomorrow. . . .'

'Oh, but come out in the air, man!'

'No, Johnny. Let me sleep here, or I think I'll tumble down and die.'

I had no coat since it was in the pawnshop, but I took up my scarf and started for the door.

Hamilton opened up one eye. 'Those Jumbles, Johnny,' he said. 'That Pew and Pace people you used to see. Can't you raise loot from them?'

'I have some pride.'

'You also have your digestion, Johnny, to consider.'

This Immigration Road is quite the queen of squalor. And though back home we have our ruined streets, they haven't the scraped grimness of this East End thoroughfare. I half shut my eyes and headed for Mahomed's café, which, though quite miserable, has the recommendation that it's open both the night and day.

This is due to the abundant energy of Mahomed, an Indian who once worked high up in a rich West End hotel, and serves you curried chicken as if you were a rajah loaded up with diamonds. His wife is a British lady with a wild love of Spades, and a horrid habit of touching you on the shoulder because she says 'to stroke a darkie brings you luck'. But you can forgive this insolence if she supplies some credit without the knowledge of Mahomed.

The Café's frequented by human dregs, and coppers' narks, and boys who come there hustling and making deals. The first face I saw, when I went in it, was the features of Mr Peter Pay Paul.

'What say, man,' I asked him. 'You still peddling that asthma cure?'

He gave me his spewed-up grin.

'I'm legitimate now,' he said. 'I sell real stuff. You buy some?'

'Roll me a stick, and I'll smoke it at your expense.'

'That's not a good business, man.' But he started rolling.

'What sentence did you get that day?'

'Case dismissed. What do you know?'

'That C.I.D. Inspector, that Mr Purity. He didn't press the charge?'

'He not in court, man—was quite a break.'

'You small beer to him, Peter, it must be.'

'If that's true, man, it's lucky. That Mr Purity looked cold hard.'

He handed me the weed.

'Peter, where you get this stuff?' I said. 'Who is your wholesaler?'

'That is my private secret, man.'

'Suppose that you cut me in on it?'

'Well, I might do . . . if you show some generosity. . . .'

'Man, I'm skinned just at present. Make a friend of me, and you won't repent of it.'

'I'll consider your request, Johnny Fortune. Give me some drag.'

Mahomed came up and bowed as he always does: this because he likes to win the affection of violent Spades who can help him if ever trouble should arise.

'An English gentleman was here looking for you, Johnny.'

'What name?'

'He tell me to say Montgomery was asking for you.'

'Ah, him. What did he need?'

'Johnny, isn't that a copper? His name was quite unknown to me, you never tell me he was a friend of yours, so I sent him farther on east down Limehouse way.'

'I don't live there.'

'To confuse the man. I said to call at 12 Rawalpindi Street, but so far as I know there isn't any such address.'

Mahomed gave us a sly, silly smile to prove his clever cunning.

'Mahomed, you're too smart. If that man calls here again, please tell him where I live.'

'He's a friend, then?'

'Is a friend, yes.'

'Oh, I apologise. You eat something?' I shook my head. 'On me, said Mahomed, and cut out behind his counter with another little bow.

I saw an old African man was watching us. 'Who is that grey old person?' I asked Peter Pay Paul.

'That old-timer? Oh, a tapper. He's always complaining about we younger boys.'

'I no tapper,' the old gentleman said. 'But all I can tell you is you boys spoil honest business since you come. Before the wartime, before you come here in all your numbers, the white folks was nice and friendly to us here.'

'They spat in your eyes and you enjoyed it, Mr Old-timer.'

'You go spoil everything. You give me some weed.'

'Blow, man. Go ask your white friends for it.'

After Mahomed's sodden chicken, we walked down the Immigration Road, Peter Pay Paul holding his weed packets in his hands constantly inside his overcoat pockets as these weed peddlers do, ready to ditch them at the slightest warning.

'I must cut out of this weed racket soon, Johnny,' he said. 'No one lasts more than three months or so, because the Law puts the eye on you before too long goes by.'

'How will you live, man, if you give it up?'

'There's the lost-property racket, but there's not much loot in that. . . . You go round lost-property offices asking for brief-cases, say, or gold-topped umbrellas, and claiming the nicest object you can see.'

'They give them to you without any proof?'

'You speak some very bad English, and act ignorant and helpless to them, when they ask for explanations. They end by yielding up some article which then you can sell. . . . If only I could get a camera from them, though.'

'To take street photograph?'

Peter Pay Paul stopped and laughed.

'Man,' he said, taking me by the scarf, 'you're crazy. No. Hustling with Jumble queers. You get yourself picked up by them, taken home, then photograph them by flashlight in some dangerous condition and sell them the negative for quite a price. Or sell a print and keep the negative for future use. . . . Or else beat them up and rob them, but that's dangerous, because sometimes they turn round and fight you back. . . .' Peter walked on again. 'No, straightest of all, man, is finding sleeping accommodation and company for G.I.s, or buying cheap the goods they get from PX stores, but for this you need quite a capital. Best of all, of course, is poncing on some woman, but I haven't got the beauty enough for that. Why don't you try it, Johnny?'

'My sex life is not for sale.'

'Ah, well . . .'

We turned down a side street through an alley-way into a big empty warehouse. We climbed up some wooden steps, and Peter Pay Paul knocked on a three-locked door.

'Say who!' a voice cried inside.

'Peter, man. Let me in.'

The door opened two inches, and we saw an eye. 'And this?' said the voice behind the eye.

'My good friend Fortune, out of Lagos. Let us both in.' And he whispered to me: 'A Liberian—beware of him.'

This wholesale weed peddler was a broad-chested cripple, who dragged his legs when he moved about the room, never keeping ever still. His eyes were very brown-shot inside their purple rings.

'Good morning, Mr Ruby,' said Peter Pay Paul. 'Perhaps I could introduce you a new customer.

3

Pew and Fortune go back west

I MEANDERED ABOUT LIMEHOUSE DOCKS an hour or more before I realized that Indian had made a fool of me: there was no Rawalpindi Street. So I walked back, through the ships' masts and abandoned baroque churches of Shadwell, in the direction of the Immigration Road. On the corner of a bombed site, surviving by the special providence that loves brewers, I found a pub called the Apollo Tavern. Coloured men inside were dancing softly with morning lassitude, and behind the counter there was an amiable Jew. I asked him for a Guinness, and he said: 'One Guinness stout, right, I thank you, okey-doke, here it is, one and four, everything complete.' His wife, if she was, a grim-faced Gentile, gazed at me with the rude appraisal only women give.

I sat down. A voice said: 'So you's come movinx into this areas of London eastern populations?'

It was the Bushman. I shook his hand. 'And how is your instrument?' I asked him.

'Sold, man. Bisnick is bads juss at this mominx.'

'I, too, have been unfortunate of late. This doesn't seem to be our lucky month.'

There was a gentle tap on my shoulder, and a black hand protruded holding two double whiskies in its fingers. 'Who are these for?' I asked the Bushman.

'For you, man, and for me.'

'But who is this kind person?'

'Is my tribesmans. He offer some drinks to his sief's son and to his sief's son's friend.'

I turned and looked round. The donor was joining three others, all neatly dressed, who raised their glasses politely to the Bushman.

'But who are they, Mr Bushman?'

'I tells you: is my tribesmans. I come to this Immigrasions Roats for some tribal tributes. Here they will pay some offerinx to their sief's son.'

The Bushman caught me eyeing his soiled and greasy clothes.

'Soon they will takes me out to eat him foots,' he said, 'and make me comfortables and give me presinx. Stay, now, and you will enjoy them toos.'

'But why don't you speak to them, Mr Bushman?'

'When I reaty, I spik to them. They waits for me. Then I spik.'

The offer of liquor was repeated several times. After the third double, I gave up. 'Your father,' I said, 'must be a very powerful man.'

He grunted with satisfaction. 'And one day I. Then I invites you to my jungle home, and you stays with us for evers.'

'I look forward immensely to it.'

'Stay with us for evers, or we puts you in a pot.'

'I'm bony—only good for soup.'

'All him sames, we eats you as special favour.'

'Thank you so very much. Goodbye now, my kind friend.'

The Bushman shrieked with laughter, and, as I went out, I saw the tribesmen approach him with deferential smiles.

Possessed now by that early morning drunkard's feeling which suspends time by making all time worthless, and gives the daylight a false flavour of the dark, I sauntered up the Immigration Road. A girl's voice hailed me from a ground-floor window. It was Johnny Fortune's young friend Muriel.

'Come in,' she said, opening the door, 'I want to speak with you.'

Muriel was cooking something cabbagey. The boy Hamilton was snoring on a bed. She wiped her hands on her skirt, told me to sit down, and gave me a cup of very sweet thick tea.

'Johnny will be coming in for his dinner,' she said, 'and I know he'd like to see you.'

'Oh, I've been looking for him. He lives here now?'

'Yes, here with me. I work round the corner, and cook him all his meals.'

'And Hamilton?'

'Hamilton has no room just now, so he's staying here.'

She sat down too, and leaned across the oil-cloth. 'Can't you do something to help Johnny?'

'In what way, Muriel?'

'With money.'

'Surely he has some . . .'

'It's all been spent.'

'Oh. Can't he work?'

'Johnny won't work for less than twenty pounds a week. I tell him only clever men get those jobs, and he says he is a clever man. But he doesn't get one. . . .'

'I could lend him something. . . .'

She stirred a cup. 'If only we could get married,' she said. 'I'd help him in any job he wanted.'

'Can't you get married?'

'He doesn't want to.'

She began to cry. Women are so immodest in their grief. Even when you don't care for a woman much, to see her misery openly expressed is painful.

'These boys are all the same,' she said. 'Never anything fixed or steady, they just drift . . .'

There was a clatter at the door, and in came Johnny with Mr Peter Pay Paul.

A change had come over Johnny Fortune. His body still had its animal grace and insouciance, but his face wore at times a slanting, calculating look. And though the charm was as great as ever, he was more conscious of it than before. He greeted me with what seemed genuine affection.

'Where have you hidden yourself, Johnny?' I asked him.

'Oh, times have been difficult, man. And with you? You look sharp—real smart!' And he fingered my third-best suit.

'With me, times have been disastrous.' And I told him about my exit from the Welfare Office.

'That is one big pity,' he said gravely, 'because I thought perhaps you could help me with some new business.'

'What is it? Perhaps I can.'

'Come on one side.'

He led me over to the window, though he stood away from view of the street in the half light.

'This pack,' he said, pulling a large oblong piece of newspaper from inside his shirt, 'is wholesale weed. Five pounds' worth, which

I can sell in small packs for ten to twenty pounds if I can find five pounds now for Peter Pay Paul.'

'Here they are, Johnny. Are you going to earn your living that way?'

'Thank you, man. Well, what else can I do? I know no trade, no business . . .'

'Wouldn't your father send you money?'

'No, Montgomery, I cannot tell my Dad my loot is gone and that I'm not studying meteorology. Also, he has sent loot at my request to Muriel's mother. But my brother Arthur, so I hear, has stolen it away from her . . .'

'Perhaps the time's coming, Johnny, when you should think of going home.'

'Not till I make some fortune from this city, man. To go empty-handed home would be my shame.'

He gave the notes to Peter Pay Paul and, after removing a handful of weed, pushed the paper package up the chimney.

'And how is Miss Theodora?'

'Missing you, Johnny.'

Muriel heard this.

'She'd better keep on missing him.'

'Who spoke to you, Muriel?'

'Aren't you going to give me some of that money? How do you think we'll live?'

'Be silent, woman. Go on with your cookery.'

'I'm not an African, Johnny. You can't treat me like I'm a household slave.'

He shrugged his shoulders. 'Come, Montgomery,' he said. 'This woman troubles me with her yap, yap, chatter, chatter, chatter.'

Muriel clutched his arm. 'But don't you want your dinner, Johnny? It's all cooked.'

'I have had chicken. Hamilton, wake up! We leave this sad East End to go up west.'

But Hamilton kept snoring, and Muriel wept again into the steaming pot as we went out.

4

Coloured invasion of the Sphere

MONTGOMERY AND ME left Mr Peter Paul at the Aldgate station, and started the long bus ride through the City to the west. I chose the special seat which bus constructors made for those who smoke hemp (I mean the private seat, top floor at rear, which nobody can overlook), and there, while Montgomery grew more nervous, I folded up little saleable packets of my weed. 'I must kick my heel free of this miserable life,' I told Montgomery. 'I must climb back again into prosperity.'

'You might marry a fat African lady whose father owns acres of groundnuts,' he said to me.

'Oh, I could do that, perhaps, you know. But I want to go back home well loaded from this city. . . .' I folded a little packet and said to him, 'Has Miss Theodora money?'

I saw he didn't approve of this request of information, though a natural one, I thought, among two men.

'She's only her salary, I think,' he told me. 'But you mustn't play about with Theodora's feelings.'

'Why not? She likes me—no?'

'And you her?'

'I could do, if it should prove necessary. . . .'

'I'd rather you ran a whore, like Billy, than do that. Business and no pretences. . . .'

What did my nice English friend know about that kind of life? 'I may come to do just that,' I said to him.

'I hope you don't mean it. . . .'

'This Dorothy pursues me some time now. Pestering and giving me no peace at all. She wishes to leave Billy, and for me to take possession.'

'From what I can understand,' Montgomery said, 'it's the woman who takes possession of the man. She can sell him down the river any day she likes.'

Well, that was true enough from all I know of how those bad boys live—trembling, however brave, at every knock of the front door, and so afraid of the loot their women give them that they throw it all away in gamble-houses as soon as they've snatched it from her handbag. 'Oh, yes,' I said, 'these whores are always masters of their ponces. One word to the Law, and the lucky boy's inside.'

Montgomery sat looking sad, like the Reverend Simpson. 'I don't like to think of you in that miserable world,' he said.

I smiled, and patted on his anxious back. 'No real ill luck can come to me, Montgomery,' I told him. 'Look!' And I opened my tieless shirt and showed him the wonderful little blue marks tattooed upon my skin by Mum's old aunt, who knows the proper magic, and also the mission school badge I wear around my neck upon its chain. 'These will protect me always,' I explained.

'You believe that, Johnny?'

'So long as I believe it,' I said to him, 'they will protect me.'

Though it was well after morning opening time when we reached the Moorhen public house, we were surprised to find it absent of any Spade. 'There must have been some raid,' I told Montgomery. But no. A strange old Jumble man he knew, who looked at me as if I wasn't there, said all my race had left the pub and moved to another further down the road, one called the Sphere.

'But why have they gone?' Montgomery asked him.

'Because they've shut the dance hall opposyte—and high time too.'

'The Cosmopolitan? Why did they do that?' I asked.

'Moral degeneracy,' the old man said fiercely at me. 'Didn't you read it in your Sunday paper?'

'Good heavens!' I cried out. 'Have these Jumbles no mercy on our enjoyment?'

'This place is improved out of all recognition now,' the nasty old man informed us.

Dismal, dark, dreary, almost empty, I suppose that was improvement to his eyes.

We found that this Sphere was a small pub divided into more segregated sections than is usual even in these English drinking dens. Boys flitted in and out from one box to the other, and the publican, I could see, was not used to our African habit, which is to treat such places like a club, with no dishonour to be there even if you have no loot to spend. The barman, a young boy with a face like cheese, seemed worried also; and as I held my lager beer, casting my eyes around, I spoke to him freely of his look of great mistrust.

'But those lads over by the pyano,' he said to me. 'They come in here for hours and never buy a thing.'

'Why should they not? This is their meeting-place, for exchange of gossip, information, and other necessities of life.'

'But if they come in here, then they should spend.'

'Man,' I explained, 'you will find when they spend, they *do* spend. You will make more profit from them in one evening than of your bitter-sipping English customers in a whole week.'

He seemed to doubt me. 'The guv'nor tried turfing them all out at first,' he said, 'but he's given up the struggle.' He leaned across the counter. 'Tell me something,' he went on. 'You don't mind me asking?'

'Speak, man. I listen.'

'How do you tell which is which among you people?'

'You mean we all look the same like sheep?'

'No, not exactly. I mean, which is African, and which is West Indian—all I can tell is the Yanks, and then only when they open up their mouths.'

I shook my head at such enormous ignorance. 'Do you know,' I said to him, 'my grandmother cannot tell any one Englishman from another?' I left Montgomery with his whiskies, and went round into the larger bar to look for customers.

And there I caught sight of many quite familiar faces: Ronson Lighter, playing the pin-table, and Larry the G.I., and also my brother Arthur, who I was not all that pleased to talk to because of the theft of all that loot my Dad sent his Mum, and also, lurking away in an evil corner underneath the stairways, that one-time champion boxer, Jimmy Cannibal.

'What say, man,' I said to Ronson Lighter. 'Long time no see.'

'Well, look now, who's here! Where you been hiding yourself, Mr Fortune? Somebody here's been searching out for you.'

'Called what?'

'A seaman from back home who won't tell his real name, but says just to call him Laddy Boy. He has a letter for you from your sister Peach.'

'He's in here now, this seaman?'

'I haven't noticed him around yet, but if he calls, I'll hold him for you.'

'Thank you, my man. And tell me now. I'm in business, Ronson Lighter, in this article,' (and I showed him some). 'You interested at all?'

Ronson put his body so as to hide mine from the general view. 'Be careful of that little white boy Alfy Bongo,' he advised me. 'He comes here to meet our African drummers, so he says, but I think he's a queer boy, and you cannot trust them.'

I looked at this blond and pimply creature, chatting and giggling to some West Indians, and I made a clear note of his skinny, feeble frame in my recollection.

'I'll take a stick or two,' said Ronson Lighter.

'Here, man. How's our Billy?'

'I'm worried about that man, Johnny, and so is he. He thinks the Law has got the eye on him real hard. The house is being watched, we know.'

'Why should they turn the heat on Billy after all this time?'

'Is averages, Johnny. Six months they turn you loose, then one month they turn the heat. Nobody knows why. Perhaps you're next man on their Vice Department list, that's all. Or perhaps somebody been talking. Cannibal, say.' (And Ronson Lighter looked across at him.) 'Or maybe even Dorothy.'

'Not Dorothy?'

'I don't know why, man, but I believe this Dorothy plans to cut away from Billy, and she thinks the best way is to get him put inside. Perhaps,' said Ronson, lighting up his charge, 'it is because of you, who she prefers to Mr Whispers.'

'I'm not even slightly interested in that chick.'

'Oh, I believe you man, if you say so, of course.'

Ronson was dragging now, but still hadn't paid me any money. I touched on his arm and gently held out my hand.

'Will you take one of these instead?' he asked me.

They were pawn tickets for various articles. All city Spades hold pawn tickets, and if the man's honest they're quite as good as money, often better if you can get them with the discount. I took my pick.

'And Hamilton,' said Ronson Lighter. 'How does he keep?'

'Bad. He's using all his dope allowance now, not selling any. Even buying more of that poison whenever he can.'

Ronson lowered down his voice. 'You know who put him on the needle and supplied him? It was that "Nat King" Cole.'

I said to Ronson: 'Was it only Cole who did this injury to my friend? No one else you know of who was the person?'

'Who else could it be, man? No one else.'

'I thought maybe you could tell me who.'

Ronson was silent. 'No man, not me,' he said.

By now my brother Arthur had detected me, and over he came, as happy as a smiling hyena. 'How's Muriel?' was how he greeted me.

'She's well.'

'Ma's told the Law you've taken her.'

'She's not under sixteen, is she?'

'She's a minor, brother, in need of care and protection. Ma wants her sent off to a home.' Now he approached me closer. 'Johnny,' he said, 'do something for me. Lend me loot.'

'You spent all that which you took away from Mrs Macpherson?'

He smiled at me some more: I grew to hate that smile. 'All gone,' he said. 'The gamble-house way, like you did. It sure goes so fast away in there.'

'You get no more from this side of the family, Arthur.'

'Listen, now,' he said. 'I see you's selling weed. I'd like I go partners with you. I'd get you customers.'

'Thanks, brother. I prefer I operate alone.'

'You're wasted, Johnny. No good to me at all.'

I saw the human being called Alfy Bongo standing just behind me. 'What can I do for you, mister?' I said nasty.

He answered me in a great whisper, with a lot of winks. 'They tell me you've got some stuff.'

'I don't like your face,' I said to him. 'And if you speak to me again without you're spoken to, they'll have to send you into some hospital or other.'

This didn't seem to be my lucky day for gay society, because the next person who accosted me was no one less but a well-known idiot from back home called Ibrahim Tondapo, a thoroughly gilded youth who, just because his Dad owns two small cinemas that regularly catch on fire and burn up portions of the audience, allowed himself in Lagos great airs of class distinction, earning hatred and laughter everywhere around. He looked at me up and down and shook his body in his expensive suit as if he was shivering cold water off it. So 'Hullo, chieftain,' I said to him. 'How is each one of your six mothers?' (this being a reference to his not knowing really who his mother was, because his Dad is volatile, and he quite unlike any of his brothers.)

At which this foolish man spat on the floor.

I ought not to have said what I did, of course, but nor ought he to spit—is an unhealthy habit. So I slapped him on his face, and a fight began, and I was seized on by eight people and thrown out through the doors. Stupid behaviour, with my pockets stuffed with weed, but poverty and misery cause you to act desperately, as all know.

'You and I,' I shouted back at Tondapo through the door, 'will meet each other shortly once again.'

Out in the street, the boys were charging in the light of day, a habit dangerous in this city, where now the notable sweet smell of this strong stuff is well known to curious nostrils. So I crossed the road to where some builders were erecting a new construction, and among them I was surprised to see a tall West Indian toiling, one that I'd known in gamble-houses in my prosperous days. We gazed at each other quite politely, and he came over to say his word to me.

'Just look at me,' he said. 'A member of the labouring classes.'

'If a brick falls on your head, man, you'll certainly go straight up to heaven for this honest labour.'

'Yes, man, that's authentic. But wouldn't I much rather be sitting there in the Sphere consuming Stingo beer or something of that nature.'

'You're Mr Tamberlaine,' I said to him. 'I see you round some time ago, you may remember. Introducing people one to the other was your speciality.'

'Yes, that's exactly so. Pimping about the city, as you might call it, if you wanted to.' And he gave me his harmonious smile.

'And that's all over now, that kind of business?'

'Oh, no. I'm still in the market in the evenings, but find it prudent, don't you see, to have some part-time occupation in the days to justify my movements and existence if there's any police inquiries.'

'Wise, man. You's real educated.'

'There's something,' he said, 'as might interest you at a party taking place this evening, which is an exhibition by some boys from Haiti that I know of their special voodoo practices. So if your luck's not all you've been aspiring to, you've only to come and ask them for their kind assistance to alternate your fate.'

While I said yes, that I'd accept this invitation, Ronson Lighter called to me from the public house. 'This seaman's here,' he shouted out. 'This Laddy Boy.'

He was a muscle man, this individual, his arms like legs, his legs like elephants', and with a lot of rings and gold teeth and a happy look about him that these strong men have, especially when they're loaded up with loot, as merchant seamen always seem to be. He gave me the note from Peach, which, when I opened it, said this to me:

'Macdonald, what is this we hear? Bad news has reached us, by boys returning home, that you have engaged yourself with evil company, and thrown away money that Dad gave you, and broken the sequence of your serious studies. Dad says, "He'll find his feet." But I do not believe this, nor does Mum, and she will send you the fare home (paid to care of the travel company, not in cash to you), if you agree that is what's sensible to do, which our brother Christmas also thinks it is. Be wise, Johnny, and return among your own people for all our sakes that love you as you know we do.

'I tell you, your younger sister Peach is worried. And if you do not return home before New Year, let me tell you of my intentions. They are to come out to England there, to train as nurse, which full enquiries prove can be arranged. And if I do, you know you will have me watching you each second I am not on duty, which will make you ashamed of yourself before the other men.

'But come back freely, Johnny. It would be so much better for us all.

'Dad says he thank you for what you discover of those Macpherson people. He has done what he can and will do no more at all.

'Mum adds: a cable, and you have the fare home in a fortnight.

'Your sister, and you have no other,

Peach.'

'You saw my sister?' I asked Laddy Boy.

'Your family entertained me very kindly, Johnny, at your home.'

'They're all of them well back there?'

'They're well, man, but a little worrying about you. You know why. Is not my business, countryman, but you know why. . . . You take a drink?'

'I'm barred inside that pub.'

'Not with me, you're not, man, no. You're not barred in any public house that I go into.'

He took me inside, and there was no more reference to my recent wild behaviour. While I sipped my drink, I thought quite deeply. Yes, home would be beautiful again, but surely my duty was to try to rescue myself by my own efforts before seeking family aid?

In the nearby bar, I saw Montgomery talking with Larry the G.I. This gave me a new idea of how to raise some loot quickly in a last attempt, before throwing in my sponge and going back to Lagos tail between the legs.

I went to the phone box and asked for the radio corporation of the B.B.C., and for Miss Theodora Pace. After some secretaries, her voice came clear over the line towards me.

'Miss Theodora, this is Johnny Fortune.'

'Oh. One minute, please.' I heard some mutter, and a door close. 'Yes, how are you? What can I do for you?'

'You remember those radio talks we spoke about, Miss Theodora? With me as possible performer in them?'

'Yes. . . . Why've you not contacted me again?'

'Oh, there have been things, you know, so many. But this is to say I'm willing now, though there is one stipulation I should like to ask about.'

'Yes?'

'Would your officials consider a small payment in advance? Of twenty pounds?'

I knew, of course, that this was asking Theodora for the loot, but it seemed a way of doing so that could satisfy both our dignities.

'When do you want it?'

'Today. The soonest would be the best.'

There was quite a pause here before she said: 'I dare say that could be arranged. Come to the building, and ask for me at Reception, please.'

The Sphere was now closing for the afternoon, and the Spades were scattering all over town on their various errands, from this their daily joint collecting-point. I went off myself quite quietly, without telling Montgomery of my personal intentions.

5

The southern performers at the Candy Bowl

THOUGH LARRY THE G.I. had been wonderfully entertaining (telling me of how it was back home in Cleveland, Ohio, with Pop and Mom and his six young brothers, including the one who was in love with horses), I began to miss Johnny; and explored all the Sphere's bar cubicles, until I met Ronson Lighter, and learned he'd already left. These sudden disappearances I was by now used to, so I went back to Larry and suggested we both have lunch. 'Man, here's no food,' he answered. 'So why don't we go down to the Candy Bowl?'

He said this was the club most preferred by coloured Americans, and he told me he had two swell southern friends of his he'd like to have me meet—performers in the Isabel Cornwallis ballet company, now visiting the city, and stirring up a deal of excitement in balletic and concentric circles.

How little one ever knows of one's home town! I'd been in that courtyard a dozen times, but never sensed the presence of the Candy Bowl: which, it is true, looked from outside like an amateur sawmill, but once through its doors, and past a thick filter of examining attendants, it was all peeled chromium and greasy plush, with dim pink and purple lights, and strains of drum and guitar music from the basement. G.I.s, occasionally in uniform, but mostly wearing suits of best English material and of best transatlantic cut, lounged gracefully around, draped on velours benches, or elegantly perched upon precarious stools.

Sitting at a table by the wall, writing letters, were two boys in vivid Italian sweaters. 'That's the pair of them,' said Larry, '—Norbert and Moscow. Norbert you'll find highly strung, but he's quite a guy. Moscow's more quiet, a real gentleman.' We drew near to their table. 'I want you to know my good friends Norbert Salt and Moscow Gentry,' Larry said. 'Boys, this is Montgomery Pew.'

Norbert Salt had a golden face you could only describe as radiant:

candidly delinquent, and lit with a wonderful gaiety and contentment. His friend Moscow Gentry's countenance was so deep in hue that you wondered his white eyes and teeth weren't dyed black by all the surrounding blue-dark tones: a face so obscure, it was even hard to read his changes of expression.

'Montgomery,' said Larry, 'is mightily interested in the ballay.' (Not so: I've never been able to take seriously this sad, prancing art.)

'I've not seen your show yet,' I told them, 'but I look forward immensely to doing so.'

They gazed at me with total incredulity. Clearly, anybody who'd not yet seen their show was nobody. 'If you wish it,' said Moscow Gentry, 'we'd be happy to offer you seats for the first house this evening.'

'Alternatively,' said Norbert Salt, 'we could let you and Larry view a rehearsal of our recital if you'd care to.'

'Man,' said Larry, 'that's something you certainly should not miss. If these boys don't shake you in your stomach, then I'll know you're a dead duck anyway.'

I asked them about Miss Cornwallis and her balletic art.

'Cornwallis,' said Norbert, 'isn't pleased with the British this trip so very much. Two years back when we were here, we tore the place wide open, and business, as you know, was fabulous. But this time there's empty seats occasionally, and that doesn't please Cornwallis one little bit.'

'She's having to kill chickens once again in her hotel bedroom,' said Moscow Gentry.

Even Larry didn't quite get this.

Norbert Salt explained. 'Cornwallis believes in voodoo, even though she's a graduate of some university or other in the States. So when business isn't what it might be, well, she gets her Haitian drummers to come round to her hotel and practise rituals that bring customers crowding to the box office.'

'And it works?'

'Man, yes, it seems to. At lease, it's not failed to do so yet.'

'And is Miss Cornwallis's style Haitian, then?' I asked.

'Oh, no—she choreographs a cosmopolitan style,' said Norbert. 'Being herself Brazilian by birth, and internationally educated by her studies and her travels, her art's a blend of African and Afro-

Cuban, with a bit of classical combined. It makes for a dance that's accessible to cultured persons on every civilized continent.'

'And has your art been well received in Europe?'

'In Rome-Italy and Copenhagen-Denmark,' Norbert told me, 'we found they still liked us this trip as particularly as before. But as for here, I guess with all your thoughts of war you British haven't so much time for spiritual things.'

'Our thoughts of *war*?'

'Oh, yes,' said Moscow Gentry. 'You English people are constantly crazy about war.'

'Besides which,' said his friend Norbert, 'you don't appreciate the artistry of what we do. In Rome or Copenhagen, or even Madrid-Spain, we get all the top people at our recitals. But here, it's only the degenerates who really like us.'

'Can you fill a theatre in this city with degenerates for several weeks?'

'Oh, sure,' said Norbert Salt.

'Well,' I told him, nettled, 'you should be thankful to our degenerates for not thinking about war as you say the others do.'

'We don't thank anyone, sir. We perform, that's all, and if they like us, then they pay. We don't have to thank them for patronizing an entertainment that they're willing to pay for.'

I offered them a drink: they took lemon squash and tonic water. 'And this rehearsal,' I enquired. 'It takes place soon?'

'It takes place,' said Norbert, looking at a gold watch two inches wide, 'in forty minutes from this moment. I guess we should all be going to the theatre. In the Cornwallis company, we're always dead on time.'

The two young Americans made a royal progress down the streets that lay between the Candy Bowl and the Marchioness Theatre: catching the eyes of the pedestrians as much by the extravagance of their luminous sweaters and skin-tight slacks as by the eloquence of their bodily gyrations, shrill voices and vivid gesticulations; and did anyone fail to look at them, his conquest was effected by their bending down suddenly in front of him or her to adjust an enamelled shoe, so that the recalcitrant bowler-hatted or tweed-skirted natives found themselves curiously obstructed by an exotic, questioning behind.

There was some opposition to our entry at the stage door—which was manned (as these doors are) by a person who would have been disagreeable even to Sir Henry Irving. But his rude rudeness was outmanœuvred by an abrupt and devastating display of bitchiness by our two hosts. 'These ain't no stage-door gumshoes, they're *my friends*,' hissed Norbert, after an ultimate nasty salvo. He led us past the doorman's corpse to a narrow lift of the alarming kind that receives you on one side and ejects you on the other. Norbert and Moscow preceded us along a clanging concrete corridor to their dressing-room, where they immediately stripped naked, and started painting their faces and bodies in improbable jungle hues. 'The number we're rehearsing's African,' said Moscow. 'Cornwallis wasn't pleased with our performance of last evening, and she's called this rehearsal to get us in the ripe primeval mood.'

'Come and meet the girls,' said Norbert, and, still in nothing but his paint, he stepped down the corridor, and flung open the door of a larger dressing-room in which a dozen resplendent coloured girls were gilding the lilies of their beauty. He passed rapidly from one to the other, fondling each with gestures of jovial obscenity, and capering at times to the music of a portable radio they had. 'Say hullo to Louisiana,' he called out to us from a far corner. 'Boys this is Louisiana Lamont, our *ingénue*.'

She was a succulent girl with radiant eyes that positively shone. She smiled at Larry and me as if we were the two men in the world she'd most been waiting for, and said, 'My, ain't you both quite a size.'

'Just average,' said Larry, who was gigantic.

'Louisiana is our baby,' Norbert told us. 'She's just turned seventeen and she shouldn't really be travelling outside her country yet.'

'Why, Norbert! Where I come from, we's *married* at twelve years old—that was the age my Mom had me at. Why, honey, we's *grandmothers* before we're *your* age.' She offered us some sponge fingers from a paper bag. 'I do appreciate your British confectionery,' she said to me.

'Together with marmalade, meat sauces, and some cheeses,' I answered, 'biscuits are the only thing we make that's fit to eat.'

Louisiana paused in the biting of the sponge. 'Why, Montgomery!' she cried out in amaze. 'You said that just like an Englishman.'

'But I *am* an Englishman, Miss Lamont,' I told her. 'I am one.'

'I know you are. But you said it just like they do.' She appeared entranced.

A sharp bell rang.

This was the signal for a scattering and caterwauling of coloured boys and girls, racing out of dressing-rooms, tumbling downstairs in a brown and gold cascade, their voices shrill and laughing-screaming, then suddenly, with a last cry and clatter, silent. Larry and I were left alone with their memory, their odour, and little scraps on the floor of their costumes' straw and feather. He said: 'We'd best follow them down and see.'

We reached the wings in near darkness, and saw the company sitting on the stage in an oval, staring up at a woman standing in their midst who slowly revolved, talking to one and then the other, like the axis of each one of their destinies. 'That heavy piece,' said Larry, in a whisper, 'is Isabel Cornwallis herself in person.'

Miss Cornwallis was saying to her audience:

'I want you to understand. All I want is just that you understand me. Why I bring you dancers here to Europe is for a purpose. You think it's for the money I may make: well, if you think that, will you speak to my accountant, please, or else my lawyer? They'll tell you, no. It's for my art and for my people that I bring you here. The dance is an old, old art, since the days of pre-anthropology and those things. It's not just shaking your asses round like you children seem to imagine that it is. It's uplifting, and an honour to participate. It's also a source of advancement to our people. White folk imagine all we can do is jungle numbers, and ritual dances, and such. That's why I've choreographed our African and Caribbean dances in with classical European and other sources. It shows them we're up to the highest tones of their endeavour—Norbert, will you stop scratching there in your arm-pits?'

'It's an itch, Miss Cornwallis.'

'I don't want no itches in my company. I thought you understood what I'm telling to you, Norbert. You and Moscow and Jupiter here and Huntley are some of my older performers, my stars. It seems like I'm superfluous if you scratch your arm-pits during my conversation. Which reminds me to tell you what I've often said before. Dancers are desiring in their thousands to join the Isabel Cornwallis company. So I don't have to stay with you, and you don't have to stay with me, unless each party feels we want to. We're not obligated to each other in any way. But so long as I have my company, I'm going to keep up my standards of achievement.'

On and on she went, like a playback from a tape recorder. It was clear they had heard all this a million or so times before; yet were none the less fascinated by her flow.

The boy called Jupiter, a creature of breath-taking dignity and beauty, who sat in serene repose like a work of art more than one of Nature, said, in a high, squealing, petulant voice, 'Miss Cornwallis, some of the younger performers smell so bad of their perspiring it's unbearable.'

'They should use perfume, Jupiter, like you do, and I do, and all self-regarding human beings do.'

'I wish you'd tell them, Miss Cornwallis. They just stink.'

'I am telling them, Jupiter, as you can hear.'

Now it was the turn of the boy called Huntley: a slender, graceful light-skinned youth with a Roman rather than a Negro profile.

'Some of the young performers, Miss Cornwallis,' he said, in weary, spiteful, yet mellifluous tones, 'are saying I'm impolite to them when I take class. Now am I the ballet master here, or am I not? That's what I want to know.'

'You are, Huntley, since it's there in your contract that you are, but the man who's master never need be unpolite. And that reminds me, too, Huntley. You're getting so pale in this land of sunshine you look almost like a white boy now. You must have some sun-lamp treatment, Huntley, or else use a coloration lotion on your body. This is a coloured company, remember, with all that it implies.'

Larry the G.I. nudged me. 'The crazy old bitch,' he said in dangerous *sotto voce*. 'How does she get away with it? If it was me, I'd slap her down. And do you know, man? She's getting so fat only two boys of the whole company can catch her when she flies through the air like a ton of frozen meat. The others, she knocks them flat.'

Miss Isabel Cornwallis was off again. 'Just one more thing,' she said. 'These parties you've been going to, that I've heard about. I understand the gay folk, and the rich folk that you meet, and I approve of this association—it's good for the reputation of the company you should move in high society. But you, Norbert, and you,

Moscow, have been seen in peculiar assemblies, so I hear, with people of evil reputation.'

'If you're speaking of last Saturday a somebody may have told you or, Miss Cornwallis, it was at a prominent lawyer's house, and bankers and military officers and also a chief man of police were present there.'

'Now, please don't argue with me, Norbert.'

'If a party's suitable for the police chief, what can be so wrong with it as that?'

'It's not parties I'm talking about, Norbert—it's how you spend your leisure time when you're not dancing. You should be visiting the picture museums and cultural centres of which this city's provided very freely.'

'All right, Miss Cornwallis, we'll visit picture museums and study pictures.'

'Please don't argue with me, Norbert. It's not necessary.'

My trance-like fascination was interrupted when a pair of arms clasped me gently, but firmly, round the waist. I turned and saw a short, lissom figure standing on tiptoe, gazing up as if adoringly, and, beside him, a tall slender companion, holding two tapering elongated drums.

'There are the Haitian boys, the drummers,' Larry said. 'That's Hercule La Bataille who's trying to seduce you, and Hippolyte Dieudonné is this one here.'

I greeted them, disengaging myself with difficulty from the encircling arms.

'These boys,' said Larry, 'will be doing their bit of voodoo at the party tonight.'

'I turns you into hen, and eat you,' said Hercule with an abominable smile.

Hippolyte was expressionless, but gave six sharp taps on one of his drums.

'You turn this Limey into a hen, and I slit your throat,' said Larry, suddenly producing an enormous knife from inside his clothing, and brandishing it (though sheathed) before the faces of the Caribbeans.

'Larry, do be careful,' I cried out. 'Why on earth do you carry that dreadful weapon?'

'I'm never without my knife,' said Larry. 'Not in any circumstance whatsoever.'

6

Theodora lured away from culture

THE PRICE Miss Theodora made me pay for that twenty pounds she gave me at the radio corporation building was quite heavy: it was to take me that selfsame evening to a theatre, and show me a play by a French man about nothing I could get my brain to climb around. At a coffee, in the interval (for this theatre had no liquor in its sad bar), I said, 'Miss Theodora, I know this kind of entertainment is suitable for my improvement, but don't you think we could now step out into the air?'

'I did hope you'd like it, Johnny.'

'Quite over my comprehension, Theodora. Please—can't we go?'

I could see she was sad that I didn't rise up to her educational expectancies; but to hell with that, and by some violent smiles I managed to get her up into the street away from that bad place. For compensation of her feelings, I took her by the hand and pressed and rubbed it nicely as we walked along the paving-stones. Then what should I hear, rising up from underneath my feet, but the sound of real authentic African song and drumming. A door said, 'The Beni Bronze', and I pulled Miss Theodora down the steps before she quite knew what.

Just think of my pleasure when I found it was a genuine, five-drum combination, and hardly had I parked Miss Theodora on a seat beside the bar when I stepped across the floor through all the dancers and asked the band leader (who was bald on his head as any ostrich egg) if I could sit in at the bongos for a moment, at which I am quite a product. He gave his permission with a weary smile, and I asked the young bongo player, as I wedged his sweet instrument between my thighs, what this leader's name was. 'Cuthbertson,' this boy said. 'Generally called Cranium.'

I think to their surprise my performance gave some pleasure, and as soon as we'd ended I asked this Mr Cranium to come over to the bar. Theodora, I could see, was not very glad at the use I was making of the wad of notes she'd given me, and tried some attempt to pay herself, which I soon avoided. (I do hate those women fishing in their handbags. *No* woman will ever pay a drink for me—unless I hold her money for her beforehand.)

'And how is our African style appreciated in this country?' I enquired of Mr Cuthbertson.

'Just little,' he replied with sorrow. 'Only our people like it, and some few white; but West Indians and Americans—well, they like something less artistic and dynamic.'

'So you've not done so well in England, Mr Cranium?'

'I tell you something, Mr Man. Before I leave home five years ago, I dream that one day I have a lovely wife, three lovely children and a lot of money.' Here he pulled out some snapshots from his hip. 'Well, I got the lovely wife, the beautiful children too, as you can see, but, man, that loot just fails to come my way.'

This gave me a wonderful idea.

'What you require,' I said to Cranium, 'is contacts in the highest type of Jumble high-life. Well, tonight this lady here and I are going to a most special voodoo party, and why don't you come along with us and play some numbers that will win you good engagements?'

Cuthbertson thought this was a rare idea, full of brilliant possibilities; but Theodora was not pleased to hear I planned to take her to a party without asking her approval. As I waited for the club to close, I had to surmount all her oppositions by pouring gins in heavy sequence down her throat.

The address that Tamberlaine the West Indian had given me was in the fashionable area of that Marble Arch: but there's fashion and there's fashion, and none of us quite expected such a glorious block of similar flats. The doorman examined our little group, especially Cranium's combination, carrying their instruments, and would possibly have been an obstacle if Theodora (who has just that haughty way some Jumble ladies use back home to drive our people mad with hatred) hadn't kicked him round the hallway with her tongue, and got us all into a lift built to hold only five. The boys rubbed up against her in their gratitude for her display.

'Who is our host, Johnny?' she asked me.

'Theodora, if only I knew that!'

But no need to worry. It was that kind of party that once you're there, and look glamorous or in some way particular, they welcome you with happiness and push a bottle in your hand. As soon as they'd tanked themselves up a bit, the boys led by Cranium went into action, and Tamberlaine got hold of me to introduce me to our host.

'This man's a counsel in the courts of law,' he told me, 'called Mr Wesley Vial. Observe his appearance—like an eagle. Very precarious to be his victim in the dock, man, but full of charm and generosity as a hostess.'

'A hostess, Tamberlaine?'

'Well, you understand me, man.'

Mr Vial was fat, too fat, his flesh was coloured cream, his eyes sharp green, his hands most hairy and his feet small as any child's. He wore a pleated shirt that was some shirt, and when he shook my hand he held it up and looked at it like it was some precious diamond.

'You've lovely finger-nails,' he said.

'My toe-nails also have been much admired,' I told him.

'You're a witty boy as well as handsome. Now I do like that!'

The other guests of Mr Vial's were strange and fanciful—the whites very richly dressed, whether men or women, and the coloured so splendid I guessed they'd be Americans in show business at least. And this I soon learned was so, when Larry the G.I. appeared with some of this star material from the bathroom. 'Huntley,' he said, 'is going to act a dance.' And out came a naked boy wrapped round with toilet paper, who pranced among the guests and furniture, which most seemed delighted by—not me. These Americans!

A fierce voice said into my ear, 'Now listen, Johnny! Why have you brought Theodora here?'

This was Montgomery, bursting with fire and indignation.

7

Voodoo in an unexpected setting

'MONTY,' HE SAID, 'you really must cease to act the elder brother to me. I have one already, called Mr Christmas Fortune.'

'Don't call me "Monty".'

'Then what is all this, please, Mr Montgomery?'

'You're playing on Theodora's feelings to no purpose.'

'Well, if you say so, man.'

'And sponging on her too, for all I know.'

'Man,' said Johnny sullenly, 'you beat my time. What can I say to calm your interference?'

'And please,' I went desperately on, 'don't use those awful English phrases they taught you in Lagos high school.'

'Lagos high,' he said, 'is maybe better than is Birmingham low.'

'I must warn you, Johnny, if you trifle with Theodora, I'll take steps.'

'Oh, you win, man. What is it you'll do to me—you make me one dead duck?'

And away he went, indifferent and debonair, to rejoin Theodora, who, crouched like a flamingo on a cushion, was holding a little court of coloured boys lying round her, relaxed, inquisitive and amused. She was treating them to a display of mental pyrotechnics which delighted them as an athletic performance, however little note they took of what she said. And though her questions and observations were outrageous, they took no offence because they recognized in Theodora what I had never thought her to be—a natural.

Her chief interlocutor was a bland West Indian called Tamberlaine; who said:

'Oh, calm you English are, certainly, Miss Theodora, like a corpse is, and reliable, as you say; but always reliable for what no man could desire: like making sure he pays his income tax instalments highly punctually.'

'But what you haven't got,' said Norbert Salt (reluctant to see this

West Indian steal his American thunder), 'is the social graces and spontaneous conduct we're renowned for. Also,' he said, rising to his feet and clasping Moscow Gentry by the hands, 'you've not got our glorious beauty. See now, what a beautiful race we are!'

The pair posed in an arabesque, like the bronze group above the entrance to some splendid building.

'I'd like also to rebuke you, if you'll permit me,' Tamberlaine went on, his voice rising higher to attract eyes from the arabesque, 'for the peculiar observations you English make to we people in public houses, omnibuses, and elsewhere.'

'For instance?' said Theodora, resolutely impartial, her spectacles aglint.

Tamberlaine ran to the door, and reappeared wearing a bowler hat and an umbrella. 'Now I shall show you,' he announced, 'a conversation between myself and some kind English gentleman. This gentleman, he say to me' (Tamberlaine's accent became the oddest mixture of West Indian and deep Surrey) ' "I do envy you fellows your wonderful teeth." To which I reply in my mind, if not with my voice' (Tamberlaine removed the bowler), ' "Well, sir, me don't envy you your yellow horse-fangs, and if you look clearly down my throat, you'll see most of me back ones anyway is gold." '

The performance was applauded. 'Go on,' said Theodora, seemingly unmoved.

'Or else,' Tamberlaine continued, 'he come up to me and say' (bowler on), ' "Don't you miss the hot weather over here?" '

'Oh, no, man, no, not that familiar saying!' cried several voices.

'Sometimes,' the West Indian dramatist proceeded, 'this Englishman is a more serious person, with a feeling of sorrow for past wrongs committed. In this case, he will raise his hat to me and say, "I think, sir, that conditions in the Union of South Africa are a scandal." To which I inwardly reply, "Then please go there and tell Mr Strijdom of your sentiments." Or else he will look very sad and sorrowful and tell me, "You may find, sir, that there is sometimes a certain prejudice in England, but believe me, sir, that some of us are just as worried about it as you." '

Laughter and renewed applause.

'Let me tell you,' cried Norbert, snatching the stage from Tamberlaine, 'what's the craziest thing of all they say. Is this.' He wheeled, returned with a mincing step, torso rigid, legs flaying like mad stilts, stopped dead, and said, ' "I like coloured people, myself." '

'That one,' said Moscow Gentry, 'wins top prize for pure impossibility.'

Theodora was displeased: even saddened, I thought, as if at last minding more for generosity than for justice.

'You're all very unfair,' she said. 'You must remember our people often mean well, and are only shy. Often they *do* like you, and want to help you if they can, but just don't know how to tell you.'

Tamberlaine looked slightly vicious: he no doubt felt he'd got her on the run.

'Well, lady,' he said, 'all that may be. But please remember this. We're not interested in what your kind ideas about us are, but chiefly in your personal behaviour. We even prefer the man who doesn't want to help us, but is nice and easy with us, to one who wants to lecture us for our benefit.'

There was a loud clap of a pair of hands. Mr Vial stood on an occasional table in the middle of the room, supported round the hips by willing hands of manicured white guests and long Caribbean fingers.

'Miss Isabel Cornwallis,' he announced, 'has telephoned to say she can't be with us.' There were polite, disappointed cries of 'Ah!' Mr. Vial hung his head as if dejected; then, raising it up, with a bald, beaming glare, he cried, 'But the voodoo will take place all the same!'

The lights went out.

A hand took mine. 'It's all right, hon',' the voice said. 'I'm Louisiana.'

'What's going on?'

'You'll see. Sit down here. Cornwallis never meant to come—this party's not up to her degree of expectation.'

'How does she know it's not?'

'I called her up at her hotel to say so. I'm her spy, you see, in the company. I keep her informed of what's going on.'

An Anglepoise lamp, operated by the dim, green cheeks of Mr Vial, shone on the naked torso of the dancer Jupiter, who stood immobile. Hercule La Bataille and Hippolyte Dieudonné entered, carrying what looked to be a cat in a waste-paper basket. The two

Haitians knelt on either side of the basket (which they had up-ended, cat inside), and, with Jupiter towering motionless above, began chanting. It was wonderful to look at for a while, but it went on, and on, and on, and on, and on. The white guests, and even the West Indians, became restive. A Caribbean voice said, 'When you going to slay this pussy, now, man? We want some whisky down our throats.' Unmoved, the Haitians chanted. 'It usually lasts an hour,' Louisiana whispered, 'before they kill the animal.' Really, I thought! Even for the sake of higher mysteries, I can't allow that; and was about to do something inelegant and British, when I was anticipated by Theodora, who strode briskly from the floor, seized cat and basket from between the Haitians, and stumbled off into the gloom.

The three performers looked nonplussed and shocked. The lights came on, and our host Mr Vial, his face really 'distorted with fury', as they say, cried out, 'What does that bitch think she's doing?'

'She ain't no bitch, she's my lady,' said Johnny Fortune. 'Is me who bring her here.'

'You little bastard,' said Mr Vial.

Johnny reached up and pulled the knot of Mr Vial's blue bow tie undone. 'You sure you not say, "little *black* bastard"?' he asked the lawyer mildly.

Mr Vial bulldozed his face into a smile. 'Just little bastard,' he said gently.

'Oh, well, I'm legitimate, so there must be some mistake,' said Johnny. 'I see you again some day soon, my mister.' He followed Theodora out of the room.

There was a pause in the proceedings, and a certain amount of hard looks and shuffling. 'I guess everyone,' said Larry the G.I., 'is behaving most peculiar. Why don't we put on some discs and dance?'

I found myself sitting next to the star performer Huntley, who had removed the lavatory paper he had pranced in, and attired himself, instead, in a pair of Austrian *lederhosen* he had found in his host's bedroom. 'These niggers,' he said. 'It's always the same when you have them at a party.'

'But, excuse me, you . . .'

'Oh, I work in a coloured company, sure, and half of me belongs to them, I guess, but they're just so dreadful! So hopeless, so dreadful! There's always this confusion whenever they're around. Man, they can't even *work*—and I should know, I'm their ballet master. "Work like niggers"—whoever thought up that one?' He drank a glass of neat whisky and arose. 'I just can't bear them,' he said. 'I'm going back to sleep at my hotel. I've bought me a marmoset here in this city, and it's better company to me than they are.'

The party, it seemed to me, was deteriorating. I rose to go also, but was overtaken by Norbert Salt and his friend Moscow Gentry.

'Moscow and I,' said Norbert, 'have been thinking. And what we think is, it would be cheaper for us if instead of spending money at our hotel, we moved in with you. Now, you've got an apartment, haven't you?'

'That is, if it's not too far out from the city centre,' said Moscow Gentry.

I handed them the keys. 'If I ring the bell,' I said, 'I hope you'll be kind enough to let me in.'

'Oh, sure.'

'And thanks.'

In the hall there was a white boy in a barman's jacket, reading an evening paper and sipping a glass of wine. He looked up.

'I think I've seen you earlier,' he said.

'Yes? I don't remember.'

'My name's Alfy Bongo.'

'I don't remember you.'

'I work here for Mr Vial on special evenings,' said this person, taking me with two fingers by the arm. 'He's a very much nicer man than you might think.'

'And so, I'm sure, are you,' I said to Alfy Bongo, as I opened the mortice lock of Mr Vial's front door.

8

Theodora languishes, not quite in vain

THIS MISS THEODORA! Outside the Vial man's flat, I found her with the cat, two legs in each hand, searching the late darkness for a taxi. 'Let me take it for you, please,' I said to her. 'You don't want it to scratch you on your nylon blouses.'

'They're not nylon,' she said to me, and I saw she was in tears.

I took the animal.

'We walk a bit together, you and me,' I said, 'and get the fresh air in our weary choke-up lungs.'

'You'll catch cold without a coat on.'

'Me? I'm hearty! Walking warms up the circulation.'

After a silent while, she said, 'I suppose you think I oughtn't to have done that, Johnny.'

'Is for you to judge. Each man is jury of his own actions—even women.'

'I didn't mind all that much about the cat, but I couldn't bear them all enjoying themselves so much.'

This cat was wriggling, so I shoved it inside my shirt and buttoned it. 'Ju-ju is ju-ju,' I replied. 'Surely, is best to stay away from watching it, or, if you come, not interfere.'

'But you took me there to see it.'

A remark how like a woman!

'African ju-ju, or Haitian voodoo,' I explained to her, 'is not to be despised like you do through your ignorance. Medical science is, of course, a European discovery, as we know when we buy our spectacles, or have the appendix out. But living and dying is also very much a mystery of the mind that ju-ju understands.'

With my conversation, and the night air, she was recovering her usual sharp brain. 'According to what I read,' she said, 'the latest European opinion bears you out.'

A taxi sailed by, cruising cautious, slow, and eager for custom like a prostitute would do. I hailed it, and opened up the door. 'Here is your quadruped,' I said. 'What will you call it?'

'You choose a name.'

I took the cat beneath the taxi headlamps to examine it for sex. 'Tungi,' I said, 'is a nice name for a boy.' I handed it back, but she grabbed my arm as well as Tungi when I did so. 'Come home with me, please,' she asked, 'just for a while.'

I know what 'for a while' means, once a chick's got you inside her front door . . . and I wasn't eager for any close association with this not so young, young lady. All the same, she'd given me the twenty pounds, and perhaps she might be helpful to me on some later occasion. I climbed in and took the cat again, to make sure I had a good excuse not to hold whatever else that might be offered.

'And how is Muriel?' she said, in that voice women use to hide their disapproval.

'Muriel is well. Her health is good.'

'Are you fond of her, Johnny?'

' "Fond of" is not some words I use. Either is "love" or "not love" in my language.'

"So you love Muriel, then.'

'Well, yes, I do. She makes me quite mad with all her practical remarks and weepings, but I have some love for Muriel, that's certain.'

'So you'll get married soon?'

'Who said I would? Did I say so?' The cat was wriggling once more—I slapped it. 'Any conversation about loving a woman,' I exclaimed, 'ends up always with some talk by her of marriage.'

'Excuse me, Johnny.'

'Oh, I excuse you, naturally.'

This argument gave me excellent reasons for saying my farewell to her once delivered safely at her address; but when the cab stopped, she asked me to dig some earth up from the little garden there outside the rails. 'For the cat,' she said. 'He'll need a tray upstairs. Just bring it up, will you, when you've done? I'll leave the door open.'

This woman beats my time! I gathered up two handfuls, kicked the door closed behind me, and climbed three steps up at a jump, leaving trailings and spots of dirty earth upon the landings. Inside her room, the lights were already on, the radio in operation, and she was pouring out some drink in quite a hurry.

'Where is this tray?' I cried.

'What tray?'

'For Tungi your dear cat, Miss Theodora. Or shall I lay this soil upon this sofa?'

'Oh, don't be so angry with me, Johnny. I know men don't like being asked to do a menial task.'

Didn't that make it worse? She handed me some drink. I gulped it, then said, 'Goodbye, Miss Theodora, Montgomery would not approve if I should stay.'

'Him? He's nothing to me! He'll be out drinking somewhere, anyway.'

'Nothing to you, you say. Am I then something?'

This chilly lady, all skin and eagerness and spectacles, now flung herself upon me like some jaguar, and covered me in tears and kisses. I could not speak even until I'd wrestled her away. 'It's not always Spades, then,' I shouted out, 'who try to seduce white ladies, like they say.'

At this remark of mine, which I agree was not a gentleman's, like it wasn't meant to be, she stood up, smoothed all her body down, and said, 'Accept my apologies. I'm making myself just a little cheap.'

'If you say so, lady—but I didn't.'

'Don't call me "lady"!'

She was so pale and furious. 'All right, all right, Miss Theodora.'

'Or "Miss" anything.'

'Okay, Theodora. Just play cool.'

She picked up her spectacles from the floor, where they had fallen, and propped her lean body against the fireplace.

'All right,' she said. 'You know I'm in love with you, and you're not with me, and I'm not fool enough not to know that makes me just a nuisance. All that I ask you, though, is . . . that if I promise there will be no more scenes like this one, you'll stay a friend of mine.'

'Of course. I'm everybody's friend.'

'Oh, don't be so cruel! After all, I've helped you once already, and it's possible—in fact, it's very possible—I may have to do so once again.'

I got up.

'You gave me loot, yes,' I said. 'You want it back? Well, I'll have to owe it, because I need it.' And I went towards the door.

'Oh, come back,' she said. 'Let's stop quarrelling, and have a drink.'

This seemed quite reasonable to me. We clicked both our glasses, and both sat politely down.

'Even if you don't marry Muriel . . .' she began.

'Must we still speak of that?'

'Yes, because a practical matter's involved. Even if you don't marry her, she may have children.'

'One child she certainly will have.'

'Already?'

'So she has said to me.'

She frowned like some prime minister. 'When you people get independence,' she said sharp, 'we'd better change our immigration laws. Otherwise we'll soon have a half-caste population.'

'Like in the West Indian Islands, or even in parts of Africa.'

'People here don't understand what's happening.'

'Then when they do, what splendid opportunities they will have! Always you preach in England against colour bars in other countries! Now you can practise what you preach at home.'

'They just don't realize that you're here to stay. They think you're all here just temporarily.'

'Then they must learn.'

'I suppose we must.'

She reached for a note-pad and made some note on it. 'For your radio programme?' I enquired.

She nodded. 'Why won't you marry Muriel?' she said.

'For many reasons. Is a bad family, is one.'

'You mean her sister Dorothy?'

'For example, her: I do not wish a sister-in-law who is a prostitute.'

'How did she become one in the first place?'

'How should I know? Ask Mr Whispers. These boys meet some foolish chick at a dance. They take her home and give her the good time. Then suddenly—the smiles all disappear, also the money. The chick is afraid to go home to her mother. And so she accepts to step out on the streets and be agreeable . . .'

'And what do they earn?'

'The girls? Now, Theodora! Are these informations also for your broadcast programmes?'

'No, I'm just curious. Don't tell me if you don't want to.'

'A hundred pounds a week or more, if she is sharp. . . . If less than twenty a day is brought, the man will beat her.'

'What man?'

'The ponce. Her man.'

'Does he take everything?'

'If she keeps even one shilling from him, he will beat her.'

'But in return, he protects her?'

'No—not at all. She does not do her business in the house where they both live. . . . What happens outside is not his concern at all. His only thought is to be where they live at daylight to collect his loot. . . .'

'Then what does she get out of it all?'

'She? Love, so she thinks. Also the power to hold him, through fear of the Law, even though he takes everything from her.'

'And he?'

'He gets the good time: nice suits, and drinks, and taxi fares, and money to gamble all way. They never save it.'

'And can they separate if they want to?'

'The one who first will wish to leave will be the partner who is stronger. If the chick is making a good business, she can turn her eye on a new boy. Or the man may grow up to be a fashion among those women, and all then will try to steal him from his girl. Dorothy, for example: she now wishes to leave Billy Whispers, so I hear.'

'To go to whom?'

'I have been kindly suggested by her.'

'You'd not do that. . . .'

'Me? No, thank you. I have my family to think of, and my blood.'

'What will Billy Whispers do if she should go?'

'Use the razor on Dorothy, I should say. Unless she first shops him to such police officers as Mr Inspector Purity.'

'But if she does, the case must be proved in court?'

'With the woman as witness, that is not difficult at all. But when the man comes out of his jail again, that chick should leave town by the first train she can catch.'

I finished my drink, and held out my hand to thank her. 'Telephone me, Johnny,' she said. 'You've got the number.'

'I will.'

'You promise?'

'I do.'

'Kiss me goodbye.'

While holding her, I thought of Dorothy and Billy, and whether I should not go down to Brixton and advise that little Gambian to turn his Miss Dorothy loose before the trouble started. These serious thoughts were interrupted by Miss Theodora, who was saying in my ear, 'Won't you just once, Johnny? I promise I'll never ask you ever again. . . .'

Oh dear, this female person! Where was her modesty? 'Oh well, if you feel so bad,' I said to her. 'Where is it you keep your bedroom in this flat?'

9

The Blake Street gamble-house

When I left Mr Vial's party, I wandered across the silent reaches of Mayfair, which, in the middle night, looked like crissed-crossed canals where the water of life had drained away. In a vast, sad, dramatic square, I paused in the lamp- and moonlight, and gazed at the blue foliage of huge, languishing trees. I took out a cigarette. 'Light, Mr Pew?' said someone. 'You don't remember me?' the voice continued. 'I thought we'd be meeting again before too long.'

'You're acting mysteriously, whoever you are. You must be a member of the secret service.'

'As a matter of fact, that's what I thought you might possible be.

I turned, and saw Detective-Inspector Purity of the C.I.D. He was wearing a tuxedo with a considerable air, had his hands in his coat pockets, and an empty pipe clenched between his teeth. 'I'm out and about around the clubs tonight,' he said. 'Routine check-up, that's all it is. As I was saying. I know it's not my concern, but I thought you were doing special work of one kind or another.'

'Did you?'

He came rather nearer and put the pipe in his breast pocket. 'It stands to reason, Mr Pew, that someone from the service must be keeping an eye on these coloured folk, and I saw at once an official like yourself wouldn't be mucking in with them like you did that night we picked you up, unless you had your cover story ready. . . .'

'If I were what you suggest, of course I wouldn't tell you.'

'Naturally . . . though I could always try to check. . . . But it's clear as daylight someone is watching these colonials—the troublesome elements among them. First the Maltese come, then the Cypriots, and now this lot! They don't make the copper's task any the easier.'

'You find that colonials are more trouble than the natives?'

'What natives? Oh, I see what you mean. No, I don't suppose so, really . . . but it's a new problem. When they come unstuck, of course, they get more publicity in the Press than ours do. But I don't suppose their criminality is out of all proportion. . . . It's just that they're there, you see.'

'I'll say good night to you.'

'Yes, I thought we'd be meeting again,' Inspector Purity said, falling in alongside as I moved away. 'You've been to a party, I expect?'

'That's right.'

'Good one? Jolly? There are some very nice flats around the Marble Arch . . .' He stopped a minute. 'By the way, you didn't mind me asking you what I did?'

'About my job? I've left the Colonial Department, as it happens.'

'Yes, I heard that—word gets around.' He sounded pleased. 'And now you're just a private person.'

'That's it.'

'Doing nothing so very special at all, you'd say. Well, that's interesting to know.'

We went on some way in silence. He had the art which coppers have of inserting his personality, unwelcomed and uninvited, into your own.

'And how's young Mr Fortune?'

'Who?'

'Come on, now. You know who I'm speaking of.'

I stopped. 'Is this an official interview?'

'Not exactly. No, I wouldn't say so.'

'Then good night.'

'So you have seen something of him? I thought perhaps you had. He's a nice boy, in his way.' Mr Purity took his hands from his pockets and slapped his flanks. 'I have my duty to get on with,' he said briskly. 'We never rest.' He walked on ahead and turned the corner. When I reached it, there was no sign of him.

I crossed the neutral ground of Regent Street into the upper regions of Soho. The eighteenth-century houses looked graceful, mouldering and aloof. Beside an electric power station, that had intruded itself among them, I stopped: and wondered whether the time had not now come to 'cut out', as Johnny Fortune might have said, from the society of the Spades. They were wonderful, of course—exhilarating: the temperature of your life shot up when in their company. But if you stole some of their physical vitality, you found that the price was they began to invade your soul: or rather, they did not, but your own idea of them did—for they were sublimely indifferent to anything outside themselves! And in spite of their *joie de vivre*, in any practical sense they were so impossible! 'They're dreadful! They're just quite dreadful!' I shouted out aloud, above the slight hum of the dynamos.

I turned some corners, and under a lamp saw Africans squatting on their haunches on the pavement. I stepped out on the street to make a circuit, but was hailed by one who ran crying after me, 'Lend me two pounds, man, or even one!' It was Johnny's half-brother, Arthur.

'Hullo, Arthur. What goes on there?'

'We're throwing dice. I lose a bit . . .'

'Here in the street?'

'What's wrong with here?'

'Doesn't anyone interfere?'

'Oh, we take care. We're barred at Mr Obo-King's, you see, and can't play there.'

'Mr Obo-King?'

'He owns the Blake Street gamble-house. You'll find some people you know there, if you go.'

'What number in Blake Street is it?'

'I forget the number, man, but here on this envelope it's written.' He pulled out a crumpled one on which I saw:

> Mr Arthur,
> by the Blake Street Gamble-house,
> London, Soho.

The postmark was from Manchester.

'Somebody wrote this to you there?'

'Yes, man, a friend. He plays clarinet Moss Side.

'And this got delivered?'

'Oh, everyone knows the gamble-house. It's raided regular weekends.'

'Don't they ever close it?'

'Why should they, so long as Mr Obo-King pays his fines, and makes his little presents to the Law? Mr Obo owns several places, and they're never closed. The Law likes to keep them open, so it knows where to look for everybody.'

I gave him ten shillings. 'Best of luck,' I said.

He snatched it, and cried: 'Never say "Good luck" to any gambler! You not know that?'

'No. Sorry.'

'You see my brother Johnny?'

'Earlier on.'

'I must get to meet him again soon. This man owes me everything. I feel real sore about him.'

He ran back to the circle without thanks.

I went on to Blake Street; and only then realized that Arthur's envelope, after all, had no number on it. I walked up and down, and could find no sign of what looked to be a club, when out of the area steps from a basement I saw a coloured man cautiously emerge and, as he walked towards me, recognized Larry the G.I.

'Man, that sure was some bum evening at Mr Vial's,' he said. 'I pulled out fast when I saw how it was shaping. They was having an orgy when I left, but me, I don't care for these pig-parties or gang-bangs whatsoever.'

'Where have you been just now, Larry?'

'In and out of the gamble-house, to get me some bit of loot.'

'Did you play in there?'

'What, me? Among all those Africans when they're throwing dice? Man, are you crazy? They'd eat me. A soldier can tell dynamite when he sees it.'

'But you went in there alone?'

'Oh, no, that Tamberlaine came with me. West Indians I can partly understand, but not these African ancestors of mine.'

'How did you get the money, then?'

'Sad—but I had to sell my knife. No other way to get myself back to base. But I'll find me another there.' He shook my hands. 'So I'll be seeing you,' he said. 'Norbert and Moscow has given me your phone number where they're moving in.'

I walked up the road, and went down the gamble-house steps. The door in the area was open, and there was no one inside to stop you going in. At the end of a dim-lit corridor was another door. I was going to open it, when from inside came shouts and clatterings, two men ran out and started fighting in the area. There was a horrid scream and whimper, and quick, noisy footsteps on the metal stair up to the street. Someone had fallen at the foot of them. I ran over. 'Can I help you? Are you hurt?' I cried out.

By the light from the inner door, I could see this man was bleeding. He tilted his face, and I saw Jimmy Cannibal. He gave me a look of intense dislike, crawled to his feet, and lurched slowly up the stair. A voice from behind me said, 'Who's you?'

I turned, and saw a very fat man in a fur-lined jerkin.

'That boy's been wounded. What should we do?'

He said nothing, and struck a match under the stair. I saw him pick up a knife. He looked at me, still holding it. 'Who's you?' he said again.

'A friend of Johnny Fortune's.'

'I think I hear about you. What did you see out here?'

'You know what I saw. A fight.'

'Is best you saw nothing.' He picked up a piece of newspaper, and wrapped the knife in it. 'Who did attack him? You saw that?'

'No. It was too quick.'

'Is best you saw nothing, then. You come inside now?'

'I don't think I will.'

'Best you come in till they scatter up there in the street. Give them the time to scatter.'

He propelled me in, and shut the outer door. We stood in the dim corridor.

'How's Johnny? That boy got some loot again just now?'

'Not much.'

'He ought to get some, then. A boy like him could make some easy, and then lose it all to me.' He let out a laugh as big as his body. 'And you, are you loaded?'

'I have some money, yes.'

'Come inside, then. I give you some good excitement before you say goodbye to it.'

'Are you Mr Obo-King?'

'That's what they call me. They should so, is my name.'

He led the way into a large room with little chairs and tables where chicken and rice and foo-foo were being served. Some boys were playing a juke-box, and Mr Obo-King called to one of them, 'Take a bucket out there, man. There's some mess to wash away.' He turned again to me. 'The gambling's through here. In this next door.'

'I'll come in later. I want to eat.'

Mr Obo-King looked at me. 'Then come later. I give you some good excitement before I skin you.'

I sat down, asked for foo-foo, and looked around. Some of the men and women were dressed like birds of paradise, so that you'd turn and look at them in the street; though down here they seemed right enough, in spite of the resolute squalor of the place, and even though other customers were in the last degrees of destitution. A few seemed to have camped there for the night, for they'd kipped down on window-shelves and tables, snoring, or dreaming, possibly, of 'back home'. A short boy with a pale blue-green pasty face and enormous eyes came up and said, 'Buy me a meal, man.' As I called for it, he suddenly lifted his sweater and showed me, on his naked stomach underneath, an enormous lump. 'Hospital can do nothing—what is the future?' he said, and carried his plate away. From time to time customers emerged, always disconsolate, from the gambling room, and started long public post-mortems on their disasters. Soon the West Indian Tamberlaine came out, and said to the company in general, 'Well, I not had much, see, so I not lose much.' He spotted me, and accepted an offer of coffee. 'So voodoo is not for you,' he said. 'Perhaps you like this place better.'

'Who comes here mostly, Mr Tamberlaine?'

'If white like yourself, they's wreckage of jazz musicians, chiefly, a lot on the needle and full of despair; if coloured, well, ponces and other hustlers like myself.'

'You're a hustler, then?'

'You might say I pimp around the town, picking the pounds up where I can. I don't often gamble, though, because the winner is the table, and like all these boys I never know when to stop if fortune does the bitch on me like she do. But coloureds like gambling, don't you see—it's part of our care-free nature.'

He gave me a sarcastic grin. 'Who gambles mostly?' I said. 'Africans or West Indians?'

'What! You recognize some difference? Ain't we all just coal-black coloured skins to you?'

'Don't be offensive, Mr Tamberlaine. Like so many West Indians I've met, you seem to have, if I may say so, a large chip sitting on your shoulder.'

'Not like your African friends? They have less chip, you say?'

'Much less. Africans seem much more self-assured, more self-sufficient. They don't seem to fear we're going to take liberties with them, or patronize them, as you people do.'

'Do we now!'

'Yes, you do. Africans don't seem to care what anyone thinks of them. So even though they're more clannish and secretive, they're easier to talk to.'

Mr Tamberlaine considered this. 'Listen to me, man,' he said. 'If we's more sensitive like you say, there's reasons for it. Our islands is colonies of great antiquity, and our mother tongue is English, like your own, and not some dialects. So naturally we expect you treat us like we're British as yourself, and when you don't, we suffer and go sour. Why should we not? But Africans—what do they care of British? For African, his passport just don't mean nothing, except for travel, but for us it's loyalty.'

I couldn't resist a dig. I'd had, after all, to take so many myself in recent months. 'I think,' I said, 'it's easier for them than it is for you. They know what they are, and you're not sure. They belong much more deeply to Africa than you do to the Caribbean.'

'My ears is pointed in your direction,' said Mr Tamberlaine, sipping his coffee, 'for some more ripe instruction.'

'Here it comes, then. They speak their own private tongues, their lives are rooted in their ancient tribes, so that even when they're lonely or miserable here they feel they're sustained by the solid tribal past at home. But you, you're wanderers, cut off by centuries from Africa where you first came from, and ready to move off again from your stepping-stones strung out across the sea.'

'Our islands is stepping-stones? Thank you now, for what you call them so.'

'Wouldn't you all move on to North or South America, if they'd let you in?'

'Well, yes, perhaps we would, the way they treat us here, and how it is back home.'

'You see, then. You're not sure what you are—African, Caribbean, or American—and so you're quite ready to be British.'

'Thank you for the compliment to our patriotism. So many of our boy who serve in R.A.F. would gladly hear your words.'

I saw the conversation wasn't a success, and apologized to Mr Tamberlaine. 'I'm just saying what I think—excuse me if it gives offence.'

Mr Tamberlaine smiled politely. 'Is no offence, man. You say what's in your mind, and that's your liberty. What's certain, anyway, is that we're different, Africans and we. We don't mix much, except when we stand shoulder to shoulder against the white.'

He got up, put on his tailored duffel coat, and said, 'Now I must get out in the cold and do me pimpin'. You're not interested in anything I have to offer, I suppose?'

'Such as what, Mr Tamberlaine?'

'A little coloured lady for you? You go with her, and add to your education of these different races.'

'All right. Is it far?'

'We go down Brixton way, man, and see there. I hope you have money for the taxi, there's no all-night bus.'

10

In Billy Whispers' domain

TAMBERLAINE WAS BORED AND SILENT on the journey, except for occasional altercations with the taxi driver, to whom he gave a succession of imprecise addresses ('take us just by that football ground, that's by that Tube station, cabby, and then I'll tell you . . .'). We reached the area of chain-store windows, parks fit for violations, and squat overhanging railway bridges, all bathed in a livid phosphorescent glare, when Tamberlaine rapped the glass and shouted, 'Here now! Here!', as if the driver should have known our final destination. Tamberlaine strolled away, leaving me to settle, while the driver exhaled his spleen. 'These darkies should go back home,' he said, 'and never have come here in the first place.'

'They tip well, don't they?'

'Either they do, or they run off without paying. But it's the way they speak to you. Calling me "cabby"!'

Tamberlaine had turned a corner, and I followed him into a tottering street of late Victorian houses, where lights, despite the lateness of the hour, were shining through many a green or crimson curtain. 'This is your London Harlem,' he said to me. 'Our Caribbean home from home. We try this one,' and he climbed some chipped steps beneath a portico, knocked loud, and rang.

A head and shoulders protruded from above. 'Is Tamberlaine,' he shouted. 'Gloria, is she there?'

'No, man. Is here, but not available.'

'Aurora, now, is she there?'

'No, man. You come too late to see her.'

We tried at several other houses, without success, till the vexation of a wounded professional pride was heard in Tamberlaine's voice. 'Is nothing more to do,' he said, 'but go back to the north of London —unless you don't fear to call upon an African, which after what you say, you shouldn't.'

'If you don't, why should I?'

'This house is one of Billy Whispers', who's the devil.

'Oh, I know him.'

'You do, now?' Tamberlaine seemed mildly impressed. 'Come, then, let we go.'

It started to snow, and my West Indian Mercury pulled the hood of his duffel up over his head, drove his hands deep in the pockets, and walked on just in front of me, like some Arctic explorer heading resolutely for the Pole. After twists and turns, of which he gave no warning, we reached a bombed lot with some wreckage of buildings on it. Tamberlaine plunged down the area steps, and beat with his fingertips on the window. A voice cried, 'Say who!', and when he did, Mr Tamberlaine walked inside, and left me standing there.

After five minutes of waiting in the area, and five more strolling round the street outside, I decided to call it a day, and started off up the street. But steps came running after me. I heard a cry of 'Hey, man!', and turned to see not Tamberlaine, but Mr Ronson Lighter. He shook hands, caught me by the sleeve, and said, 'Is all right, you can come. There is a party to celebrate one boy come out of prison, but Billy say you welcome when you come.'

We climbed two floors into a large room, festively crowded, that overlooked the street. Ronson dragged me to a buffet where, under the watchful eyes of a bodyguard of three, stood piles of bottles in disarray, and plates of uninviting sandwiches. 'Give this man drink,' said Ronson. 'Is Billy say so.' One bodyguard, aloof until these words, poured out a beer glass full of whisky.

Some of the guests I knew by sight, and others even better still: there were Johnny's former landlord, 'Nat King' Cole, and the African youth, Tondapo, with whom he'd quarrelled at the Sphere, and little Barbara, the half-caste girl of the memorable evening at the Moonbeam club; and also a contingent from Mr Vial's disrupted party, among them Mr Cranium Cuthbertson and his musicians, and the dubious Alfy Bongo. Arthur was there, strolling from group to group unwelcome, with his restless smiles; and enthroned on a divan, surrounded by fierce eager faces, his handsome, debauched half-sister Dorothy. Alone by the fire, as if a guest at his own entertainment, was Billy Whispers; and Mr Tamberlaine, like a suppliant at the levee of the paramount chief, was deep in conversation with him.

Mr Ronson Lighter led me over. 'Good evening, Mr Whispers,' I said, raising my voice above the clamour. 'It's very kind of you to ask me in.'

'My party is for this boy,' said Billy Whispers, pointing with glass in hand to a huge and handsome African, who positively dripped and oozed with mindless masculine animal magnetism and natural villainy, and who now was dancing, proud and sedate, round the room with Dorothy.

'He came out yesterday,' said Tamberlaine. 'This is his home-coming among his people, but the boy is sore. His girl was not true to him while he was away; but as you can see, he's a type of boy who soon will find another.'

Billy Whispers was looking at me closely: with those eyes which fastened on your own like grappling-hooks, and lured and absorbed your psyche into the indifferent, uncensorious depths of his own malignancy. 'Tamberlaine say to me,' he remarked, 'that earlier you see Jimmy Cannibal.'

'Yes. There was a fight at Mr Obo-King's.'

'You see who fight him?' asked Ronson Lighter, with an excess of indifference.

'No. Do you know who it was?'

'I? Why should I know?'

'You not tell nobody you see this?' said Billy Whispers.

'No, not yet.'

'Is true, I hope.'

There was a crack like a plate breaking, and a yell. Whispers went over to a group. Someone was hustled out. 'To fight at a sociable gathering,' said Mr Tamberlaine, 'is so uncivilized.'

Dorothy stood in front of me, posturing like someone in an historic German film. 'Hullo there, stranger,' she said. 'Long time no see. How is my little sister Muriel and her boy friend?' I smiled at her, and didn't answer. 'Oh, snooty,' she said. 'Sarcastic and superior,' and she stalked off in a garish blaze of glory.

During this conversation, I saw Alfy Bongo eyeing me in his equivocal way: with all the appearance of deviousness and cunning, yet openly enough to let you see he knew you realized he was up to something. He sidled over and said, 'We meet again, Mr Montgomery Pew. Two fishes in the troubled water.'

He sat down beside me. 'The rumour about me with those who

just don't know,' he went on, as if aggrieved (and I'd aggrieved him), 'is that I'm working for the coppers: a nark, like. But do you really think these boys would let me come here if they thought that lie was true?'

'How should I know?'

'The Spades trust me, see? They trust the little queer boy because we're both minorities.'

'How old are you?' I asked him.

'Seventeen.'

'You're much too old for your age.'

He sighed and smiled, and looked at me appealingly. 'I've had so hard a life—if you but knew! I was brought up by the Spades—did you know that?'

'No.'

'Yes, by them. Fact. I was an orphan, see, and brought up by Mr Obo-King.'

'Is this true, or are you making it all up?'

'Why should I lie to you—what's the advantage? Yes, by Obo-King I was brought up, till I set out on my own.' He looked sad, and wizened, and resigned. 'It's all the same,' he said, 'if you don't believe me. I do odd jobs for Mr Vial and other gentleman, that's what I do. Make contacts for them that they need among the Spades.'

'Why bother to tell me?'

He sighed again. 'You're suspicious of me—why?' he said archly. 'Anyway, I'll do you one favour, all the same. You'd better be going, because there's trouble in store tonight for someone.'

'Why?'

'Oh, you *do* want to know?' He rose, assumed a bogus American stance and speech and said, 'Stick around, man, and you'll see.'

A complete stranger, wearing a dark blue suit and spectacles, said, 'Come now, sir. She wait for you, Miss Barbara. Come now with me.'

I followed him to the next floor, where he opened a door with a polite inclination, and shut it after me. Barbara was sitting by a gas fire, reading a 'true story' magazine. 'Oh, hi,' she said, finished a paragraph, then went on, 'Tamberlaine said you want to talk with me.'

'That's right, Barbara.' I sat down too.

'Do you ever read these things?' she said, handing me the book. 'But they don't know nothing about life as it really is.'

'They say truth is stranger than fiction, don't they.'

'Eh? All I know is, if you've been a kid like me in Cardiff, and seen what I seen, there'd be more to tell than you could put in any *book*. I just haven't had the life at all. Everyone uses me, white like coloured. If you're Butetown born, down Tiger Bay, your only hope is show business, or boxing if you're a boy. But me, I can't even sing a note straight.' She got up. 'Well, shall we get on with it? I don't want to miss the party.' She began taking clothes off in an indifferent casual way. 'Yes,' she went on, 'my only hope is to marry me a G.I., and get right out of this. Or maybe a white boy if he has some *position*, that's what I want, a *position*. I'm sick of these hustlers with their easy money! And do you know—I couldn't tell you who my Dad is, even if you asked? Even my Mum don't know, or so she says, can you believe it? Can you imagine? Not even to know who it was created you? Why do you leave your socks on last? It makes you look funny.'

'The linoleum's cold.'

Billy Whispers and Ronson Lighter came, without knocking, into the room. 'Go out now, Barbara,' said Ronson. 'We talk to this man alone.'

'But I'm not dressed.'

'Dress yourself on the landing, out the door. Go, now.'

I began putting clothes on too, but Ronson Lighter snatched away the essential garments, and sat on them on the bed. 'Just wait now a minute,' he said. 'We want to talk with you.'

'You're always pinching things, Ronson Lighter. One day somebody will hit you.'

'Like you will, perhaps?'

I'd noticed a kettle on the gas fire. I edged nearer.

'We give these clothes back when you speak us what you know,' said Billy Whispers.

'Don't be so *African*, Billy. You're so bloody cunning you'll fall over yourself.'

With which I grabbed the kettle and flung it at Ronson Lighter. It missed, but drenched him splendidly in scalding steam. He yelled, and held his eyes. Billy Whispers lowered his head and butted me in the stomach, which was so horribly painful that I grabbed him in the only grip I remembered from gymnasium days, the headlock,. twisted his skull violently, and fell with him on the floor. His face was uppermost, and his killer's eyes glared with a hunger for death that was beyond hatred or cruelty—a look almost pure. I hung on, he seized me in the most vulnerable parts. I howled: then suddenly he let go, when fingers were thrust into his throat and nose. I saw beyond the fingers the arms and fierce face of Johnny Fortune. Ronson, prancing with rage and agony, cried, 'You take the side of this white man? You enemy of your people?' Johnny increased the pressure. 'You stop now, Billy? You stop and tell me what is this you think you doing?'

11

Back east, chastened, in the early dawn

WHEN BILLY WAS NEAR DYING, I let him just breathe, but not till he loose his tight hold of Montgomery. I stood back and waited, ready, in case these two Gambians might start some fight again. But all three in the room—Billy and Ronson Lighter and Montgomery—was rubbing themselves silently in different places. 'Put your clothes on, Montgomery,' I said. 'Is never a good choice to fight without your garments.'

These ponces' celebration parties! Always they end up in struggles. But when I came down from Theodora's flat to visit Billy and, I thought, do him a favour by my warning, I did not expect to find this sort of battle. Perhaps soon someone would tell me the reasons of this strange argument.

'I'm glad to see you, Johnny,' said Montgomery, when he was more clothed. 'Who told you I was up here?'

'That Alfy Bongo. So of course I didn't believe him, but I came upstairs to check, and heard from little Barbara you was here. Will someone now please explain to me?' I added, giving cigarettes around, for I wished to show what friendship I could to Billy and to Ronson Lighter, and not make them think the white man could rely on me entirely, always, and for everything.

Ronson speak first. 'This Jumble shop us,' he cried out. 'He sell us to the Law, and come here spying the effects.'

'What *is* all this, Ronson Lighter?'

'I tell you. Tonight we punish Cannibal in the gamble-house. Is I who do it, with the knife I buy. This Jumble see it, and go tell the Law about me.'

'So it was you, Ronson,' said Montgomery.

'You know was I. Tamberlaine tell us what you see in there.'

'But I didn't know it was you with the knife,' Montgomery said. 'And I haven't told anyone about it.'

'A-ha! Can we believe this word?' cried Billy Whispers.

'Whether you do or not, you might have asked me before you both attacked me.'

'Is you who attack us,' cried Ronson, 'with this your kettle.' He picked it up and waved it fiercely. I took it from him.

'I do not know,' I said, 'what my friend Montgomery see. But that he tell the Law, I don't believe. If he do that to you, then why he dare come here after?'

'To spy!' said Billy. 'To put the eye on us.'

'You's foolish, Billy,' I said to him. 'If anyone tell the Law of Ronson, it will be Cannibal.'

'Cannibal not dare to. He know I end his life if he start yapping.'

'Ronson try to end his life anyway, man. That takes away his fear of speaking to the Law.'

Billy Whispers looked at me as if a knife was all I was fit for too. 'Fortune, I know you's not my friend,' he said. 'You never was my friend at any time.'

I looked hard at this Gambian, to show I did not fear him. 'Billy,' I said, 'if I am not your friend, there can only be one reason. It is the drug you give to *my* friend Hamilton Ashinowo, that kill him dead and steal his life away.'

'Who say I do that?'

'Cole. I catch him at your party here downstairs and talk to him. He put the blame on you and run away.'

'And you believe that man?'

'Is true, then?'

'And if is true? I sell that stuff to Hamilton. He buy it; he want it; I give it. I satisfy his need.'

'Then do not wonder, Billy, I am not your friend.'

'So you betray me. You put the Law on me as well.'

'Billy,' I said. 'What puts the Law on you is your life here with Dorothy. Why don't you cut out, man, go up to Manchester Moss Side, or go back home?'

Billy rubbed on his throat and said, 'This is where I stay, here in this city. I fear of nobody. The man who makes me leave town is my master.'

'All right, Billy Whispers, is your life, is not mine. Now what say we go downstairs and drink a drink and soon forget all this unfriendliness?'

The room was now empty of many of its guests, especially Tamberlaine and 'Nat King' Cole. But Cranium and one of his boys was still playing on their drums, and Barbara and Dorothy was yap-yap-yapping by the fire. And shooting dice up on the floor was my brother Arthur and Alfy Bongo, and that gilded man Tondapo with who I had not yet had my explanation of his earlier behaviour to me. 'Give us some tune, Cranium,' I said. 'Come, Billy. Forget your suspecting everyone, and pour some drink.'

'Drink for you who attack me?' Billy said to Montgomery and to me.

'Oh, come now, Billy. Don't spoil this pleasant evening, or, if you like, we have to go.'

So he poured these drinks. Dorothy she came and stood by Billy, hands on hips, looking so very foolish. 'What's all this fighting?' she cried out. 'What sort of home do you think you've given me?'

Billy gave Dorothy no drink. 'Be careful, now,' he said. 'Be careful what you say to me. Be careful what you say to anybody. The one place for your trap is shut.'

Cranium Cuthbertson beat sweetly on, trying. I could see, to give some harmony to everyone's emotion. Also, he began to sing: a chant like to himself, in his own tongue, about a boy who leave the coast beside the sea and walks all his life right up to Kano, looking for blessings of his ancestors, who came from there. The boys stopped shooting dice, and all began clapping softly to the rhythm, and singing the 'Ay-yah-ah' chorus to Cranium's good song.

But the door came open, and I saw Inspector Purity of the C.I.D. and three more of his dicks. Billy had leapt quick under the table, which had a cloth. 'Stay where you are, everybody,' this Purity man said. 'I want a word with Mr Billy Whispers. Where is he?'

No one spoke. Though did I see my brother Arthur smile at Purity and look across the room towards the table?

As feet approached it, Billy did a brave and foolish thing: he rushed and jumped right through the window, glass and everything. Dorothy screamed. Two dicks ran downstairs, one stayed beside the door, and Mr Purity stepped over to the window.

We all stood still, though Cranium beat a note or two upon his drum. Purity shone down a torch. 'Got him?' he shouted.

There was a shout up back.

'What?' Mr Purity cried out. 'Well, carry him over to the car. I'll be right down.'

Dorothy ran up to Inspector Purity and caught hold of his hair. 'What are you doing to my husband?' she screamed out. He pushed her off on to the floor. 'So he's your husband, is he?' said Purity. 'I think he's living off your immoral earnings.'

'Is that the charge? Is that the charge you make?' said Ronson Lighter.

'Resisting arrest will be one charge,' said Purity, 'and no doubt there'll be others. Well, let's take a look at you all and see who we've got. Stand up, everyone, with your hands on top of your heads. Come on!'

Everybody stood up except Dorothy, and all put their hands on their heads except Montgomery and myself. Detective Purity walked round inspecting all the party, like a general, and to some he spoke.

'So you're here, Alfy,' he began. 'One day we'll have to find a little charge for you. Any suggestions, lad? I've got one or two ideas. And you,' he said to my brother Arthur. 'You getting tired of life outside the nick? Maybe we could help you back inside again. Dice, eh? That's gambling. Hullo, Barbara. Aren't you in need of some care and protection? We'll introduce you to one of our lady coppers, she'll see you home to Cardiff. Good evening, Mr Pew, or is it good morning? You keep some strange company, don't you. And you weren't altogether frank with me earlier on about your young friend here . . . Mr Fortune. How are you, son? Do you know something? We're going to nick you for peddling weed one day soon, so don't you think you'd better get aboard a ship? No, don't bother to turn your pockets out this time, we know you've put it on the fire. And you!' He'd stopped in front of Ronson Lighter, who thought he had been missed. 'You'd better come along with us as well. There's been some malicious wounding, and perhaps you can tell us something more about it. Your friend down there seems to be unconscious, and they think he's broken some legs.'

'You bastard!' Dorothy cried out from the floor.

He didn't look down, but said to her, 'We'll be sending for you, Dorothy, when we want you. Don't leave London just at present, will you? Come on now, you!' he said to Ronson. And this boy, though if it was a fight he would fear nothing, like so many of our men when big misfortune falls upon them, was quiet and quite helpless in the copper's hand.

Inspector Purity stopped by the door. 'I needn't tell you all to watch your step,' he said. 'There's not a man or woman here we haven't got a charge for when the time comes, and we feel like paying you a visit.' Then he went out with Ronson and the other copper, who had stood there waiting and not said one word.

When the door closed, Dorothy scrambled up, opened it again and cried down the stairs, 'You bastards!' Then slammed it, turned to us all and shouted, 'Somebody's shopped Billy!'

'Would it be you, Dorothy?' I said.

'Me, Johnny Fortune! Call me a whore if you want to, but I don't shop nobody. Someone here has spoken with the Law. Somebody's shopped Billy!'

Faces all looked at faces.

'Come now, Montgomery,' I said, when looking from the window I saw the Law car drive away. 'Is time to go.'

Dorothy and Barbara were weeping on each other's shoulder. 'I have my car outside,' said Ibrahim Tondapo, like some emir. 'I offer you a lift.'

I made no reply to this vain man, but went with the others down the stairs. This Ibrahim insisted foolishly on our company, so we came up to his limousine. Place in the car was refused by me to Arthur and to Alfy Bongo, who walked away chattering in spite together. The passengers I allowed were Cranium and Montgomery in the back seat, and I by Ibrahim Tondapo's side.

'Where to?' he said.

'East End for me.'

'I'll see you home, Johnny,' said Montgomery.

'For me, please, a drop-out at the Trafalgar Square,' said Cranium Cuthbertson.

Tondapo drove elegantly but too fast, anxious to demonstrate his skill. In the central city we turned Cranium loose, and drove on across the commercial area of the city's wealth, this Ibrahim trying to make eager conversation with Montgomery and with me. But I silenced my Jumble friend, and would say nothing to this African, for whom I still planned a vengeance for his earlier action in the

Sphere. So when we came to the dockside poverty of the Immigration Road, I asked him to take two turnings and then halt.

'Thank you,' I said.

'You welcome, man. Bygone is bygone.'

'Your tyre is flat.'

'No, I not think so, man.'

'I tell you is flat: your motor rumbles.'

We all got out. Montgomery noticed my intention.

'No, no, Johnny,' he cried out. 'Not any more!'

But I had heaved this Tondapo against the wall and battered him. He fight hard and bravely, but had eaten too much throughout his comfortable life. When I had laid him low, I lifted him and put his groaning body in the back seat of his vehicle.

Montgomery was in rages with me. 'You must learn to control yourself,' he said.

'And you! Fighting with two Africans in your nakedness.'

'That was a misunderstanding.'

'Let us not argue, Montgomery. There have been arguments enough.'

We walked through the dim and silence of these evil streets: all tumbling: all sad.

'Who *did* betray Whispers?' said Montgomery.

'It was not you, then?'

'Oh, don't be absurd, Johnny. Why should I?'

'That Alfy Bongo?'

'I don't understand that hobgoblin. I don't think he's working for the Law. . . . Excuse my asking, but had Arthur anything to do with it, perhaps?'

'Perhaps so. Or more perhaps is really Dorothy who spoke.'

'She didn't act like it.'

'Dorothy is tired of Billy. Maybe she's glad to see him go inside for some other charge than laying his hands upon her earnings. If she told the Law about this wounding, and of nothing else, then she will not have to appear in court against him.'

'Isn't the simplest explanation that Jimmy Cannibal told them about the attack himself? That Ronson did it, and Billy was behind it?'

'Could be so. When the court case comes, then we shall see. By the witnesses, we shall see. But what is sure is that Billy will suspect us all—you for what you saw in the gamble-house, and Dorothy that she wants to leave him, and also me.'

'Why you?'

'Because Dorothy's foolish hope is to come and live with me. I must keep clear of that evil little chicken.'

We crossed the Immigration Road.

'Inspector Purity was asking about you earlier on,' Montgomery said, and told me of that meeting. 'Be careful, Johnny.'

'I am always careful.'

'You had no weed with you tonight?'

'None left. Though if they want to take me, they would not mind if I had weed or not.'

'If that's so, why didn't they arrest you there and then? Or any of the others except Ronson?'

'The knifing was their business this evening. One operation at a time is the Law's slow and steady way. Perhaps there were also too many witnesses for the frame-up. They have their skill and patience, Montgomery, have the Law.'

Outside my sweet-shop, I said goodbye to him. 'Do not come in, Montgomery. Muriel and Hamilton will be sleeping. I telephone you.'

'You promise? Keep in touch, now, won't you.

'I speak to you on the phone tomorrow.'

'Take care, then. And thank you, Johnny, for helping me with those two boys.'

Helping him! Had I not saved his skin entirely?

'Is nothing,' I said. 'Good night now, Montgomery. I shall see you.'

He walked away, and turned and waved, and I waited till he shrunk right out of sight. Then I went indoors to my misery.

Muriel was up, in spite of it was morning. I kissed her, but she turned her face away.

'Hamilton's gone,' she said. 'They've taken him off to hospital in the ambulance. He had delirium.'

'It was real bad, this what Hamilton have?'

'I don't think he'll live, Johnny.'

I sat down by her side.

'Let us go sleep now,' I said to her. 'A great many troubles have come my way today.'

'You're bleeding, Johnny. Let me wash you.'

'Wash me, then. But I must sleep.'

She wiped the blood off from my face and fists, and gave me a cup of warm-up tea. 'You're back so late. Always back to late,' she said, taking my clean hands.

'But I am back, Muriel. Come, we go sleep.'

'I have to go to work in a few hours.'

'Before you go to work, Muriel, you sleep with me.'

12

Splendour of flesh made into dream

FOR SEVERAL WEEKS, my life in the flat had been transformed: Norbert and Moscow had made themselves at home. 'It sure is Bohemian here,' Norbert said, 'and we'll not be in your way.' They hardly were, indeed; for so much did they overflow about the place, flinging heady articles of clothing everywhere, singing naked on the stairs down to the bath, entertaining, at all hours, their wide circle of acquaintances, that I became almost the interloper in my dwelling, and feared to inconvenience them, rather than they me. Yet though so entirely heartless, and so rigorously selfish, they radiated such *bonhomie*, were perpetually so high-spirited and so amiable, laughed, danced and chattered so abandonedly, that even Theodora was won over. 'Of course, I prefer Africans,' she said, 'they're more authentic. But these young Americans certainly have charm.'

Carrying her cat Tungi, she was paying me a morning visit (such as, in earlier days, she'd never made) while my lodgers were out at their rehearsal. 'I only wish,' I said, 'they wouldn't use the telephone quite so recklessly. I caught Norbert calling up Jackson, Mississippi, yesterday, and really had to put my foot down.'

'"Put your foot down"!' Theodora irritated me by repeating with superior disdain. 'You're quite unable to say no to them about anything.'

'And you, my dear Theodora?' I could not resist asking. 'Have you not succumbed, despite your initial indifference, even hostility, to coloured people?'

'My feeling for them is selective, just as it would be with one of us. I don't admire coloured people in the mass, like you do.'

'You mean you've fallen in love with one individually, and I haven't.'

Theodora, touched on the raw, assumed her severe departmental manner. 'For some time now, Montgomery,' she told me, 'I've been wanting to say just what I think. And it's this. Your interest in these people is prompted by nothing more than a vulgar, irresponsible curiosity.'

'Thank you, Theodora.'

'You like to be the odd man out, and lord it over them.'

'I'm happy with them. It's as simple as that.'

'If you call that happiness.'

'I do.'

She shifted, woman-like, her ground.

'It's the crude animal type that attracts you most of all. It's simply another form of *nostalgie de la boue*. You've taken the easy way and are losing face, even with them. Do you see anything, for instance, of the intelligent types? The coloured intellectuals?'

I decided a dressing-down was due. 'In the first place, I'd remind you, Theodora, that I see much of Mr Karl Marx Bo. I listened to him addressing a meeting only last Sunday in Hyde Park, and we had a long and angry conversation afterwards. As for you, my dear, and *your* predilections, would you really describe Johnny Fortune as an intellectual?'

'He's most intelligent.'

'I don't deny it; but not lacking, I would say, in animal attraction.'

'He's handsome, in the way they are—yes.'

'Theodora, I don't wish to be unkind, but you're pathetic. Why not admit you love him?'

She looked at me long and hard. 'Because I'm ashamed to,' she said at last. 'Not ashamed because he's coloured, or, as you say, animal, or anything else, but because it's a feeling so strong I can't control it. I'm not used to that, and I can't cope.'

I ventured to pat her on her unyielding shoulder. 'Perhaps that's good for you,' I said. 'Perhaps one should not be able to dominate every situation. . . .'

She looked to be crying, so I considerately turned away. 'They're so appalling!' she said at last, quite softly. 'So tender and so heartless. So candid and so evil!'

It was my turn now, I felt—from the depths of what was, after all, a wider experience than her own and, so I thought, one more dearly won—to lecture her.

'I don't think you must take,' I said, 'a *moral* attitude towards these people: or rather, a moral attitude within the English terms of reference. I don't think you must suppose, if they seem to you such charming sinners, beyond good and evil (or before it, rather), that the devil has therefore marked them for his own.'

'Why not?' she said, rather sulkily.

'Use your historical sense, Theodora—one certainly far better documented than my own. Remember, for instance, that in parts of Africa not a soul had ever heard of Christianity less than a hundred years ago. . . .'

'Where hadn't they, precisely?'

'Don't be pedantic. In Uganda, for example. May I go on?'

'But Johnny doesn't come from Uganda.'

'Who said he did? Can't we move, just for a second, from the particular to the general?' I was quite exasperated.

'Go on, then.'

'I shall. You should therefore remember that if coloured men seem, to your eyes, more happily amoral than we are, they have other spiritual ties, quite unknown to us, and very different from our own, that are every bit as strong.'

'Such as?'

'Don't interrupt. They have sacred tribal loyalties, for instance, of which we feel absolutely nothing that's equivalent. If Johnny had been a Gambian like those boys who set on me that evening, and of the same tribe as they were, he certainly wouldn't have helped me, however close our friendship.'

'The more fool he.'

I restrained myself. 'There's another thing,' I went on. 'The family. We think our family ties are precious, or, at any rate, that we should feel so. But they're nothing at all to theirs. Have you noticed, when an African makes a solemn promise, what he says to you?'

'I can't say I have.'

'He says, "I swear it on my mother's life." '

'And probably breaks his word.'

'Oh, no doubt! Just as we do when we swear upon our gods, or on our sacred books. The point I'm trying to convey, though, to the frosty heights of your Everest intelligence, dearest Theodora, is that there are entirely different moral concepts among different races: a fact which leads to endless misunderstandings on the political and social planes, and makes right conduct in you, for instance, seem idiotic to Johnny Fortune, and some gesture of his which he believes necessary and honourable to seem foolish, or even wicked, in your eyes.'

'Don't bully me, Montgomery,' she said. 'You're as bad as he is.'

'I'm sorry, Theodora. Let's have some coffee in the kitchen, if I can find my way through the provocative underclothes my lodgers have hung there in festoons.'

She put Tungi down and came and helped me make it, turning thoughtfully over the gossamer vests and pants that rested on the lines.

'Have you seen Johnny lately?' I asked, as I handed her a cup.

'Yes, several times, and he telephones. But I'm worried about him, Montgomery! If only he'd work!'

'He's a lazy lad, I fear.'

'Like you. How is your free-lancing going?'

'It's not.'

'I thought it wasn't. And Johnny does absolutely nothing—only stays with that squalid woman.'

'If you knew Muriel better, you'd not call her so.'

'At all events, her sister's little friend is now in jail.'

'Billy Whispers' being sentenced has nothing to do with Muriel, Theodora. Do be consistent. And don't gloat.'

'Johnny said he got six months.'

'For being an accessory to a wounding, yes. But the evidence against him was given by a Mr Cannibal—the sentence had nothing to do with Dorothy, even less with Muriel.'

She pondered and sipped her coffee. I saw her eyes become transfixed by a peculiar garment. 'What on earth's this?' she said.

'It's what the French call a "slip" or, more accurately, a "zlip". The boys wear it when they dance. Which reminds me. There's a matinée this afternoon. Would you like to come?'

'No.'

'Don't be so ungracious, Theodora. You ought to see them. After all, my guests are courteous to you round about the house. . . .'

'Oh, very well, then. I could do with a day off—and the Corporation owe me plenty. I'll call my secretary.'

For a matinée, the place was crowded, principally with males, and with a fair peppering of coloured admirers of the Isabel Cornwallis company. I noticed, and greeted in the foyer, Mr Lord Alexander, to whom Theodora, once she heard who he was, behaved most graciously—she had apparently become a collector of his records; and also Mr Cranium Cuthbertson, who did not please her possibly because, poking her in the ribs and bending double with amusement, he cried out in a familiar fashion, 'You's the hep-cat what stole Mr Vial's puss-cat!' Bells rang, and we went inside the auditorium to see how the Cornwallis company would achieve that most difficult of theatrical feats—the creation of illusion just one hour after the midday meal.

Although I'd seen the show so often before (almost nightly), I marvelled once again at the complete transformation of these bitter, battling egoists, with their cruel jealousies and bitchy gossip, their pitiless trampling ambition, and their dreadful fear of the day, some time so near in their late thirties, when they could dance no more—into the gracious, vigorous, sensual creatures I saw upon the stage. By Miss Cornwallis' alchemy, the sweaty physical act of dancing became an efflorescence of the spirit! True, there were tricks theatrical innumerable, but Isabel Cornwallis was wiser than she knew: because her raw material, the dancers, possessed an inner dignity and nobility, of which even she could hardly be aware, but knew, by instinct, how to use. These boys and girls seemed incapable of a vulgar gesture! And as they danced, they were clothed in what seemed the antique innocence and wisdom of humanity before the Fall—the ancient, simple splendour of the millennially distant days before thought began, and civilizations . . . before the glories of conscious creation, and the horrors of conscious debasement, came into the world! In the theatre, they were *savages* again: but the savage is no barbarian—he is an entire man of a complete, forgotten world, intense and mindless, for which we, with all our conquests, must feel a disturbing, deep nostalgia. These immensely adult children, who'd carried into a later age a precious vestige of our former life, could throw off their twentieth-century garments, and all their ruthlessness and avarice and spleen, and radiate, on the stage, an atmosphere of goodness! of happiness! of love! And I thought I saw at last what was the mystery of the deep attraction to us of the Spades—the fact that they were still a mystery to themselves.

'I can't take any more,' said Theodora at the interval. 'They're too upsetting.'

'Can't you stick it out until the end? We could meet them at the stage door and have some tea.'

'You stay: I'll go back to the office.'

We went out in the foyer. 'Be sure you say something nice to them back at the flat, Theodora,' I said to her. 'You're so parsimonious with your praise.'

'I won't know what to say.'

'Just praise them. It's all they want.'

I saw her to a taxi. Hurrying back into the theatre, amid clanging bells, I was detained by the odious Alfy Bongo.

'You again!'

'Yes, it's me. Ain't they the tops?'

'Of course. I want to see them, though, not you. Farewell.'

He plucked at my arm. 'You heard Billy Whispers and Ronson Lighter have gone inside?'

'Yes, yes.'

'They should have got a good lawyer. It's hopeless without. I told them, but they wouldn't listen.'

'Look! I want to see the show.'

He followed me into the theatre, already dark. 'They should have gone to Mr Zuss-Amor,' he whispered. 'Remember the name—it's Zuss-Amor.'

13

Inspector Purity's ingenious plan

Often I had tried for many weeks to visit Hamilton in his hospital, but they were not eager to allow me near him on account of his condition being critical. But on this present visit I was called in immediately to the Sister.

'The patient is a relative of yours?' she said.

'No, he is my friend.'

'Has he relatives in this country?'

'I know of none. Why?'

'In Africa, you know his family's address?'

'Hamilton did not tell it to you?'

'He refused to . . .'

'If he did not tell you this, I do not wish to. He has his reasons that his family should not know.'

This practical woman put on her kind face. 'Your friend is very ill,' she said. 'He's on what we call the danger list. Surely he would wish his family to know?'

'I may speak with him?'

'Yes. But not for long.'

That Hamilton would soon die was certain by his waste-away appearance, and also by his special situation convenient to the door. My friend also knew that this was to be his fate, for his first words were to tell me of his understanding. He spoke without fear of this, as you would expect of Hamilton, but very sadly. I did not deny what he foretold, nor would I agree to it, but sat by him and held his bony hands.

'Speak to me of your life, Johnny. Tell me what happens to you now.'

'I must not tire you, Hamilton.'

He smiled a very little. 'What is the difference, Johnny Fortune? Speak to me. How is Muriel?'

'Muriel is gone. I also have left our house.'

'Why?'

'Dorothy has come to live there now.'

'To stay with you?'

'No, man, no—I will explain. Muriel have sickness with her coming baby, and could not work. We owed rents to the landlord, and had no loot. Dorothy, without asking us, go see the landlord, pay over our arrears, and get the rent-book for herself. Then she say to Muriel and me that we can stay there if she stay there too.'

'And you say yes?'

'No, we say no. But where could we go to? Even I began to work, Hamilton, at labouring. But before I get my first week wage, we had no other place to go, and stayed on there with Dorothy. Even after that first week, we stay some while to make some little savings.'

'And then?'

My friend's eyes showed me he guess what happen then.

'I keep away from Dorothy, Hamilton, like you would think. But one time when Muriel was out . . . well, this thing happen between me and she. Foolish, of course, I know, but a cold evening and we left alone together. . . .'

'And Dorothy tell Muriel of this happen?'

'I think no: but Muriel she guessed. A woman can always tell it, Hamilton, when you betray her. How so, I do not know; but they can tell.'

My friend turned slowly in his bed. 'And then Muriel leave you, Johnny?'

'Yes. She go back to her horrible Mrs Macpherson mother, and will not see me. She say to me, "If is Dorothy you wish, not me, then you can take her."'

'But you do not wish for Dorothy?'

'No. She ask me, of course, to stay and live off what she earn. But I wish for nothing of that woman. Though foolishly I stay in the house some weeks more for sleeping.'

'For private sleeping, Johnny?'

'Alone. Then we have quarrel, Dorothy and I, and I leave these rooms entirely. And now I stay this place, that place, with boys I know, till I can get my room.'

Hamilton thought about my story, 'These Jumble friends of yours,' he said. 'You could not stay with them?'

'Oh, you understand me, Hamilton! When Jumbles do the favour, always they ask some price. For payment of their deeds, they wish to steal your private life in some way or another.'

'And you will not return again with Muriel at any time?'

'She say to me, Hamilton, that if I do not marry her, now that she soon has the child, she does not wish to stay with me at all. But how can I marry such a woman? What would they say back home?'

Hamilton, he understood this. 'The best thing, Johnny Fortune, is certainly for you to sail to Africa. Do not leave this too late, as I do, or you will find yourself in misery like me.'

What could I say to my old friend—but that I hope the days of both of us would soon be rather brighter? I said goodbye to him, and still Hamilton would not let me tell his home address to the people in the hospital.

So I leave that sad place behind me, and walked out in the dark winter East End afternoon: no use to go back now to my labouring job, whose foreman would not give me time off to visit Hamilton, and now would certainly dismiss me for my absence. I thought of Mahomed and his café, and how a free meal of rice would give me strength, and there, playing dominoes, I meet the former weed-peddler, Peter Pay Paul.

'Mr Ruby,' he tell me, 'ask why you come for no more business.'

'I cut out that hustle too, man. I cut right out of peddling like you say is best to, when the months go by. And you, what do you do now, Peter?'

'Good times have come to me, Johnny. I doorman now at the Tobagonian Free Occupation club, and this is a profitable business.'

'Tell me now, Peter. I have no room at present. May I sleep in your cloakroom for this evening?'

'What will you pay me, man?'

'Skinned now, Peter Pay Paul. You do this for your friend.'

'Just this one night, then, Johnny. Do not please ask me the next evening, or word will reach the ear of this Tobagonian owner and I lose my good job.'

Peter supplied me with one coffee. 'Arthur is down East End,' he said. 'He asks for you from several people.'

'I do not wish to see that relative of mine ever again.'

A great pleasure came to me now, which was the arrival in Mahomed's of the seaman Laddy Boy, he who had brought the letter from my sister Peach. His ship had been sailing to the German ports, and he told us of the friendly action of the chicks he'd met in dockside streets of Hamburg.

'I see some Lagos boy there, Johnny,' he told me now. 'In a ship coming out of Africa. He tell me some news about your family that you should hear.'

Almost I guessed what Laddy Boy would tell me. 'Your sister Peach,' he said, 'has sailed to England now to train as nurse.'

'This news is certain of her coming? I wish it was some other time she choose.'

Laddy Boy said to me: 'Tomorrow, come meet my quartermaster, Johnny. Speak to him and see if you can sign on our ship, to have some serious occupation for when your sister reaches England.'

'I have no knowledge of a sailor—will he take me?'

'We speak to him together, man. I know some secrets of his smuggling that have helped him raise his income to his benefit.'

When the half-past-five time came at last, Laddy Boy took me for some Baby Salt at the Apollo tavern. We sit there drinking quietly, I thinking of home and Lagos, and of Peach and Christmas and my Mum and Dad.

But what spoils these thoughts is Dorothy, when she come in the saloon bar with a tall G.I. She send this man over and he say to me politely, 'Your sister-in-law ask me, man, to ask if you will speak with her a minute.'

'No, man, no. Tell her I busy with my friend.'

He went back to Dorothy, but come to me once more. 'She says is important to you, what she have to tell.'

I went with Dorothy in one corner of the bar. 'Now, Dorothy,' I said. 'Please understand I do not wish to mix my life with yours. Do not pester me, please, with your company, or I turn bad on you, and we regret it.'

She was high with her drink, I saw, but quieter and more ladylike than I know her ever before.

'Look, man,' she said. 'I know the deal I offered you means nothing to you, but can't we still be friends?'

'I do not wish to be your enemy or your friend.'

'Why are you so mean to me always, Johnny? You know how gone on you I am.'

'Keep away from me, Dorothy, is all I ask you.' I got up, but she called, 'Just one thing more I want to say to you.' She got that far, then stopped, and when I waited, said, 'Get me another drink.'

'Is that it? More drink?'

I moved finally to leave her, making from now a rule that never would I answer her again. She grabbed my arm suddenly and pulled me down towards her, and said so close my ear I smell her whisky breath, 'If I leave the game, Johnny, and get off the streets for good, will you marry me?'

I pulled my arm away. 'Your life is your life, Dorothy. Do not try to mix it in with mine is all I say.'

I left this woman, and returned to Laddy Boy. When she went out some minutes later, she stopped as she passed by and said to me, 'I'll mix in, Johnny Fortune, if I want to. I always get my own way in the end.'

The G.I. shook hands to show his dislike of her behaviour, and they both left. 'That woman should drink tea,' said Laddy Boy.

I made the arrangement with him for the meeting next day with his quartermaster, and then went to see my overnight home at the Free Occupation club. Peter had not yet come back to his duty, so I waited in the hallways, where I saw a big poster of the Cranium Cuthbertson band, which said they would play at the Stepney friendly get-together where white and coloured residents were invited to know each other rather better.

'Hullo, bra,' said some voice, and it was Arthur.

'"Bra" is for Africans, not for Jumbles,' I said to him.

'Why you always insulting me, Johnny? Would our same Dad like it, if he knew?'

'Blow, man, before I do you some violence,' I said to him.

He walked back to the door, and said out loud, 'He's here!', then scattered quick. The C.I.D. Inspector Purity came in with another officer.

'We want you, Fortune,' he said. 'We'll talk to you at the station.'

These two men grabbed me, though I made no resistance and said nothing. Each held an arm, and tugged me across the pavement to their car. Peter Pay Paul came up at just this moment, and stopped still when he saw me. 'Telephone, Peter, to the radio B.B.C.!' I cried out loud. 'Speak to Miss Pace. Pace! B.B.C. radio headquarter!'

They dragged me inside the Law car. The journey was short and fast, and they did not speak. In the police station, they took me beyond the public rooms, and then, from behind me, Mr Purity struck me on the neck and I fell on the concrete. I got up, and they pulled me into a small room.

'Finger-print him, Constable,' said Purity to the other officer.

'I have no wish to be finger-printed.'

'Shut up. Over here.'

'You cannot finger-print me. I have no conviction on my record.'

The two looked at each other, then at me. The Detective-Constable, whose face was pale and miserable, came close and said, 'You're not going to co-operate?' Then he beat me round about my head.

I know the great danger of hitting back against the Law, so sat still with my hands clenched by my side. This beating went on. 'Don't bruise him,' said Mr Purity. The Constable stopped and rubbed his hands.

'Our bruises do not show in court so well as white man's do,' I said. 'This is the reason why you hit us always harder.'

Mr Purity smiled at this funny remark I made. He asked me for details of my name, and age, and this and that, and I gave him these. Then they searched me and took away every possession. Then he began asking other questions.

'In English law,' I said, 'do you not make a charge? Do you not caution a prisoner before he speaks? This is the story that they tell us in our lessons we have back home on British justice.'

Mr Purity raised up his fist. 'Do you really want to suffer?' he said to me.

'I want to know the charge. There was no drug in my possession—nothing.'

'We're not interested in drugs at present,' said Mr Purity. 'We're charging you with something that'll send you inside for quite a bit longer, as you'll see. You're a ponce, Johnny Fortune, aren't you. You've ponced on Bill Whispers' girl.'

This words were such a big surprise to me, that at first I had no speech. Then I stand up. 'You call *me* ponce?' I shouted.

'Nigger or ponce, it's all the same,' the Detective-Constable said.

I hit him not on the face, but in the stomach where I know this blow must hurt him badly, even if they kill me after. They did not kill me, but called in friends and kicked me round the floor.

After this treatment, I was left alone and even given a kind cigarette. An old officer in uniform and grey hair then visited me, and spoke to me like some friendly uncle. 'You'd better do what you're told, son,' he said, 'and let them print you. Tomorrow they'll oppose bail in court, and the screws can print you in the nick at Brixton.... You don't want to fight the whole police force, do you? You can only lose....'

'Mister, this battle is not ended,' I said to him. 'Outside in this city, London, I have friends.'

14

Mobilisation of the defence

THE MESSAGE REACHED THEODORA, in a highly garbled version, through an agitated secretary who boldly interrupted an inter-departmental conference at Broadcasting House on a projected series of talks to be called, provisionally, 'The Misfit and the Body Corporate: a survey of contemporary un-integrated types.' Theodora, scenting mischief, had asked the D.A.C. (Programmes) if she might be excused, and had parliamented with the secretary in an airless corridor outside.

'I'm sorry if I did wrong, Miss Pace, to barge in on the meeting,' the secretary whispered, 'but it sounded urgent. This person said this person was "in big trouble"—those were his words.'

'Which person?'

'The one who phoned said it. I think he must have been a native.

'You mean the African who telephones me sometimes?'

'No: an illiterate sort, Miss Pace. I could hardly understand a word he spoke. But he did say to tell you "the Law have put the hands on she Spade friend"—those were the exact words he used.'

'Thank you, Miss Lamb,' said Theodora. 'You did quite right. Please go in and tell the D.A.C. I'm called away on urgent family business. A sudden case of sickness.'

All this Theodora told me, in calm, shrill tones, over the telephone to the flat, where I was helping Norbert Salt iron the ruffles he'd sewn on to the front of a silk shirt he planned to wear with his tuxedo at a gala.

'It sounds, Theodora, as if Johnny's been arrested.'

'Of course it does. But where? And why? How does one find out?'

'Telephone the police station.'

'Which one?'

'Well, try the East End ones first. Would you like me to do it?'

'No, I'll work from here. I'll call you back when there are developments.'

'Just a minute, Theodora. Lay your hands on some money if you can—it always come in useful. And what about a lawyer?'

'I'd thought of all that. I'll call you later.'

I waited half an hour, then telephoned the B.B.C. Theodora had gone and left no message. I wondered what to do. I opened the fourth volume of the telephone directory and looked up 'Zuss-Amor'.

Though the hour was late, a female voice replied. Yes, Mr Zuss-Amor was in, but what was it about? I started to explain, but clickings in the line suggested to me someone listening on an extension. 'Look,' I said. 'May I please speak to Mr Zuss-Amor direct? Tell him I'm a friend of Alfy Bongo's.'

Immediately a male voice said, 'What sort of case is it, Mr Pew?'

'I don't know yet, my friend's only just been arrested. We're trying to find out why. He's an African.'

'Oh. Then we know what the case will probably be, don't we. I can see you here tomorrow at half-past-five.'

'But Mr Zuss-Amor, that'll be too late. Won't the case come up in court tomorrow morning?'

'He'll be formally charged tomorrow, yes, but you can take it from me, if the case is at all serious, the police will ask for a remand. There's nothing I can do till I've heard some facts from you and from the client: that is, if I agree to take the case, of course, and he agrees to me.'

'What should I do tomorrow morning?'

'Where was your friend arrested?'

'I don't know yet. He lives down in the East End.'

'It'll be Boat Street magistrates' court, most likely. Go there, try to see him, and try to get the magistrate to grant bail. I doubt if he will, though.'

'Why?'

'The police usually oppose bail in the kind of case I think it's likely to be. See you tomorrow, then, Mr Pew, and thanks for calling.'

I had a lot more to say and ask, but Mr Zuss-Amor hung up on me. The moment I put the telephone down, the bell rang, and it was Theodora.

'I'm at Aldgate, Montgomery,' she said. 'I couldn't get any sense out of the police over the phone, so I took a taxi down here and went to the station.'

'Yes, yes. And?'

'He's been arrested, but they won't tell me where he is or what the charge is.'

'Why?'

'They wanted to know what they called my "interest in the matter". I said I was willing to go bail, but they told me that was a matter for the magistrate. Then I tried to get through to Sir Wallingford Puke-Drew——'

'Sir who?'

'He's my family solicitor: the one who advised us on the eviction trouble; but there's no one in his office.'

'I've got a solicitor, Theodora. A Mr Zuss-Amor.' And I told her of our conversation.

'But what do you know about this person, Montgomery?'

'Nothing. But he's seeing me tomorrow, isn't he? We must get things moving.'

There was a slight, agitated pause. 'Suppose they convict him tomorrow before we have time to get legal advice?'

'They can't possibly do that. He has the right to apply for legal aid.'

'But does he *know* that?'

'He's not an idiot, Theodora.'

'If only I knew what it was all about.'

'Well, stop fussing, and come back here and talk about it. There's nothing else to do now that I can see. Would you like me to come down there and fetch you?'

'No. I've kept the taxi waiting.'

She arrived back, battered and dismayed as I had never seen her before. I gave her a glass of vodka (a present to the household from Moscow Gentry), and she recovered something of her poise.

'I've been thinking, Montgomery,' she said, 'and it must be one of three things. Either some act of violence, or else having that disgusting hemp in his possession, or else . . .'

'Yes?'

'You don't think this woman Muriel was a prostitute, do you?'

'I'm certain she wasn't. She wouldn't know how.'

'Would he have lived on any other woman of that type?'

'You can never be certain, Theodora, but I really don't believe he would.'

'What can you get for having Indian hemp?'

'I believe on a first conviction it's only a fine—unless they could prove he dealt in it as well.'

Theodora poured out another glassful. 'I'll have to cook up some story for the office,' she said. Then, draining it down, 'I wish I knew more about the world!'

Next morning saw us driving down to Boat Street in a taxi—I in my best suit with an unusual white shirt, and Theodora in her severest black. She opened her bag as we drew near the East End, and made herself up rather excessively. Then she took a small yellow pill, and swallowed with difficulty. 'Dexedrine,' she said. 'Want one?'

'No thanks.'

'Good for the nerves. Tones you up in an emergency.'

'Like hemp, apparently.'

'But if you've got a kind doctor or chemist, perfectly legal.'

'White man's magic.'

'No wonder they think we're hypocrites.'

The public waiting at the court were not prepossessing: though even Venus and Adonis would have looked squalid in this ante-chamber of the temple of justice, built in Victorian public lavatory style. When the sitting began, we squeezed in among a considerable throng, and watched a succession of small, grim cases—on all of which two dreadful old men beside me throatily passed whispered comments, invariably derogatory to the accused. Somebody nudged me. It was Mr Laddy Boy, the seaman I'd met earlier in the Sphere. He shook hands, and pursed his lips as if to say, 'I'm here, and you're here—so there's nothing to worry about at all.'

When Johnny Fortune was brought in, he looked a little shrunken and shop-soiled, but preserved, I was glad to see, his habitual buoyancy. He immediately glanced round to where the public were, saw us, nodded slightly, and then faced the magistrate.

This was one of those old gentlemen who look so amiable, but in such a neutral, meaningless sort of way that one really can't tell very much about them. The clerk read the charge, which, as I'd feared, and all the time secretly believed it would be, was one of living on the immoral earnings of a common prostitute, to wit, Dorothea Violet Macpherson. To this odious charge, Johnny Fortune pleaded not guilty in ringing, confident tones.

'Fucking ponce,' whispered one of the disgusting old men.

'These black bastards,' said the other.

Laddy Boy trod accidentally on their feet. There was some slight scuffling, and the usher turned and frowned severely.

Through watching this, I did not at first see Inspector Purity until he stepped into the box. My heart sank. He gave evidence of arrest in a clear, manly, honest voice and immediately asked for a remand.

'For how long, Detective-Inspector?' said the magistrate, as if asking a neighbour how long he wanted to borrow the lawn-mower.

'We should be ready in a week, sir.'

'Very well. What about bail?'

'We oppose bail, your Worship. The accused showed violence when under arrest, and we fear intimidation of the prosecution's witnesses.'

'I see. Have you anything to say?' the magistrate asked Johnny.

As soon as Johnny spoke, the court stiffened slightly, and all of them—audience, Press, lawyers and innumerable coppers—glanced curiously towards the dock. This was evidently not the ordinary African.

'I wish to ask that you grant me bail, sir, in order that I take law advice, prepare my case, and see my witnesses to defend me. Two white friends of good reputation are here in the court to bail for me.' (Everyone looked towards the public box.) 'I undertake no violence to anyone, unlike what has been stated by the police evidence.'

The magistrate mused, then turned. 'What do you say, Detective-Inspector?'

'An additional reason that we have, your Worship, for opposing bail, is that the prisoner refused to have his fingerprints taken. We also know the accused consorts with coloured merchant seamen, and have reason to believe he may try to stow away and leave the country without standing trial.'

Laddy Boy muttered something in African.

'Why wouldn't you have your finger-prints taken?' the magistrate asked Johnny, as if he had thereby deprived himself of a curious and amusing experience.

'My belief, sir, is that here in this country no man is forced to have prints taken of his fingers unless he has been convicted of some crime, which in my life I never have been at any time for any reason.'

The magistrate contrived both to frown and raise his brows. 'But don't you think you ought to help the officers in their enquiries?' he said, in a mild and fatherly way. 'You know, of course, I could always make an order for you to have them done.'

'If, sir, you say I must submit to finger-prints, I will. But what is most important to me is that you give me bail, because in my cell I cannot fix to be defended as I should be. I am not a stowaway, and came to England here as proper passenger paying my own fare; and shall not wish to leave in any other way before I stand my trial.'

This speech of Johnny's seemed a little too voluble, and syntactically unsound, to please the magistrate.

'No, I don't think so,' he said finally. 'You'll have every opportunity to prepare your case and take legal advice in custody. Bail refused.'

I turned in a rage to Theodora, but found she'd gone. I went outside the court with Laddy Boy.

'They put him in Brixton for remand,' the African said. 'We go and see him there and bring him liquor.'

'In prison?'

'Port wine is allowed for only on remand, but not some spirits,' he told me. 'We also take some chicken.'

This seemed to me so irrelevant to the major problems that I wanted to clout Laddy Boy. 'The thing is to get him a good lawyer and get him out!' I said crossly.

'Oh, yes, lawyer,' said Laddy Boy. 'You fix him that.'

Theodora reappeared, red-faced and furious. 'They wouldn't let me see him,' she exclaimed. 'But I spoke to the jailer. He says we can go down to Brixton this afternoon and see him there.'

We walked out in the chilly sun, breathing great gulps of air. I stopped Theodora on the pavement.

'Doesn't one thing stick out a mile?' I said.

'What sticks out a mile is that the magistrate's a moron.'

'Forget about the magistrate, Theodora! Isn't it obvious that if we can get Muriel to go into the box, he's free?'

'Why?'

'Why? Because if he lived off her moral earnings in the shirt factory, he couldn't have been living off her sister Dorothy's immoral earnings on the streets.'

'*He* could persuade Muriel—but can we? That's why they refused him bail,' cried Theodora. 'Why isn't Muriel here, anyway? She's ratted on him.'

'You speak of Muriel?' said Laddy Boy. 'She leave Johnny some many weeks now.'

'And who's he been living with since?' asked Theodora sharply.

'Sometimes Dorothy, I think, but he leave her too.'

'My God!' cried Theodora. 'The imbecile!'

'Laddy Boy,' I said. 'You don't think he *did* this with Dorothy, do you?'

The sailor looked vaguer than ever. 'Thing is to get him free,' he said. 'What he do, not matter. What matter is get him free.'

'We'd better go and see Muriel, anyway, and find out,' I said.

'Muriel, she with her mother now, Johnny tell me,' Laddy Boy said, rather indifferently.

We had a not very agreeable lunch together at a fish-and-chip place. Laddy Boy went out shopping, and, when he came back, spent much time making mysterious little bundles of what he'd bought.

'These Africans are *hopeless*,' said Theodora in a whisper like a scream.

'What *are* you up to, Laddy Boy?' I asked.

'I tip out the port wine from the bottle, and put in whisky,' Laddy Boy said proudly. 'He like that better. And in these chicken wing, I put some weed beneath the skin of it.'

'Good heavens! Don't they examine everything?'

'Oh, yes. But I do it very clever.'

'Let's hope to God you do.'

We set off to Brixton in dejected silence, only Laddy Boy undismayed. He pointed out landmarks on the way. ('That the Oval station, there,' for example.) Outside the prison gates, the taxi driver was facetious. ('Don't stay in there too long, mate, will you?' etc.) We were kept waiting in the waiting-room inside by a jailer whose face had to be seen to be believed. Laddy Boy carefully handed over his parcels, which the warder dumped like offal in a cardboard case. At last, behind the partitioned wire-netting that ran down one half of the room, Johnny Fortune made his sad appearance.

And it was sad: the buoyancy had dropped, and for the first time since I knew him I thought he looked afraid. He wasn't much interested in Theodora and in me, and talked most of the time to Laddy Boy in African. Theodora grew increasingly enraged. 'We *must* get the information out of him, Montgomery. Do interrupt that wretched African, and *talk* to Johnny.'

'The lawyer will see him for all that, Theodora. Don't be angry—just try to cheer him up.'

Almost at once, the warder said, in tones like a funeral bell, 'Time up!' At this Laddy Boy seemed suddenly overcome with hysteria and, clutching the wire-netting, cried, in English, 'My brother! Bless you, my brother! Oh, my brother!'—and tried to kiss Johnny through the grille. The warders tore him away, and Johnny was marched off. 'Any more of that,' the jailer said, 'and you'll be coming inside to keep him company.'

Out in the street, as soon as we'd turned the corner, Laddy Boy let out a roar of laughter. 'I do it!' he cried. 'I do it.'

'Do *what*, you idiot!' Theodora shouted.

'Theodora!'

'The five-pound note, he get it! I kiss it to him through the bar!'

When the ingenious seaman's mirth abated, he told us he'd screwed the note up in a ball, put it in his mouth, and passed it through the grille into Johnny Fortune's. 'But is money all that much use when you're in jail?' I asked the sailor.

Laddy Boy stopped in his tracks, and said: 'Man, in that place, loot is *everything*. You can buy *anything* if you have loot.'

'It'll make him more cheerful, then. He didn't look too happy, did he.'

'Understand me, man,' said Laddy Boy. 'It is his family he think of. Wounding or even thieving, that is nothing; but this charge they put upon him is the top disgrace.'

Nearby Lambeth town hall, Theodora insisted on entering a phone box to call up again Sir Wallingford whoever-it-was, her family solicitor. I was not surprised when she came out and told us, 'He wasn't there, but his chief clerk says it's not the sort of case they handle.'

'Very helpful. Let's stick to Zuss-Amor.'

'You want me to come with you to see him?'

'Not unless you really want to. I think it'd be much easier if I call on him alone. But first of all I'm going to try to contact Muriel. I know where her mother lives in Maida Vale.'

'I shall come too.'

'No, Theodora, you will not. The last thing likely to encourage Muriel to help Johnny is to hear a rival pleading for him to her.'

'What else can I do, then?'

'Go to your office and write some enormous memos. I'll call you as soon as I've seen Zuss-Amor.'

'I might ask the Corporation to let me appear in court as a witness to his character.'

'Suppose he gets convicted, Theodora.'

'He won't get convicted. He's innocent.'

'Yes, but if he were convicted, and you'd appeared in court, you'd lose your job.'

'I wouldn't. No one is ever dismissed from the Corporation.'

'No doubt; but I can't believe you'd rise to any further dizzy heights there if you got mixed up publicly in this case.'

'You've no guts, Montgomery. No moral fibre.'

'Oh, SHUT UP, Theodora. You're beginning to get on my tits.'

'Easy now,' said Laddy Boy.

I seized his hand, shook it, waved to Theodora, and leapt into a taxi on the rank. Then, remembering I had no money for the lawyer, had to climb ignominiously out and borrow it from her. I set off northwards in a rage.

But I got no help from the Macpherson family. A horrible old woman who admitted to being the mother refused to let me in, and though I shouted through the door for Muriel, she wouldn't come.

'She's finished with him—finished!' Mrs Macpherson yelled, sticking her face and body out at me like the figurehead of a ship. 'I don't care if they hang him for what he's done, my daughter wouldn't lift her little finger for him!' And she banged the door.

15

Wisdom of Mr Zuss-Amor

MR ZUSS-AMOR DIDN'T RECEIVE ME at the appointed hour: he kept me waiting in a corridor upon a kitchen chair, with nothing to regale me but yesterday's daily newspaper. The typist with ornamental spectacles who'd let me in vacated her cubby-hole from time to time, stepped indifferently over my legs, and went through a door of corrugated frosted glass inscribed in black cursive letters with the name of this man on whom we now pinned our hopes.

I was reduced to reading the opinions in the leading articles when the glass door was opened from inside and a voice said, 'I'm ready for you now. Quite ready.' When I went in, the door closed and a man stood between me and it, looking me up and down. He was wispy-bald, clad in a rumpled suit of good material, cigarette ash smothered his lapels, and his hands dangled by his sides. His face, which looked battered, sharp and confident, wore a tired and hideous smile. 'I'm your guide, philosopher and friend from now on, Mr Pew,' this person said. 'Come and tell me all about it.'

I did. He listened silently till I had nothing more to say.

'Have a fag,' he said, offering me one from a battered pack. 'I chain-smoke myself—that's why I don't like appearing in court. I prefer the work here.' He lit my cigarette. 'Right. In the first place, you should understand I can't be instructed by you. You're not the accused, fortunately. It's his instructions I have to take, you see.'

'But he asked me to come here.'

'I don't disbelieve you. But if I accept this case, I'll have to send someone down to the jail to see our friend. And whatever *he* wants me to do, I'll have to.'

'Am I wasting my time, then?'

'No—nor mine either, altogether. The more I know about the background in a case like this, the better. So. A point. What is the relationship between the accused and you? I mean the *exact* relationship?'

'I am his friend.'

'For what reason?'

'Because I like him.'

'*Like* him?'

'That's what I said.'

'You like him. Oh. What I mean is—is there anything at all I ought to know you haven't told me?'

'I don't think so.'

'I see. Another point. Why did you come here to me?'

'I told you. Mr Alfy Bongo gave your name to me.'

'Alfy. He told you I was a snide lawyer, I suppose?'

'He said you were a solicitor who wins cases.'

'Flattering! Right. Now, most important of all. Have you got any money?'

'Yes. Some.'

'Pay twenty to my secretary when you leave, will you? That'll do nicely to go on with. In notes, please—no cheques, or I can't fiddle my taxes.' He gave me a frosty grin, folded his fingers, and said, 'Very well, then. From what you've said, I can practically guarantee you something: which is that your friend will lose this case.'

'Why will he? He's innocent.'

'Oh, I don't doubt it! I don't doubt it one little bit! But these cases are always lost before they go to court. Believe the expert.'

'Then we might as well have no defence?'

'Not at all—why shouldn't you? I'm here to advise you. For example. You don't always have to fight a case, Mr Pew. You can also buy it.'

'Sorry . . .'

'Though it may be expensive. You say that two police officers were involved?'

'Yes. . . .'

'And they'll have their chief to remember. . . .'

'Do you mean . . .'

'That's just exactly what I mean.'

'But they've already brought the charge.'

'I know they have. You wouldn't be here if they hadn't. But for a consideration, they might not press it in the courts. There's evidence and evidence, you know.'

'What sort of consideration?'

'I'd have to see. But you'd better be thinking in terms of hundreds: not more than two, though, I dare say.'

'Can you arrange that?'

'It can be arranged. I haven't said by whom.'

'But if they got the money . . . wouldn't they double-cross us??'

'Why should they? It's not an important case to them. And they know if they do they'd lose good business of the same description in the future. . . .'

'I see.'

'I know what's in your mind: you think I'll take a cut.'

'Well, I suppose you would, wouldn't you?'

'How right you are, Mr Pew! Think of what's involved! Professional conduct of a disgraceful nature, and so on and so forth. I'd be quite reasonable, though. I'd not kill the goose that lays the golden egg. . . .'

Mr Zuss-Amor's dentures gave me an amiable, impatient smile. He clearly had other interviews in his diary.

'I'm not sure I can raise that much money all at once.'

'Oh. We can forget it, then.'

'And in any case, I think it's better to fight them.'

The solicitor ran his hand up and down his waistcoat buttons. 'It's not exactly you who's fighting them, but your friend,' he said. 'All the same, I think your decision's perfectly right.'

'Oh? Why do you?'

'If you take it to court, you'll almost certainly go down, as I've told you, though there's always a chance, if slight. But if you give these gentlemen a little something, they'll see to it you give them some more sooner or later. And probably sooner.'

'I don't get it, I'm sorry, Mr Zuss-Amor.'

'I've no doubt your life is blameless, Mr Pew. All the same, if they decided to scrape around and look for some dirt, they'd possibly find you'd done something or other. We all have, at one time, I expect. Even the bench of bishops have a blot on their consciences somewhere, I shouldn't be surprised.'

'But how would they know it was me the money came from?'

'Now, Mr Pew! Don't underestimate the Law! They know you're the friend of the accused, they've seen you in court this morning, they know—well, I dare say they know quite a lot of things.' He took off his spectacles and wiped them with his fingers. 'Or perhaps,' he went on, 'you think *I*'d tell them who paid up. Well, even if I did, I wouldn't have to: they'd just know.'

'So that's ruled out, then.'

'Very good. Right. So we go to court. The question arises: which court do we go to?'

'Isn't that automatic?'

'To begin with, yes, it is. Everyone appears before a magistrate initially. Even if you murdered the prime minister, that's where you'd first appear. But you needn't be tried by the magistrate if you don't want to be.'

'What else can you do'

'You can elect to go before a judge and jury.'

'And which is better?'

'There are naturally pros and cons in either case.'

'Well, tell me the pros and cons.'

Mr Zuss-Amor leaned back with his hands behind his head. 'My God!' he said, 'how often I've had to explain these simple facts! Don't laymen know *anything*?'

'Perhaps, Mr Zuss-Amor, it's to your advantage that they don't.'

'Oh, quick! Below the belt, but excellent! Right. Here we go. You elect to go before the magistrate. Advantages. It's over quicker, one way or the other. Less publicity, if that should happen to matter. The sentences aren't so high as a judge can give, if you're convicted.'

'And the cons?'

'No appeal—except to the bench of magistrates. From the judge, you can go up to the House of Lords, if all is well, but as you've not got the cash, the point's academic. Trial by jury takes much longer: it may be weeks before your young friend's face to face with my Lord and his merry men. Also, it'll cost you more. There'll be more for me, of course, and we'd have to get a barrister.'

'If we went to the magistrate, we don't need one?'

'Ah—you're catching on! Correct. Solicitors can appear before the beak. Though even in the magistrates' court, a barrister can be a help if he waves his law books at the old boy without antagonizing him unduly.'

'What does a barrister cost?'

'As you'd expect, it depends on who he is. If he's any good, it won't cost you less than fifty at the least—with refreshers, of course, that you'll have to pay if the trial lasted more than a day.'

'Is it likely to?'

'I don't suppose so, but we might come on late in the afternoon and get adjourned.' He paused. 'Well, have you made up your mind?'

'I don't know yet, Mr Zuss-Amor. You'd better tell me what you advise.'

'Advise! If I say, "Go to the judge," you'll think it's because I want more money.'

'Why should I?'

'You'd be a bloody fool if you didn't. . . . But all the same, there are certainly big advantages. Though, before I tell you what they are, I should repeat what I said just now—I think in this case you'll go down anyway.'

'Why are you so sure?'

'Because, my dear man, when the Law frames a case, they make a point of seeing it sticks. They have to.'

'I see.'

'I wish you did. You want to know why you should go to the judge and jury, then. In the first place, I don't know who the magistrate will be, but nine out of ten accept police evidence: the more so, as I need hardly tell you, when the prisoner's coloured.'

'Don't juries believe policemen, too?'

'They do, yes, even more so in a way, but there's a difference: twelve men have to be persuaded, and not one. Or twelve men and women, if we're lucky enough to have any serving. But that's not the chief consideration. What comes now is a point of legal strategy, so follow me closely, Mr Pew. You elect to go before the judge and jury. Right. That means the prosecution has to state its case, so as to get you committed. In other words, we hear all their evidence and they can't alter it afterwards much, though they can add to it if they get some nice new bright ideas. But as for you, you sit tight in the dock . . .'

'It's not me, Mr Zuss-Amor.'

'. . . All right, your friend sits in the dock and keeps his mouth shut. He says nothing.'

'But he has to speak later before the judge and jury . . .'

'Of course he has to, if he's called. But by that time we know the prosecution's case, and they don't know ours at all. And if me and the barrister, whoever it is we choose, take a good look at the transcript of the prosecution's evidence before the final trial comes on, our trained legal brains may find a hole or two that can be picked in it. Because it's not all that easy to think up a consistent story of what never happened—you'd be surprised.'

'It seems we should go to the jury, then.'

Mr Zuss-Amor gave me a sweet smile, as of one who congratulates a nitwit for seeing what was perfectly evident all the time.

'If you want to know the fruits of my experience, Mr Pew,' he said, 'I'll give you these three golden rules. Never accept trial by magistrate, unless it's a five-shilling parking offence, or something of that nature. Never plead guilty—even if the Law walks in and finds you with a gun in your hand and a corpse lying on the floor. And when you're arrested, never, never say a word, whatever they do, whatever they promise or threaten—that is, if you have the nerve to stick it out. Always remember, when they've got you alone in the cells, that they also have to prove the case in the open light of day. Say nothing, sign nothing. Most cases, believe me, are lost in the first half-hour after the arrest.'

'You mean if you make a statement to them?'

'Exactly. Tell them your name, your age, your occupation and address. Not a word more. Even then, they may swear you did say this or that, but it's harder to prove you did if you've signed nothing and kept your trap shut.' Mr Zuss-Amor arose, walked to the window, and gazed out glassily. 'It's a wicked world,' he said, 'thank goodness.' He pondered a moment. 'What about witnesses?' he asked me, turning round. 'Who can we muster?'

'I've told you this girl Muriel won't speak for him.'

'It might make quite a bit of difference if she did. And it looks rather bad, doesn't it, if she won't.'

'Why?'

'Come, now! If we say, as we're going to, that the defendant was living not with a whore, Dorothy, but with his lady-love, her sister Muriel, wouldn't the jury expect to see Miss Muriel in the box and hear her say so?'

'I'll have another shot at her. Are witnesses to character any use?'

'None whatever, unless you can produce the Pope, or someone. No, we'll have to do our best with Mr Fortune himself if we can't get Muriel. Can he talk well?'

'His only trouble is that he talks too much.'

'I'll warn our counsel. Now who will we have against us? The Detective-Inspector, of course, and his Detective-Constable, I have no doubt—and even an old hand won't be able to shake *them*.'

'But what on earth can they say?'

'Oh-ho! You wait and see! You'll be surprised what that pair saw through brick walls two feet thick! And then, of course, they may call little Dorothy.'

'They're sure to, aren't they?'

'No. . . . She's a common prostitute, don't forget, and juries don't seem to believe a word they say. I hope they do call her, though—I'd like to see our counsel tear her guts out in cross-examination. . . .'

Mr Zuss-Amor rubbed his chest with relish. I got up to go.

'I don't suppose you'll believe,' I said, 'that Johnny Fortune hasn't been a ponce. But isn't it clear, from all you tell me, that these cases are sometimes framed?'

'Oh, of course they are! Who said they weren't?' Mr Zuss-Amor stood face to face with me. 'I handle a lot of cases for the defence,' he said, 'that they don't like to see me get an acquittal for. So the police don't love me all that much, as you can imagine. And believe me, whenever I get into my car at night, I look it over to see if they've planted anything there.'

'You do?'

'Well, if I don't, I ought to. And that reminds me,' he went on, leaning his lower belly against the desk. 'If you can pay for it, we'll have to get a barrister who's not afraid of coppers.'

'Some of them are, then?'

'Most of them are. But one who certainly isn't is Wesley Vial—even though he's a junior.'

'A Mr Vial who lives near Marble Arch? A fat, hairy man?'

'You know him, I dare say. He's a friend of little Alfy's.'

'I know him slightly. And so does Johnny Fortune. We went to a party at his house. I don't think he likes either of us much.'

'Oh, really? Wheels within wheels, I see.' Mr Zuss-Amor sat down again. 'I won't enquire why,' he said, 'but I don't think it'll make the slightest difference. If Vial takes on the case, he'll go all out to win it for you. Shall I ask him, anyway?'

'What is a junior, exactly?'

'He's not taken silk. Doesn't mean a thing, though. Some of the best men don't bother, because when they take silk their fees have to go up, and they lose a lot of clients. Better six cases at fifty guineas than one at two hundred, don't you agree?'

'And Vial's the best man we can get?'

'At the price you can pay, undoubtedly. Your young friend will have to see him some time, too. And before he does, there's something else you might as well explain to him.' Mr Zuss-Amor looked at the ceiling, then with his mouth open at me, then continued: 'It's a delicate matter: one laymen don't always grasp at once. In a nutshell: to beat perjured evidence, you have to meet it with perjury.'

'No, I don't understand.'

'I didn't expect you would. However. Let me give you an instance. Suppose you walk out of this building and the Law arrests you on the doorstep for being drunk and disorderly in Piccadilly Circus while you were really talking here to me. What would you do?'

'Deny it.'

'Deny what?'

'The whole thing.'

'That's the point: if they took you to court, you'd be most unwise. When they go into the box—and remember, there's always more than one of them—and swear you were where you weren't, and did what you didn't, no jury will believe you if you deny their tale entirely.'

'So what do I do?'

'You say . . . having sworn by Almighty God, of course, like they have, to tell the whole truth, etcetera . . . you say that you *were* in Piccadilly Circus, yes, and you *had* taken one light ale, yes, but that you *weren't* drunk or disorderly. In other words, you tag along with their story in its inessentials, but deny the points that can get you a conviction. If you do that, your counsel can suggest the Law had made an honest error. But if you deny everything they say, the jury will accept their word against yours.'

Mr Zuss-Amor shrugged, flung out his hands, and corrugated his brows into deep furrows.

'So Johnny mustn't deny all their story, but simply say he never took money from Dorothy, or had sex with her.

'Particularly the former, of course. Yes, being an African, I don't suppose he'll mind damning his soul to get an acquittal. A lot of Christians do it. Is he one?'

'I believe so.'

'You can help him wrestle with his conscience, then. But do it before he sees Mr Vial. Because that's what Vial will want him to say, but he won't be able to put it so plain himself. It wouldn't be etiquette, not for a barrister. Dirty work of that nature's left to us solicitors, who really win the case by preparing it properly outside the court—that is, if it's the sort of case that can be won.'

Mr Zuss-Amor bared all his teeth at me. I got up and shook his hand. 'Thank you, Mr Zuss-Amor, you've made things wonderfully clear.'

He also rose. 'They need to be,' he said. 'Trials are all a matter of tactics. I don't know what happened, or if anything did happen, between that boy and that girl, any more than I suppose you really do. But believe me, when you listen to all the evidence in the court, you'll be amazed to see how little relation what's said there bears to what really occurred, so far as one knows it. It's one pack of lies fighting another, and the thing is to think up the best ones, and have the best man there to tell them for you so that justice is done.'

He opened the frosted door and let me out.

SECOND INTERLUDE

'Let Justice be done (and be seen to be)!'

THE TRIAL OF JOHNNY MACDONALD FORTUNE took place in a building, damaged in the Hitler war, which had been redecorated in a 'contemporary' style—light salmon wood, cubistic lanterns, leather cushions of pastel shades—that pleased none of the lawyers, officials or police officers who worked there. The courts looked too much like the board-rooms of progressive companies, staterooms on liners, even 'lounges' of American-type hotels, for the severe traditional taste of these professionals; and all of them, when they appeared there, injected into their behaviour an additional awesome formality to counteract the lack of majesty of their surroundings.

On the morning of the trial, Mr Zuss-Amor had a short conference with Mr Wesley Vial. In his wig and gown, Mr Vial was transformed from the obese, balding playboy of the queer theatrical parties he loved to give at his flat near Marble Arch, into a really impressive figure; impressive, that is, by his authority, which proceeded from his formidable knowledge of the operation of the law, his nerves of wire, his adaptable, synthetic charm, his aggressive ruthlessness, and his total contempt for weakness and 'fair play'. Mr Zuss-Amor, by comparison, seemed, in this décor, a shabby figure—like a nonconformist minister calling on a cardinal.

'Who have we got against us?' said Mr Zuss-Amor.

'Archie Gillespie.'

'As Crown counsel in these cases go, by no means a fool.'

'By *no* means, Mr Zuss-Amor.'

The solicitor felt rebuked. 'What was your impression of our client, Mr Vial?'

'Nice boy. Do what I can for him, of course—but what? The trouble with coloured men in the dock, you know, is that juries just can't tell a good one from a bad.'

'Can they *ever* tell that, would you say?'

'Oh, sometimes! Don't be too hard on juries.'

'We'll be having some ladies, I believe.'

'Excellent! He must flash all his teeth at them.' Mr Vial turned over the pages of the brief. 'There was nothing you could do with this Muriel Macpherson woman?'

'Nothing. I even went out and saw her myself. She's very sore with our young client, Mr Vial. Frankly, I think if we *had* called her, we'd have found ourselves asking permission to treat her as a hostile witness.'

' "Hell hath no fury," and so on. On the other hand, Gillespie tells me he's not calling the sister Dorothy. Very wise of him. He's relying on police evidence—which, I'm sorry to say, will probably be quite sufficient for his purpose.'

'Pity you couldn't have had a go at the woman Dorothy in the box, though, Mr Vial. . . .' The solicitor's eyes gleamed.

'Oh, best to keep the females out of it, on the whole. I'll see what can be done with the two officers. I've met the Inspector in the courts before . . . always makes an excellent impression. Looks like a family man who'd like to help the prisoner if he could: deeply regrets having to do his painful duty. I don't think I know the Detective-Constable. . . .'

'A new boy in the C.I.D. Very promising in the Force, I'm told. Man of few words in the box, though. Difficult to shake him, I think you'll find.'

Mr Vial put down the brief. 'And yet, you know, it *should* be possible to shake them.'

'If anyone can do it, you can.'

'I didn't mean that. I mean this charge: it's bogus. Just look at it!' (He held up the brief.) 'It stinks to high heaven!'

'You think this boy's telling the truth—or part of it?'

'I think he's telling the whole of it. I pressed him hard at our little interview, as you saw. And what did he do? He lost his temper! I've never seen such righteous indignation! I'm always impressed by honest fury in a defendant.'

Mr Zuss-Amor nodded, frowned, and scratched his bottom. 'Why do they do it, Mr Vial?' he said.

'Why do who do what?'

'Why do the police bring these trumped-up charges?'

'Oh, well . . .' The advocate sighed with all his bulk, and hitched his robe. 'You know the familiar argument as well as I do. The accused's generally done what they say he's done, but not how they say he's done it. The charge is usually true, the evidence often false. But in this case, I think both are phoney. . . . Well, we'll have to see. . . .'

The two C.I.D. officers were having a cup of tea in the police room. 'It's your first case with us in the vice game,' said the Inspector, 'but you don't have to let that worry you. The way to win a case, in my experience, is not to mind from the beginning if you lose it.'

'But we shouldn't lose this one, should we, sir?'

'I don't see how we can, Constable. But just remember what I told you. They'll keep you outside until I've given evidence, of course, but you know what I'm going to say in its essential outlines. If they ask any questions in examination that we haven't thought of, just say as little as possible: take your time, look the lawyer in the eye, and just say you don't remember.'

'He's rough, isn't he, Inspector, this Wesley Vial?'

'That fat old poof? Don't be afraid of him, son. He's sharp, mind you, but if you don't let him rattle you, there's nothing he can do.' The Inspector lit his Dunhill pipe. 'It's obvious what he'll try,' he continued. 'He'll make out that he accepts our story, but he'll try to shake us on the details, so as to put a doubt into the jury's mind.'

The constable sipped his beverage. 'They're not likely to raise the question of that bit of rough stuff at the station, are they?'

'Vial certainly won't—he knows no jury would believe it. But the boy might allege something, even though Vial's probably told him not to. Let's hope he does do. It'd make a very bad impression on the court. Drink up now, Constable, we're on in a minute or two.'

The constable swallowed. 'I'm sure you know best about not calling that girl Dorothy, sir. But don't you think if we'd had her to pin it on him good and proper . . .'

'Mr Gillespie said no, and I think he's right. I've told her to keep out of the way and keep her trap shut till the trial's over—and she will. You never know how it will be with women in the box: she may love this boy, for all we know, and might have spoken out of turn;

and if we'd called her for the prosecution, we might have found ourselves with a hostile witness on our hands.'

In the public gallery, a little minority group of Africans was collecting: among them Laddy Boy, who'd brought an air cushion and a bag of cashew nuts; the Bushman, who'd got a front seat, leaned on the railing and immediately gone to sleep; and Mr Karl Marx Bo, who planned to send by air mail a tendentious report on the trial to the Mendi newspaper of which he was part-time correspondent, if, as he hoped it would be, the result was unfavourable to the defendant.

Theodora and Montgomery arrived much too early, and sat in great discomfort on the benches that sloped steeply like a dress circle overlooking the well of the court. They wondered if they could take their overcoats off and, if so, where they could put them.

'It doesn't look very impressive,' said Theodora. 'It's much too small.'

'It looks exactly like Act III of a murder play. Which is the dock?'

'Just underneath us, I expect.'

'So we won't see him.'

'We will when he's giving evidence,' said Theodora. 'That's the witness-box there on the right.'

'Box is the word for it. It looks like an up-ended coffin.'

Mr Wesley Vial met Mr Archie Gillespie in the lawyers' lavatory. 'I do hope, Wesley,' the Crown counsel said, 'your man's English will be comprehensible. I take it you'll be putting him in the box?'

'Time alone will show, Archie. But if you want any evidence taken in the vernacular, we can always put in for an interpreter and prolong matters to your heart's content.'

'No, thank you,' said Mr Gillespie. 'Crown counsel don't draw your huge refreshers.' He dried his hands. 'Who's the judge?'

'Old Haemorrhoids.'

'My God. It would be.'

The lawyers looked at each other resignedly. There was a distant shout, and they adjusted their wigs like actors who've heard the call-boy summon them to the stage.

Johnny Fortune had been brought up from Brixton to the court in one of those police vans where the prisoners half sit in metal boxes, hardly larger than themselves. They'd arrived more than an hour before the case began, and the court jailer, after searching him yet again, said, 'Well, we won't put you in the cells unless you really want to go there. If I leave you in the room here, will you behave yourself?'

'Of course.'

'You want some cigarettes?'

'They not let me take any of my money.'

'Oh, pay me when you're acquitted!' said the jailer with a hearty laugh, and gave Johnny Fortune a half-filled pack of Woodbines and a cup of purple tea. 'I see you've got Vial,' he went on. 'That'll cost you a bit, won't it? Or should I say'—the jailer laughed roguishly—'cost your little lady and her customers?'

Johnny stood up. 'Mister, put me in your cells. I do not wish your tea or want your Woodbine.'

'No offence, lad, don't be so touchy. I know you all have to say you're innocent—I get used to it here. Come on, keep them—you've got an hour to wait.' The jailer patted his prisoner on the shoulder, and went over to gossip with a lean, powdered female constable in civilian dress, who, as they talked, looked over the jailer's shoulder at the folds in Johnny Fortune's trousers.

Everyone stood, and the judge came in wearing a wig not of the Gilbert and Sullivan variety, but a short one, slightly askew, that made him look like Dr Johnson's younger brother. The jury was new, and the case their first, so they had to be sworn in by the usher. Two of them were women: a W.V.S. housewifely person, and the other with a beret and a tailored suit whose nature it was impossible to guess at. A male juror turned out, when he swore, to be called 'Ramsay Macdonald', on hearing which Mr Vial made a slight histrionic gesture of impressed surprise to Mr Gillespie, who ignored him.

One of the two policemen in the dock nudged Johnny, and he stood. The clerk, a quite young man with a pink, pale face, read out the charge in a voice like an Old Vic juvenile's; and when he asked Johnny how he pleaded, looked up at him, across the court, with a pleading expression on his own wan face.

'I plead not guilty.'

Mr Zuss-Amor, flanking his advocate, twitched his shoulders slightly. You never could tell with defendants: he'd even known them get the plea wrong at the outset.

Mr Archie Gillespie's opening statement of the case for the Queen against the prisoner was as methodical as one would expect from a Scottish lawyer of vast experience and entire integrity. He had the great psychological advantages of believing the facts in the brief that he'd been given, or most of them, and of being quite dispassionate in his advocacy. He had no feeling of animosity towards the prisoner whatever, and this made him all the more deadly.

He began by explaining to the jury what living on the immoral earnings of a common prostitute consisted of. It was a distasteful subject, and a painful duty for the members of the jury to have to hear about it. But they were, he did not doubt, men and women of ripe experience, to whom he could speak quite frankly. Very well, then. As everyone knew, there were, unfortunately, such women as common prostitutes—selling their bodies for gain (Mr Gillespie paused, and gazed at a female juror, who licked her lips)—in our society; women whose odious commerce was—subject to certain important restrictions—not actually illegal, however reprehensible on moral grounds. But what *was* illegal—and highly so, and he would say more, revolting and abhorrent—was the practice of certain men—if one could call them men—of battening on these wretched creatures, and living on the wages of their sin; and even, in a great many cases—though he would not necessarily say it was so in the present instance—even of forcing them out on to the streets against their wills. It was not for nothing, said Mr Gillespie, removing his spectacles a moment, that such men, in the speech of a more robust age, had been known as 'bullies'.

The judge manifested a slight impatience, and Mr Gillespie took the hint. He explained to the jury that two police officers would tell them how observation had been kept on one Dorothea Violet Macpherson, a known and convicted common prostitute, who had been seen, on several nights in succession, to accost men in Hyde Park, receive sums of money from them, entice them into the undergrowth, and there have carnal knowledge of them. These officers would further tell the members of the jury how the said Dorothea Violet Macpherson was subsequently followed to an address in Immigration Road, Whitechapel, where she lived in two rooms with the accused. (Here Mr Gillespie paused, and spoke more slowly.) These officers would then tell how, on a number of occasions when observation was kept on the accused and on the said Dorothea Violet Macpherson, she was seen to hand over to him large sums of money that had come into her possession through her immoral commerce in the purlieus of Hyde Park.

The Crown counsel now glanced at Mr Vial, who sat looking into the infinite like a Buddha. 'No doubt my learned friend here will suggest to you,' he declared, 'that the accused was not present on these occasions or, alternatively, that the sums of money in question were not passed over to him or, alternatively again, that if they were, they were not those proceeding from the act of common prostitution.' Mr Gillespie waited a second, as if inviting Mr Vial to say just that: then continued, 'It will be for you, members of the jury, to decide on whose evidence you should rely: on that of the witness, or witnesses, that may be brought forward by the defence, or on that of the two experienced police officers whom I am now going to call before you.'

The Detective-Inspector walked in with a modest, capable and self-sufficient mien. He took the oath, removed a notebook from his pocket, and turned to face his counsel.

'Members of the jury,' said Mr Gillespie. 'You will observe that the Detective-Inspector is holding a small book. Inspector, will you please tell the court what this book is?'

'It's my police notebook, sir.'

'Exactly. Officers of the Crown, when giving evidence, are permitted to refer, for matters of fact—and matters of fact only—to the notes they made of a case immediately after they have performed their duties. Very well. Now, Detective-Inspector, will you please tell my Lord and members of the jury what happened, in your own words?'

In his own words, and prompted only slightly by Mr Gillespie, the officer related the detailed minutiae of the events the counsel had already outlined. By the time of the third, fourth and fifth seeing of Dorothy taking money in the park, and seeing her giving it to Johnny in the Immigration Road, the tale began to lose some of its human fascination, even though its cumulative substance added greatly to the 'weight of evidence'.

Mr Gillespie sat down, and Mr Wesley Vial arose.

'Detective-Inspector,' he said. 'Do you know who the defendant is?'

'Who he is, sir? He's an African.'

'Yes. Quite so. An African. But can you tell us anything about him?'

'I have, sir.'

'Yes, Inspector, we know you have. But I mean who he is? His family? His background? What sort of man the court has got before it?'

'No, sir. He said he was a student.'

'He said he was a student. Did you enquire of what?'

'No, sir.'

'You didn't. Did you know this young man's father, Mr David Macdonald Fortune, wears the King's Medal for valour which was awarded to him when he was formerly a sergeant in the Nigerian police force?'

'No, sir.'

'You didn't bother to find out what sort of man you had to deal with? It didn't interest you. Is that it?'

The judge stirred himself slightly, as if from a distant dream. 'I can't quite see the relevance of that, Mr Vial,' he said, in a melancholy, croaking voice. 'It's not the accused's father who's before me.'

Mr Vial bowed. 'True, my Lord. But your Lordship will appreciate, I'm sure, how vital it is for me, in a case of this description—that is, a case where the defendant is a citizen of one of the colonies of our Commonwealth—to establish clearly his social standing and reputation. The members of the jury' (Mr Vial inclined himself courteously towards them) 'may not be as familiar as we have grown to be, my Lord, with what very different sorts of African citizen are now to be found here in England among us: some, no doubt, with a background of a kind that might render an accusation of this nature unfortunately all too credible, but others—as I hope to show you is the case at present—in whom such conduct would be as totally improbable as it would were I, my Lord, or Mr Gillespie here, tó be said to indulge in it.'

There was a hush, while everyone digested this. 'Yes. Well, do proceed, please, Mr Vial,' said the judge.

The defending counsel turned once more to the Crown witness.

'You have, in fact, Inspector—apart, of course, from the present case—nothing to say against the defendant?'

'No, sir. He's got no police record.

'Exactly. He's got no police record. And has he, at any time, made any statement in writing, or any verbal statement concerning the charge, by which he admits his guilt in any particular whatever?'

'No, sir.'

'So we're left with what you and your officers have seen, Inspector.'

The Inspector didn't answer. Mr Vial looked up, and barked at him, 'I say, we're left with what you tell us that you've seen. Will you please answer me, Inspector?'

'I didn't know you were asking me a question, sir.'

'You didn't know I was asking you a question. Very well. Now, I want you to tell us about these happenings in Hyde Park. You saw this woman accost various men at various times on various evenings, take money from them, and disappear with them into the ...' (Mr Vial looked at his notes) '... yes, into the undergrowth, I think it was. Now let us take the first evening: the evening you tell us that the defendant later received twenty-eight pounds from this woman. How many men accosted her?'

'Five or six, sir.'

'Five—or six? Which was it? You may consult your notebook if you wish.'

'Six, sir.'

'So each man would have paid an average of four pounds thirteen shillings and fourpence for this woman's services?'

'Not necessarily, sir. She could have had some money in her bag before she went inside the park.'

'In her what, Inspector?'

'She could have had some money in her bag before she went there.'

'What bag?'

'The bag she put the money in, sir.'

'Oh.' Mr Vial picked up a document. 'But in the magistrates' court, I see you told his Worship that this woman put the money in her raincoat pocket.'

'Yes, sir.'

'Sometimes she put it in her raincoat pocket, and sometimes she put it in her bag, is that it?'

'Yes, sir.'

'I see. And then she went with these people into the undergrowth. How dark was this undergrowth?'

'Quite light enough to keep her under observation, sir.'

'Come now, Inspector. Are you telling the court a woman of this description would take a man, in a public locality like Hyde Park, into a place that was dark enough for her purposes, but light enough to be observed by two police officers—standing at a certain distance from her, I suppose?'

'We were quite near enough, sir, to see whatever happened.'

'You were quite near enough. And she never saw you?'

'No, sir.'

'On no occasion? Not once on all these evenings when you and your colleague stood peering at her while she went into the undergrowth with all these dozens of men?'

'She gave no sign of being seen, sir.'

'Not even when you followed her home?'

'No, sir.'

'What did she travel home on? A bus? A tube?'

'She usually took a bus to Victoria station, and then a tube, sir.'

'She usually did. Aren't prostitutes in the habit of taking taxis? Isn't that notorious?'

'Not all of them, sir. Not always.' The officer consulted his notebook. 'She took a taxi one night, but it's not been referred to in my evidence.'

'So you followed her by bus, or tube, or taxi to the Immigration Road—and then what?'

'We saw her go into the house, sir.'

'Saw her how? Did you follow her inside?'

'No, sir. We kept observation from the street.

'So you must have seen her through the window. Is that it?'

'Yes, sir.'

'This window had no curtains, I suppose. Is that what you have to tell us?'

'Yes, sir, it had. But they weren't always drawn over it.'

'Not always drawn across the window in the depths of winter?'

'Not always, sir.'

Mr Vial paused for quite ten seconds. 'Officer,' he said, 'if you, or I, or anyone else in his right mind were going to hand a large sum of money over to somebody else, even for a perfectly legitimate reason, would we really do it in front of an open, uncurtained window on the ground floor of a house in a busy street of a not particularly salubrious neighbourhood?'

'That's what they did, sir.'

'And if the transaction was a highly illegal one, as it would be in the present instance, wouldn't there be all the more reason to hand the money over behind closed doors and out of sight?'

'These people are very careless, sir. They're often under the influence of alcohol, and other things.'

'They'd need to be! They'd certainly need to be, to behave so rashly!' Mr Vial gazed in amazement at the judge, at the jury, at Mr Gillespie, and back again at the Detective-Inspector. 'Now, Inspector,' he said gently. 'Please understand I'm not questioning your good faith in any respect. You're an experienced officer, as my learned friend has said, and there can therefore be no question of that at all. . . . But don't you think, from what you tell us, it's possible you were mistaken?'

'No, sir. She gave him the money like I said.'

'On half a dozen occasions, a prostitute takes money out of her handbag, or raincoat, or whatever it was, and hands it over to a man in a lighted room without the curtain drawn across in full view of the general public, and does it all so slowly that anyone standing outside could count the exact number of pound notes? Is that what you're telling us?'

'Yes, sir.'

'Thank you, Inspector.' Mr Vial sat down.

The Detective-Constable was called. Examined by Mr Gillespie, he confirmed his colleague's account in all essential particulars. Mr Wesley Vial rose again.

'How long have you been with the C.I.D., Detective-Constable?'

'Two months, sir.'

'This is your first case as a C.I.D. officer?'

'Yes, sir.'

'Before you joined the C.I.D., did your duties bring you in contact with this sort of case at all?'

'No, sir. I was in Records.'

'You were in Records. Now, Constable. Since this case was first brought in the magistrates' court, you have discussed it, naturally, with the Inspector?'

'I've talked about the case in general, sir. I haven't discussed the details of the evidence.'

'Of course not. The evidence you gave is entirely your own, isn't it? But you've relied on the guidance of your superior officers to a certain extent as to how you should put it to the court?'

The judge made a slight noise. 'I don't think you should ask the witness that, Mr Vial,' he said. 'You needn't answer, Constable.'

'As you say, my Lord. I have no further questions.'

The Detective-Constable left the box and went and sat by the Inspector, who gave him a slight, official smile. 'Call the defendant,' said the usher.

Johnny Fortune left the dock, walked firmly through the court and took the oath. The assembly regarded him with a slightly increased respect; for whatever the outcome of the case, a person in the witness-box seems a very different person from one sitting between two policemen in the dock.

Mr Vial faced his client with a look stern as Gabriel's, and said: 'John Macdonald Fortune: do you know what living off the immoral earnings of a woman means?'

'Yes. I do know.'

'Have you lived off the immoral earnings of this woman?'

'No. Never.'

'Have you ever lived off the immoral earnings of any woman?'

'Never! Never would I give my blood to such a person. Never!'

Mr Vial sat down. Mr Gillespie arose.

'You say you're a student,' he began. 'A student of what?'

'Of meteorology.'

The judge leaned forward. 'What was that word?'

'Meteorology, my Lord. I'm not quite sure what it is, but no doubt we'll discover. And how long is it since you attended your last lecture?'

'Is some months now.'

'Why? Is your college on holiday?'

'No. I give up these studies.'

'So now you're not studying anything?'

'No.'

'You've not been a student for some months, in fact?'

'No.'

'And what have you lived on?'

'I work in a labouring job.'

'How long did you work in this labouring job?'

'Some few week before I get arrested.'

'Some few weeks. And at the time you were living with this woman, were you working?'

'Listen to me, sir. I live some few week when I have no money with this woman.'

'So you *did* live with her? You admit that?'

The judge croaked again. 'There's just a point here, Mr Gillespie, I think. It's possibly the language difficulty, you know.' He looked at Johnny. 'You say you lived *with* this woman. Do you mean simply that you lived in the same house, or flat, or room, or do you mean that you lived there as man and wife?'

'She not my wife.'

'We know that,' said Mr Gillespie. 'What his Lordship means is, did you have any carnal knowledge of this woman?'

'Have what?'

'Did you have intercourse with her?'

'One time I have sex with that woman, yes. One time. But I take no money from her. Never.'

'I see. You took no money from her. Who paid the rent?'

'She pay it.'

'Who bought the food?'

'She buy some small food some time.'

'So you're telling us you lived in the same room as a common prostitute, alone with her, that you had intercourse with her, that you accepted board and lodging from her, and that you took no money from her? Is that it? Answer me, will you?'

'Listen, man. I answer you. Never I take no money from that woman. Not even pennies for my bus fare.'

'You really expect the court to believe that?'

'I swear on this book here what I say will be true. And what I say is true.'

There was suddenly a yell from the public gallery. It was the Bushman. He shouted, 'God is black!' and was hustled out by a constable. The judge closed his eyes during this episode; then opened them, and said, 'Please continue, Mr Gillespie.'

'I have no more questions, my Lord.'

'Mr Vial?'

The defending counsel bowed and shook his head. Johnny went back to the dock.

The judged blinked around the court. 'Mr Gillespie, Mr Vial. Is there anything further before you address the jury?'

The counsel shook their heads.

'Then I shall adjourn for luncheon before your final address.'

Everyone rose, the judge did so rather more slowly, and disappeared beneath the rampant lion and unicorn.

Mr Zuss-Amor stood with Montgomery outside the court, waiting for Theodora. 'Well, there it is,' said the solicitor. 'I need hardly tell you that I think he's had it.'

'What does Mr Vial say?'

'He won't commit himself. But our boy made some horrible admissions. And that interruption from the gallery didn't help at all.'

'That wasn't Johnny's fault.'

'I know it wasn't, Mr Pew: but it made a very bad impression. Was that boy drunk, or what?'

'No. Just voicing his feelings, I expect.'

'I wish he'd voiced them elsewhere.'

'I didn't think the police officers were all that brilliant, anyway.'

'Oh, they're not so clever in court as they are outside it, I admit. But they do know when to keep their mouths shut.'

'The Inspector was the more convincing . . .'

'He should be, he's been lying longer.'

'I don't like that place. Everyone acts as if the wretched prisoner's the only person there who doesn't matter.'

The solicitor didn't answer that, but said, 'I wish your friend Miss Pace would hurry powdering her nose. I could do with a gin and orange.'

Crossing the corridor, Theodora was detained by a pale youth in a drape suit whose face was vaguely familiar. 'Hullo,' he said. 'I let you in at Mr Vial's party, don't you remember? They call me Alfy Bongo.'

'Oh, yes. Excuse me, please.'

'I follow all Mr Vial's cases whenever I can.'

'Please excuse me.'

'Just a minute, miss. You know your boy's going down this afternoon?'

'What do you mean—my boy?'

'He is, isn't he? I remember you two that evening. I know how you feel about him.'

'Excuse me!' She hurried on. He sidled after her. 'There's only one thing could help him, isn't there.'

She stopped. 'What?'

'If there was some other woman to speak for him.'

'What do you mean?'

'Someone like you who might have been his girl at the time they say he was poncing on that chick.'

Theodora looked at him intently.

The Inspector and the Constable were drinking Worthingtons in the saloon bar round the corner. 'I was all right, then, sir? You're not dissatisfied?'

'All right for a beginner, Constable. Cheers!'

'We'd never have had all this fuss if we could have kept it in the magistrates' court.'

'That's out of our hands, lad, when the prisoner's got the money. I wouldn't worry about the result, though, and the sentence will be stiffer here.'

'Why didn't you just take him in for hemp, Inspector? That would have been more certain, wouldn't it?'

'Of course, but he might have got away with only a fine. Even with magistrates, you can't be sure.'

'I didn't like the defending counsel. He's murder.'

'I'll get that degenerate one day, if it's the last thing I do.'

The court jailer, who'd heard how the case was going, was not quite so nice to Johnny. 'Here's your dinner,' he said, handing him a paper bag.

'I want no dinner.'

'You'd better get into the habit of doing what you're told, you know. It might come in handy after this evening.'

'He's being awkward,' said the Brixton warder.

Theodora dragged Mr Zuss-Amor away from Montgomery into the private bar. 'At this stage,' she said, 'can we call any further witnesses?'

'We could if we had one who's of any use. . . . Why?'

'I've been Johnny Fortune's mistress.'

'Go on!'

'I saw him during the time they say he was with that woman, and gave him money, and looked after him.'

'Yes. . . ? Now look, Miss Pace, it's nice of you to think of trying to help him. But can you expect me to believe that—let alone a jury?'

'I'm pregnant by him.'

'Oh. You are? No kidding?'

'Oh, don't be so stupid and familiar! I tell you I've seen the doctor!'

'Have you!'

'I love Johnny—can't you understand? I want to marry him.'

'You do?' The solicitor shook his head dubiously. 'And you're prepared to swear all this in court—is that it?'

'Yes.'

'Well . . . I'll have to see Mr Vial and hear what he thinks.'

'Hurry up, then.'

'You'd better come with me. He'll want to question you a bit.'

When the trial resumed, Mr Vial asked the judge's permission to call another witness. 'I apologize, my Lord, to you, and to my learned friend, for any apparent discourtesy to the court. The fact is that my witness, who is, as you will see, a person of irreproachable character and reputation, has felt hitherto a quite understandable reluctance to appear in a case of this description; but since the evidence she will give——'

'Is this a woman, then?' said the judge.

'Indeed, my Lord.'

'I see. Go on.'

'Thank you, my Lord. Since, as I say, the evidence she will give, with your permission, will be of capital importance in establishing the innocence of the defendant beyond all possible doubt, she has felt it her duty—greatly, I may say, to her credit— to overcome any natural scruples and appear before the court.

'Have you anything to say, Mr Gillespie?' asked the judge.

'Not at this juncture, my Lord. I think any observations I may wish to make would best be kept until I have an opportunity of hearing this witness, and of cross-examination.'

'Very well, Mr Vial.'

Theodora entered the box and took the oath. She looked firm, tranquil, dignified and womanly, though with a slight hint of the repentant sinner.

Mr Vial quickly established that her name was Theodora Huntington Pace, her age twenty-eight, her state a spinster, and her occupation that of Assistant Supervisor of Draft Planning at the B.B.C. She had known the defendant since the previous summer, when she first met him at an interview in connection with his participation in a series of radio programmes. 'Please continue, Miss Pace,' said Mr Vial.

'I got to know Mr Fortune very well,' she said, in steady, almost semi-official tones. 'I grew to admire his qualities of character and intelligence, and soon became very fond of him.'

'And this feeling of yours, Miss Pace. It was reciprocated?'

'Yes,' said Theodora. 'I think it was.'

'Please tell the court what happened then.'

Theodora slightly lowered her voice, and looked up steadily. 'I became his mistress.'

'I see. And then?'

'I asked Mr Fortune to come and live with me, but he is very independent by nature, and preferred we should have separate establishments.'

'And during the period that we have heard about in court this morning. You saw the defendant?'

'Frequently.'

'And is it not a fact that you were able to help him financially when this was necessary?'

'I know Mr Fortune comes from a substantial business family in Nigeria, and that he would have no difficulty in calling on them for money if he needed it. He is, however, I'm sorry to say, something of a spendthrift . . .' (she paused slightly) . . . 'and on occasions when he was hard up I had no reluctance whatever in lending him whatever money he might want to tide him over.'

'So that during the period in question, he was in no need of money?'

'Why should he be? No. He had only to come to me.'

'Thank you, Miss Pace.'

Mr Gillespie got up.

'Miss Pace,' he said. 'In view of what you have told the court this afternoon, why did you not come forward this morning to speak for the accused on this very serious charge?'

Theodora glanced towards the dock, then said quietly: 'Mr Fortune forbade me to.'

'He forbade you? Why?'

'He wished to face this charge alone. Knowing his innocence, and being sure of an acquittal, he did not wish my name to be mentioned in any way.'

'I see, I see. And now he's *not* so sure of an acquittal—is that it?'

'I heard Mr Fortune giving evidence this morning. English is not his mother tongue, and an African has greater difficulty in expressing himself clearly than many of us realize. With this language handicap I didn't feel he was doing his case justice, and I therefore felt I ought to appear myself, even if against his wishes, to tell the court what I knew.'

'Did you, Miss Pace! Then please tell my Lord how you account for the fact that if the accused, as you say, had only to come to you for money, he chose to live with a prostitute in an East End slum?'

'Mr Fortune, as I have said, is a very independent man, and preferred to live his Bohemian student life in a quarter inhabited largely by his fellow countrymen. He told me, of course, of his staying for a while in the same house as this woman—which he regarded as an interesting way of catching a glimpse of the seamier side of London life.

'So this man, who has admitted he was a penniless labourer, prefers living in squalor with a prostitute when he has a rich mistress willing, and no doubt anxious, to accommodate him at any time?'

'I need hardly say that I would have preferred him to live in more conventional surroundings.'

'With you, in other words.'

'Yes.'

'But he didn't. Miss Pace: you have heard the accused admit that he had intercourse with this woman. Did you know of this?'

'No. I expect he was ashamed to tell me of this momentary lapse.'

'I expect so, indeed. How old did you say you were, Miss Pace.'

'Twenty-eight.'

'And the accused is eighteen?'

'Nineteen, now.'

'Is there not a considerable discrepancy between your ages?'

'Yes, unfortunately.'

'And you ask us seriously to believe——'

The judge leaned forward. 'I don't wish to hinder you, Mr Gillespie. But as the witness has admitted her relationship with the defendant, I really don't think you need press this point any further.'

Theodora turned towards the judge, and said softly, 'I am pregnant by him, my Lord. I hope to marry the defendant.'

The judge nodded slightly and said nothing. He turned to Mr Gillespie. 'I have no more questions, my Lord,' said the Crown counsel.

Theodora left the box, and the two lawyers addressed the jury.

'You must not attribute,' said Mr Gillespie, 'any undue weight to the testimony of Miss Theodora Pace. Remember that this woman who admits—indeed, I should say, glories in—an illicit relationship with the accused, is no doubt under the domination of her obsession. Keep firmly in your minds, rather, the contrast between the evidence you have heard from the two police officers, and that of the accused himself. If there may be, in the evidence of these officers, some slight discrepancies—of which my learned friend has naturally tried to make the most—you must surely conclude that the evidence of the accused is totally, utterly incredible. It simply cannot be believed! No, members of the jury: your duty in this matter is quite clear. Banish from your minds any thought that a verdict against the defendant might be imputed to anything in the nature of racial prejudice. In a British court, all men are equal before the law: and if you believe the defendant to be guilty, as you are bound to do, you should return a verdict in that sense with the same impartiality as you would show were he a fellow citizen of your own.'

To which Mr Vial, raising himself like Moses bringing down the tablets from the Mount, rejoined:

'My learned friend has asked you to discount the evidence of Miss Theodora Pace. But is her testimony not supremely to be believed? Here is a woman—a courageous woman, I would say, whatever you may think of her moral conduct (which is not what is on trial today)—who is prepared to risk—possibly even to sacrifice irrevocably—an honoured and established position in society, to bear witness to the truth, whatever the cost! Is this mere infatuation? Is this what my learned friend has called the consequences of an *obsession*?

'But even more to be believed—yes, even more—is the evidence of the defendant. My learned friend has told you that this evidence is "incredible." But is it? Is it incredible? I have no small experience of hearing witnesses in court, and from this I have learned one important lesson.' Mr Vial, who contrived to speak not like an advocate, but like the impartial spirit of justice itself, now looked very grave. 'Only a too fluent witness, members of the jury, is to be mistrusted! Only a story that has no flaw—one which the witness, or witnesses, have carefully manufactured, polished and rehearsed—is likely to be untrue. Did you not notice—and were you not impressed by it?—that the defendant at no time sought to deny facts that might have seemed prejudicial to his case? Did you not hear how he freely admitted to some few, small, discreditable facts because he knew, in his heart of hearts, that on the major issue—the essential issue you are called upon to decide—he was without guilt of any kind?' Mr Vial stood a second, hand raised aloft. 'The defendant was an angry witness, members of the jury! He was angry because he is honest: he is honest because he is innocent!

'Have a care how you deal with John Macdonald Fortune! This young man is a guest among us, who possibly has behaved foolishly, as young men will, but who has not behaved dishonourably. In this country he is a stranger: but a stranger who, coming from a country that is British, believes he is entitled to receive, and knows that he certainly will receive, that fair treatment and equal justice from his fellow men and women which has always been the glory of the British jury.'

Mr Vial sat down. The judge, his moment come at last, began his summing-up.

When he recapitulated the case of the prosecution, which he did in meticulous and admirably balanced detail, the case for the prosecution sounded quite unanswerable; but when he came to recapitulate the case for the defence, this case sounded quite unanswerable too. It was, in fact, impossible to tell what the judge thought, or even what he recommended; though he did, at one point in his dry, interminable, penetrating survey of the evidence, look up a minute at the jury and say this:

'I need hardly remind you, I suppose, that you should attach great importance, not only to the substance of the evidence that has been put before you, but equally to the demeanour of the witnesses, and to the force, the weight, I might say, of the actual words they used. Now the defending counsel, you will remember, asked the accused at one point' (the judge consulted his notes) 'if he had ever lived off the immoral earnings of any woman. To which the defendant answered in these words: "Never. Never would I give my blood to such a person. Never."' The judge blinked at the jury. 'You will have to decide whether these words which the defendant used convey to you the impression of veracity . . . of authenticity . . .'

When the judge finished—rather abruptly and unexpectedly—the clerk put the fatal question to the jury. After some slight muttering, they asked if they might retire.

'Will you be very long, do you think?' the judge asked the foreman.

'There seems to be some considerable disagreement, my Lord,' the foreman answered, glancing round at the eleven.

'I see. Very well, you may retire.'

In the emptying court, Mr Vial strolled across to the dock, leant on its edge and, ignoring the two policemen, said casually to Johnny, 'I thought the judge's summing-up was very fair, didn't you?'

'I thought you was wonderful,' said Johnny Fortune.

In the corridor outside, Theodora stood with Mr Zuss-Amor. 'Splendid, my dear,' said the solicitor. 'I'm sorry to say the Press were scribbling busily, though. I hope you don't lose your job.'

Smoking an agitated cigarette, Montgomery was accosted by the Detective-Inspector. 'Well,' said the policeman, 'whichever way it goes, there's no hard feelings on my part for your young friend. It's only another case to us.'

As the court reassembled, the usher in charge of the jury (who had sworn publicly, before they retired, upon the sacred book, that he would not divulge a word of their deliberations), whispered, as he passed by, to the two officers guarding Johnny in the dock, what their still secret verdict was. Johnny heard it too, and one of the officers patted him gently on the back of the knee.

The judge returned, and so did the jury. They did not, despite the nature of their impending verdict, gaze benevolently at the accused as juries are traditionally supposed to do, but sat like ancient monuments on their hard seats.

The clerk asked the foreman how they found. He said, 'Not guilty.'

Mr Vial then rose and said, with infinite deference, to the judge: 'May the prisoner please be discharged, my Lord?'

'He may.'

A week later, Johnny was re-arrested on the charge of being in possession of Indian hemp. Montgomery could borrow no more money quickly anywhere, and Theodora was in hospital with a breakdown and a miscarriage. 'I'll come over to the court for free, if you really want me to,' Mr Zuss-Amor told Montgomery, 'but why don't you tell him to plead guilty and settle before the magistrate? Believe me, if they don't get him for *something*, they'll never let him alone. And it'll only be a fine.'

It was, but no one had any money, and Johnny went to prison for a month.

PART III

Johnny Fortune leaves his city

1

Tidings from Theodora

THE WORD 'FREE-LANCE', I used to think, had a romantic ring; but sadly discovered, when I tried to be one, that its practice has little freedom, and the lance is a sorry weapon to tilt at literary windmills. I'd desperately succeeded in appearing in some serious periodicals that paid little, and were seen by few; and in printing some disreputable anonymous paragraphs, cruelly chopped by the sub-editors, in newspapers I'd hitherto despised. As for the B.B.C., since Theodora's departure from it, under a lowering cloud, it would not hear of any of my rich ideas.

How I missed Theodora in the house, and how unexpectedly! True, Johnny's company, since he'd come out of prison, was some small consolation: small, because a different Johnny had emerged—a rather bitter and less kindly person, a disillusioned adult Fortune who no longer seemed to think—as Johnny always had—that everything in the world would one fine day be possible.

I opened the bedroom door and looked at him still sleeping, rolled in an angry lump, his head underneath a pillow. I drew back the curtain, and let in a shaft of reconnoitring spring sun. 'Johnny,' I said, 'it's past eleven.' He bunched the sheets closer round him, and jerked himself in a tighter, unwelcoming ball. I put on the kettle, went back to the front room, and took up Theodora's letter.

'I'd forgotten, Montgomery, how ghastly the country is until I came here to recoup. The colours are green and grey, invariably, and in the village nothing happens: nothing. I'll be glad to get back to London, and only sorry, because of you, it won't be the old flat, but I just can't face living there any longer. You *will* see about the removal of my things to the new place as you promised, won't you. (Be *practical* about all this, Montgomery, for Heaven's sake.)

'I've heard from the Corporation, as I expected, that my appeal is disallowed. Their letter is roundabout and civil—almost deferential—but very clear as to essentials. My old job is out: that's definite; and if I can't "see my way", as they put it, to accepting being kicked upstairs (or rather, kicked downstairs, it really would be, as the office of the alternative job they offer in the Editing service is in the sub-basement of a former department store), they "have no alternative but to accept my offer of resignation". They're giving me a surprise farewell bonus, though: rather nice of them, don't you think, after everything?

'In fact, I really have to admit they've behaved very decently and (unlike me) quite sensibly. I broke the written and unwritten codes, and forfeited my claim to their paternalism. As the high-up I eventually got to see quite frankly said to me, "It's not so much what *you did*, Miss Pace, as that you did it without asking anyone's permission. The Corporation can't be expected to answer publicly for its servants' actions unless it knows what they're going to be." I imagine it was most of all those lurid pieces in the Press about the "B.B.C. woman" that really got them down.

'From what I hear from kind friends who've telephoned (not, of course, on the office lines), it was a close thing, all the same. My "case" went straight to the top, then down again to an appropriate level, then up even higher to the Board of Governors, then plummeted down once more—a massive file it must have been by then, I wish I could have seen it—to the person who actually had to wield the axe, or rather to his secretary (a bitch—I knew her in the Wrens—she probably drafted the letter for him herself).

'But I don't, as they say, "regret it". Being horribly competent, I can always get a job—all I really mind is having lost a battle. And I don't regret making a fool of myself in front of everybody in the court. All I deeply regret, Montgomery (oh, how I do!—you'll not understand, however much you think you do), is losing my child in that so squalid, absurd and dreadfully sad miscarriage (my first—I mean my first pregnancy, as it happens), because though I've never meant anything to Johnny Fortune, I would still have had that . . . it—he—she: anyway, a fragment of him.

'How is he? Better not tell me. I don't want to see him again. I do, of course, but I couldn't.

'And how are you, Montgomery? If you're behindhand with the

rent, as I imagine, and, as I also imagine, up to your grey eyes in debt, please let me know, and I'll do whatever I can.

'*Later*. Just been out to buy some gin. They looked at me as if I was indeed a "B.B.C. woman", but took the pound notes promptly enough.

'What's clear to me now, Montgomery—although I know you won't agree—is that love, or even friendship, for those people is *impossible*—I mean as we understand it. It's not either party's fault; it's just that in the nature of things we can never really understand each other because we see the whole world utterly differently. In a crisis each race will act according to its nature, each one quite separately, and each one be right, and hurt the other.

'It's when you see that *distant* look that sometimes comes into their opaque brown eyes that you realize it—that moment when they suddenly depart irrevocably within themselves far off towards some hidden, alien, secretive, quite untouchable horizon. . . .'

2

Appearance of a guardian angel

SINCE MY TROUBLE COME, I do not go often to the places where I go before—it is not that I fear the Law, or what it can do to me any more, but that I do not wish to be seen there by my countrymen. To be sent to jail for weed was not the big disgrace, for everybody know they never catch me if they treat me fairly; but to have a Jumble woman who I do not love speak up in court and say she have a child of me, and hear the boys say it was this woman's lies that set me free on that first charge—this is too big a shame for me. And since the sad death of Hamilton, I have no friend, except for Laddy Boy, who was now travelling again at sea, that I would wish to speak to in this city.

So what I do, as soon as Montgomery goes out, is visit cinemas and sit there by myself, or else go practising my judo and my boxing at the merchant seaman gymnasium. For now I hear that Billy Whispers also has come out of finishing his sentence, I know this boy will one day try to make some trouble for me, because he believes from what they tell him of my trial that when he go into jail, is I who takes his Dorothy.

So I sat in the darkness of the Tottenham Court picture palace this day, thinking; when near to me a white boy asked me for a match, to light his cigarette, he say, and other silly business of holding my hand too long when I pass the box, and when he gives it back to me, so that I know what his foolish hope is, and say to him, 'Mister, behave yourself, or else you come out with me and I push your face in.'

'All right, man, I come out with you,' this white boy whispered. I thought: oh, very well, if he wants hitting, then I hit him, this will be some big relief to all my feelings; but when I see his face outside the dark, I recognize it was this Alfy Bongo. 'Oh, you,' I said to him. 'Are you still living?'

'Why not, Johnny? The devil looks after his own. Won't you have a coffee with me?'

'So you are one of these foolish men who try to mess about with Spades in picture-houses?'

'Oh, I'm a little queer boy, Johnny, that's for certain; but I didn't know that it was you.'

'One day you meet some bad boy who do you some big damage.

'It wouldn't be the first time. Let's come and have some coffee, like I say.'

'Why should I come? I enjoy this film in here.'

'Listen, Johnny. Why are you so ungrateful? Didn't they tell you how I helped you at your trial?'

'I hear of this, yes; but is much better that you leave me to fight my trial alone. If this woman you speak to not go into the box, and make her statement, I go free all the same through my good lawyers.'

'You think you would have? Nobody else does—least of all Mr Vial, I can tell you that. And, anyway, who do you think found your lawyers for you?'

'Well, what good it do me—that acquittal? They catch me the second time.'

'I wish I'd known of that. If I'd known, I'd have done something for you. . . . Why didn't anyone let me know in time?'

I stopped in the street and looked at this cheeky person. 'What is all this, Alfy, you wish to do such nice things for me? You hope you have some pleasant treatment from me one day that never come?'

'Oh, no, Johnny, I know you're square. But I just like helping out the Spades.'

'You do! Oh, do you!'

'I wish I'd been born a Spade.'

'Do you now, man!'

'Yes, I do. I tell you I *do*. You have this coffee with me, Johnny, or not?'

'Oh, if you say so: let us go.'

He took me to a coffee-bar nearby, and there, when he order it, he said to me, 'And how was it in the nick? Did they beat you in there at all?'

'No, man, I play so cool. What I like least of all is your British sanitation in that place. Man, in that jail all you turn into is not any human person, but a lavatory machine.'

'And what do you do now, Johnny, with yourself?'

'What I do now? Would it surprise you, after how they treat me in those places, if now I start up some really serious hustle?'

'Don't think of that, man. You've got a record now. Second offence, and they've got you by the you-know-whats. What you should do is . . . Man, why don't you cut out and go back home?'

'How can I now, to face my family? They speak about my Dad in court—you know of that? They talk about his bravery, which I tell my white friends as a secret, not for them to put shame on my Dad by mixing his name up with that charge they put upon me.'

'I hear Billy's out. You know what he did with Dorothy?'

'No. Where she's gone?'

'Into hospital. He cut up her face.'

'Nice. Well, I'm not surprised. That thing come her way some quite long time.'

'Better be careful—you too, Johnny. Why don't you leave town a while? Go up to Liverpool Rialto way, or Manchester Moss Side?'

'Me? For fear of that man Billy? Listen now, Mr Bongo. If he kill me, he kill me. If I kill him, I kill him. Or else perhaps nobody kills nobody. We shall see.'

This Alfy Bongo person was one I couldn't quite make out. I looked hard behind his eyes, but could not see any real unfriendliness to me, or danger there.

He looked me back. 'Well, that's not the great news, is it?' he said. 'You know you're a father now, Johnny?'

'Yes? No, I not hear. . . .'

'A boy.'

'Is it then Muriel?'

'Yes. She's called it William.'

'Well—is nice for her. I hope this William turns out a nice man like his uncle Arthur, that shop me to the Law.'

'You're not going out to see your son?'

'Why, man? Let her keep this William for her pleasure.'

'She'll put an affiliation order on you, to support it. . . .'

'Oh, well. That will be just one more misery I have to suffer.'

This Alfy handed me a cigarette. 'You're turning sour, Johnny,' he said to me. 'It's bad in London, when a Spade turns sour.'

I got up to leave him. 'Spades will stay sour, man, let me tell you, till they're treated right.'

'Cheer up—they'll be treated better soon. That race crap's changing fast, believe me, Johnny.'

'Not fast enough for me, Mister Alfy Bongo. How long you think this rubbish will go on? This big, big problem that they think up out of nothing, and is nothing?'

'Not long now, man. In ten years' time, or so, they'll wonder what it was all about.'

I got up to leave him. 'Roll on that day,' I said to him. 'But I tell you this, man, and remember it. Let them kill every Spade that's in the world, and leave but just two, man and woman, and we'll fill up the whole globe once more and win our triumph!'

He asked me to come round and see him in his room in Kensington West one day, but I tell him my life is occupied, and left him and went out and caught my bus. To sleep now would be best, I thought, and I came home to where I am staying with Montgomery. When I turn round the corner to his house, I see standing by the door an African girl, and from this distance I know it is my sister Peach.

I stopped, and think quickly. I want to see Peach, but I do not want to see Peach, so I turned and run. But she see me, come running after, and hold on my coat like she tear it off my body, and there in the street hugged on to me so tight I cannot breathe, and she say nothing.

3

Disputed child of an uncertain future

FROM Johnny's vagueness, even rudeness, I could guess something had happened, but couldn't persuade him to tell me what. There were surreptitious telephone calls, and abrupt goings and comings, and a heightened air of inwardness, of 'African-ness' about him. One evening, when I saw him eyeing me steadily in a critical, almost hostile way, I said, 'Look, Johnny. You'd better tell me what's on your mind.'

He nodded and said, 'My sister Peach is here.'

'In London?'

'As training nurse. She live now at the hostel there beside her hospital.'

'Well, I'm delighted, Johnny. When am I going to meet her?'

'I do not wish you meet with her, Montgomery.'

'Why not? Oh, all right, then, if you prefer me not to. But why?'

'Because I fear you tell some things she should not hear.'

'Well—thank you! You're a nice trusting soul.'

'You blow your top too much, Montgomery. You know you do.'

'Oh, fine. Don't introduce me, then.'

'She wish to speak with you, all the same.'

'Well, make up your mind!'

'I tell her of this child of mine that Muriel has got. Peach wish to speak to you about it.'

'Why?'

'She tell you.'

'All right. When do we meet?'

'I ask her to come round this afternoon. While she is here, I stay downstairs in Theodora's place.'

'To keep an eye on me, is that it?'

'Yes. She is my sister.'

'Look, Johnny. I'm beginning to think it's time you and I should part company. If you like, I'll move out with friends, and you can stay on here by yourself until the landlords serve the summons.'

'You should not make argument, Montgomery.'

'Oh, no! What I should do is exactly what suits you.'

'What you should do, please, is see my sister Peach this afternoon because she wish to speak with you.'

We left it at that, and when the bell rang Johnny went down and let her in, but did not come up with her beyond Theodora's floor. I greeted Peach on the stairs, and ushered her into the flat. 'A cup of tea, Miss Fortune?' I said to her. 'Or I have coffee. . . .'

'No, thank you.'

How could a girl so beautiful wear such really appalling clothes? Peach had everything, and more, of Johnny's sumptuous good looks —as feminine a version as his was masculine, but with a greater air of gravity and depth. So that if one ignored (but how could one?) the rainbow shades of royal blue, and green, and crimson that she wore, she seemed one of the loveliest creatures in creation—the more so as she had such grace of easy gesture, and such self-confident, unaffected pride.

'You are my brother's friend,' she said. 'He tell me of you, and how you are his friend.'

Her English was not as eccentrically voluble as her brother's—she seemed to speak it with some difficulty. I insisted on tea, and bustled about with host-like charm which, to my mortification, made no impression on her whatever.

'I come to speak to you of Johnny's baby,' she said.

'Yes. . . ?'

'I tell him he must take it home to Africa.'

'Oh!'

'Here it will not be happy, or be well instructed.'

'No. . . . But Miss Fortune—or may I call you Peach?' (this gambit misfired too, for she made no reply) '—in English law, the baby belongs to the mother. Unless, that is, the parents were married, and even then . . .'

'It is an Africa child.'

'Well, not entirely, is it?'

'I have no money.'

'No. . . ?' (Money again!)

'My father, my mother, they have money, yes. But they will give some to my brother only for his boat fare home to Africa.'

'Yes . . . so he's told me. But I don't see . . .'

'If he have other money, then he can buy the baby from the woman.'

'Peach! You just *can't* do that here in England. Or rather . . . she *might* agree, but then there are regulations about adoption, and emigration, and so on and so forth . . . . Hasn't Johnny told you all this?'

'He tell me many things, but I wish to hear you speaking.'

'Well, I am! We could try, of course, but, honestly, I think it's unlikely the mother would . . . and in any case, what about that money?'

She looked at me.

'My dear Miss Fortune, *I* haven't got a cent.' (Didn't believe me, obviously.) 'If you explain everything to your parents, wouldn't they give Johnny something extra to try it with?'

'No. . . . My mother, no. My father, yes, but he listen to my mother.'

'Well, then, excuse me, Peach—but why do you want to get the child? Does Johnny want it?'

'No.'

'So *you* do.'

'No. But it is my brother's child, and will not be happy here, not well instructed.'

'That's very possible, I admit. . . . Is Johnny going back to Africa, then?'

'I tell him he should do this.'

'And he agrees?'

'Yes, when I speak to him.'

'Oh. Well, Peach—what can I do? I don't know. . . . I could try to see Muriel, if you like. . . . And perhaps I could try to get some money somehow if she agrees to listen, which I very much doubt. . . .' Suddenly I rebelled against this hypnotic girl. 'Why don't *you* talk to Muriel?' I asked.

'I do not wish to see this family. No.'

'Don't you? I can't altogether blame you. Well, shall I have a word with Johnny and see what might be done?' She'd already got up. 'But I don't think there's much hope. . . .' She was near the door.

'And how do you like the hospital—and nursing? How do you like it over here?' I asked desperately.

'Is good for me to learn these things in London.'

She went down the stairs. Faint sounds of a long confabulation in African drifted up them. The front door banged, and Johnny reappeared.

'You know it's impossible, what she wants?' I said to him. 'Didn't you tell her, before you inflicted all this on me?'

'My sister believes it would be possible.'

'Does she, indeed! And you: you don't really want young William in Lagos, do you, even if you could ever get him there?'

'If I have him in Africa, yes, then I would want him.'

I just stared at him. 'Johnny! Have you, and your sister, and your entire race, ever reflected that other people in the world want things besides yourselves?'

'I go out now, Montgomery.'

'You'd better!'

By force of habit, the only thing I could think of was to tell Theodora. I called up her village on the 'phone, and she didn't seem much surprised as I unfolded by incoherent story. She even said, 'If Muriel can be bought off, one might try to short-circuit the regulations and kidnap the child. An air passage would fix it—it's been done before.'

'But money, Theodora! Money, money, money, money, money!'

'Exactly. Listen. I'll come up to town tomorrow, and we'll pay a call together on Muriel.'

'Hadn't you better leave the negotiations to me?'

'When you tried that once before, Montgomery, you weren't particularly successful. And after all, it's my money that's going to be wasted.'

As I hung up, I registered, there and then, a vow that never after this, so long as I lived, never, would I interfere in anyone else's private affairs. Never! After which, I rang Mr Zuss-Amor to check on the legal aspects.

He was discouraging. 'The babe is hers until it's a major. Even if he married the woman it still would be—unless he could sue for divorce for some reason or other later on and get the custody—but is all that likely? Why does he want it, anyway?'

'You tell me. Can anyone understand Africans?'

'Well, it's a lesson to the boy, and to us all,' the solicitor said humorously. 'It makes you realize you've got to be very careful where you put it.'

I was glad to see Theodora back in London. She refused to come over to the house, and met me (neither of us could think, in a hurry, of a better place) at the pub round the corner from the law courts of evil memory. I expected that Theodora, too, would have changed, but the surprise was that it seemed a change for the better: she was less angular and spiky, rather more relaxed, and at moments she seemed almost matronly. In the taxi she took my arm and said, 'What's the sister like, Montgomery?'

'Like him. Less of a ruffian, though.'

'Women aren't ruffians.'

'No? Well, less of the female equivalent. Very attractive indeed she'll be in her nurse's uniform—I wish I could see her in it; but then, a nurse's uniform makes everyone look attractive.'

'Even Florence Nightingale? You're not going to propose to Peach, are you?'

'I don't think so, Theodora. What would be the use?'

'And how's he?'

'Moody. Melancholy. But a lot happier now he's decided to leave for home.'

'You really think he will?'

'Well, that's the plan; but like all African plans . . .'

'Don't tell me. We must go out to Africa, too, one day, Montgomery, as tourists. See all the sights together.'

'I bet as soon as we got there, we'd meet everyone we've known in all those disreputable clubs and places. We'd find Mr Karl Marx Bo prime minister, I expect.'

'That would be too much. Is this the street?'

'It is, but do let me go and spy out the land—I really think it would be best, Theodora.'

The flat was silent, and a neighbour told me the Macphersons had all left.

'It's Muriel I want.'

'Oh, she's gone off separate. I've got the address for forwarding—you're not from the landlord, are you?'

'No, no. A friend. Honest. . . .'

Muriel's new address was not far off. We walked up to the third floor, but there was nobody in there either.

'No sounds of a baby wailing,' I said. 'Shall we wait here till she comes?'

'I suppose we'd better.'

We sat on the stairs, talking. After two hours had gone, a young girl appeared with a baby. We introduced ourselves.

'I'm from the crèche,' she said. 'Isn't Mrs Macpherson back?'

'Not yet,' said Theodora. 'Shall I look after it for you till she comes?'

'Well, if you don't drop it . . .' she said after some persuasion, and handed the infant over to Theodora.

We looked together at William Macpherson Fortune. 'My God,' said Theodora. 'They say babies aren't like their parents. Just look at him!'

'I'm very nervous, Theodora. I don't think Muriel will approve at all.'

When she came, though, she almost seemed to have expected us, and asked us straight in to the single room. 'Do you mind if I feed William?' she said. 'Then I'll get you a cup of tea.'

Was there a faint triumph in her gesture, as there was certainly more than faint envy in Theodora? 'Is he good?' she asked the mother.

'He is now, but he won't be for long if he grows up like his father.'

She put the baby in its cot, and got us tea. 'I suppose you've come to tell me something about Johnny,' she said. 'What is it?'

By one of those accidents of nature, entirely unforeseeable (especially by a man, in the case of women), Theodora and Muriel, who'd only met so briefly and so long ago, seemed to take to each other, to be suddenly on familiar terms. Without too much beating about the bush, Theodora came to the point—or points, because there were quite a lot of them.

Muriel didn't seem surprised, or hurt, by the proposition Theodora unfolded to her.

'I know I behaved bad to Johnny,' she said. 'I know I should have spoken up for him in court. I should have, I dare say, but I just couldn't do it—I just *couldn't*. I was mad about him and Dorothy, and his doing *nothing* for me—*nothing*, can you believe it?—all the time.'

'Yes, I can understand.'

'And you spoke up for him instead.'

'Yes.'

Muriel looked at Theodora rather sharply, with a sudden hostile glint. Then said, 'Well, I don't blame you, if you loved him—he's a very lovable boy, isn't he, in his way. But me, I just can't make him out. . . . He's never loved *me*, that's certain. He's never loved any of us, from what I can see. . . .'

'No, I don't think he has.'

'And now he wants William: to get rid of me, and take William. Well, that's asking a bit much, isn't it? Just tell him to forget about it, will you? And that I'll send him some snaps from time to time if he'll give me his address. . . .'

'Quite apart from what he's asked us to tell you,' said Theodora, 'could I help out financially at all? I'd be very glad to.'

Muriel reflected. 'No, it's all right, thanks. I've got me job and all the allowances, and they look after William at the crèche. . . . Later on, when he grows up a bit, you could do something for him, if you felt like it.'

'Perhaps you'd let me be his godparent, Muriel.'

'And me,' I said, vexed that I hadn't thought of this.

'Oh, I don't believe in that. . . . But if you like to help William, as I say, or send him something for his birthday . . .'

We both wrote the date down carefully. Muriel saw us to the door.

'You can't hate them, can you,' she said, 'whatever they do to you. Me, I loved Johnny, I really did, like I never will anybody else, I don't suppose. And he was sweet to me in his way, and I had good times with him. But I never meant much to him, that was the trouble. I don't believe they understand love like we do, but that's their nature. . . .'

4

Back home aboard the 'Lugard'

It was when Laddy Boy returned from sea that he tell me of this tugboat, called the *Lugard*, to be sailed empty from London Docks to Lagos, and that a deck-hand crew of five was needed to take her there. And when Laddy Boy did me the great favour to give me a forged seaman's book he buy, and tell me answers I must give to any questions, I made such a good impression on the captain by my strength and willingness (he was high, anyway—an Irishman) that he sign me on, and even though I cannot yet believe it, I am to go back home from England.

So on our sailing day, I met with my English friend Montgomery and my sister Peach at a dockside Chinese restaurant where they come to say goodbye to me. 'That is like the life,' I said to Montgomery. 'My sister Peach, who never wishes to leave Africa, is now in London till she becomes a nurse, and I who wished to live in this big city, go back home to all my family to take her place.'

'Soon I come home also,' said my sister, 'with my nurse's belt and badges. I shall not waste my time with foolishness like my brother.'

A sister's remark! 'Through Peach you will have news of me, Montgomery,' I said, 'and of all my activities at home.'

'Won't you be writing to me?' asked my English friend.

'Of course, of course—and soon you will come to Africa as well and visit Mum and Dad and Christmas and our family, and live with us in our home like I do when here with you.'

'Perhaps I'll go there when Peach has qualified,' said Montgomery. 'Perhaps we'll go out together.'

'Oh yes, oh yes,' I said (but Peach has her close instructions, and this also is her wish, that she shall not see Montgomery so often, and always, if so, in the company of the nurses' hostel).

I looked at my watch—a parting friendship present from Montgomery—and said that my time had come to go. We went in the streets, in sunshine, and I spoke first to my sister in our language, and then to Montgomery, my Jumble friend.

'Goodbye, Johnny,' he said. 'I can't think what to say, and how to thank you . . .'

'Thank me? Man, it is you who gave me so many good things that I needed.'

'Nothing it wasn't a joy to. . . . Shall we see you down to the dock gates?'

'No, no, please. We find a taxi for you take my sister back to hospital, and then I go on alone.'

I opened the taxi door, and gave my surprise gift to Montgomery: it is the mission school medal I wear on my neck on its chain since boyhood. 'For you,' I tell him. 'You keep it with you, please.' Then I tell the driver where he should go, and I waved to them as the taxi carried this two away.

I walked on quickly to the dock gates, to get a best bed on my ship before the other seamen come there. But by the river side, where our strong, dirty, little boat is by its mooring, I find that Laddy Boy is waiting for me.

He took my arm, and pulled me behind the shed. 'Listen, man,' he said. 'They sign on Whispers.'

'Sign Billy on?'

'Yes. As one of the five crew. I did not know. Shall I go see the captain and try to stop this?'

'Why, man? Why you do that?'

'Why? You know why.'

'Let him come travel home with me if he wants to. Why should I stop him go?'

'Johnny, is he stop you. This man will kill you on this voyage.'

I laughed now out loud at Laddy Boy. 'No one will kill me, countryman!' I cried. 'This is my city, look at it now! Look at it there—it has not killed me! There is my ship that takes me home to Africa: it will not kill me either! No! Nobody in the world will kill me ever until I die!'